From the Chicken House

Rachel Ward's new novel, NUMBERS: THE CHAOS, made even greater demands on my nerves than her first. Here's an author who can climb into your head, create truly believable characters, and give you a superb thriller with colossal consequences – all in one book!

Remember the scene with Jem's son at the end of NUMBERS? Spooky wasn't it? You knew he was special, I'm sure. Well, his future is even stranger than you can imagine . . .

Barry Cunningham
Publisher

NUMBERS

RACHEL WARD

THE CHAOS

Chicken House 2 Palmer Street, Frome, Somerset BA11 1DS

Text © Rachel Ward 2010

First published in Great Britain in 2010
The Chicken House
2 Palmer Street
Frome, Somerset BA11 1DS
United Kingdom
www.doublecluck.com

Jacket design Steve Wells
Interior design Steve Wells
Typeset by Dorchester Typesetting Group Ltd
Printed and bound in Great Britain by CPI Bookmarque, Croydon, CR0 4TD

The paper used in this Chicken House book is made from wood grown in sustainable forests.

3 5 7 9 10 8 6 4

British Library Cataloguing in Publication data available.

ISBN 978-1-906427-30-6

For Ozzy, my soulmate

082013 23122
82064 210420
82032 220720
3122
4206

20720

0420
20720
312
3122   23
04
22072
3122
56

22   07   2

3122
0420
2072   0
312   2
312
0420
20720 2
312
420   6
07202   0
23122
0   42
20   72   0

10420
22072
2   1   131

082032
013 23122

June 2026

Adam

The knock on the door comes early in the morning, just as it's getting light.

'Open up! Open up! We've got an Evacuation Order on these flats. Moving out in five minutes. Five minutes everybody!'

You can hear them going down the corridor, knocking on doors, repeating the same instructions over and over. I haven't been asleep, but Nan nodded off in her chair, and now she jerks awake and curses.

'Bloody hell, Adam. What time is it?' Her face looks crumpled and old, too old to go with her purple hair.

'Half-six, Nan. They've come.'

She looks at me, tired and wary.

'This is it, then,' she says. 'Better find your things.'

I look back at her and I think, *I'm not going anywhere. Not with you.*

We've been expecting this. We've been camped out in the flat for four days, watching the flood water rising in the street below. They'd warned everyone that the sea wall was likely to go. It was built years ago before the sea level rose, and it wasn't going to stand another storm with a spring tide to add to the swell.

We thought the water would come and then go, but it came and it stayed.

'S'pose this is what Venice looked like before it was washed away,' Nan said, gloomily. She flicked her cigarette butt out of the window and down into the water below. It bobbed slowly along the street towards where the prom had been. And she lit another fag.

The electricity was cut off that first night, then the water in the taps turned brown. People waded along the street outside shouting through loud hailers, warning us not to drink the water, saying they'd bring us food and water. They didn't. Instead we made do with what we'd got, but with no toaster and no microwave, and the milk going off in the fridge, we were starting to get hungry after twelve hours. I knew things were bad when Nan took the cellophane off her last packet of fags.

'Once these are gone we're going to have to get out of here, son,' she said.

'I'm not going,' I told her. This was my home. It was all I had left of Mum.

'We can't stay here, not like this.'

'I'm not going.' Statement of fact. 'You can bugger off back to London if you like. You know you want to anyway.' It was true. She'd never felt comfortable here. She'd come when Mum got ill, and stayed to look after me, but she was like a fish out of water. The sea air made her cough. The big bright sky made her screw up her eyes and she'd scuttle back inside like a cockroach as fast as she could.

'Less of your language,' she said, 'and pack a bag.'

'You can't tell me what to do. You're not my mum. I'm not packing,' I said, and I didn't.

Now we have five minutes to get ready. Nan stirs herself and starts putting more things into her bin bag. She disappears into her room and comes out with an armful of clothes and a polished wooden box tucked under her arm. She moves around the flat surprisingly fast. I feel a tide of panic rising inside me. I can't leave here. I'm not ready. It's not fair.

I get one of the chairs from the kitchen and lean it up against the door handle. But it's not the right height to wedge the handle shut, so I just start grabbing whatever I can find and building a barricade. I push the sofa over, pile the kitchen chair on top, then the coffee table. I'm breathing hard, sweating between my shoulder blades.

'Adam, what the hell are you doing?'

Nan's tearing at my arm, trying to stop me. Her long yellow fingernails are digging in. I shrug her off.

'Get off, Nan. I'm not going!'

'Don't be stupid. Get some of your things. You'll want your things with you.'

I take no notice.

'Adam, don't be so fucking stupid!' She's clawing at me again, and then someone's knocking on the door.

'Open up!'

I freeze, and look at Nan. Her eyes show me her number: 2022054. She's got another thirty years, near enough, but you'd never guess it. She looks like she could go any day.

'Open up!'

'Adam, please . . .'

'No, Nan.'

'Stand away from the door! Stand back!'

3

'Adam—'

A sledgehammer smashes the lock. Then the door itself is shredded. In the corridor there's two soldiers, one with the sledgehammer, the other with a gun. It's pointing straight into the flat. It's pointing at us. The soldiers quickly scan the rest of the flat.

'All right, ma'am,' says the gunman. 'I'll have to ask you to move that obstruction and leave the building.'

Nan nods.

'Adam,' she says, 'move the sofa.'

I'm staring at the end of the rifle. I can't take my eyes off it. In the next second, maybe less than that, it could all be over. This could be it. All I have to do is make a move towards him. If it's my time, my day to go, that'll be it. *What is my number? Is it today?*

The barrel of the rifle is clean and smooth and straight. Will I see the bullet come out? Will there be smoke?

'Fuck off,' I say. 'Take your fucking gun and fuck off.'

And then it all happens at once. The sledgehammer guy drops his hammer and shoves the sofa into the room like a rugby player in a scrum, the guy with the gun tilts it up to the ceiling and follows him in and Nan smacks me, right across my face.

'Listen, you little bastard,' she hisses at me, 'I promised your mum I'd look after you, and I will. I'm your nan and you'll do what I say. Now stop playing silly buggers. We're leaving. And mind your fucking language, I told you about that.'

My face is stinging but I'm not ready to give in yet. This is my home. They can't just take you away from your home, can they?

They can.

4

The soldiers grab an arm each and carry me out of the flat. I struggle, but they're big and there's two of them. It's all so quick. Before I know it, I'm at the end of the corridor and down the fire escape and they've put me in an inflatable boat at the bottom of the steps. Nan gets in beside me, dumps the bulging bin bag by her feet and puts her arm round my shoulders, and we're away, chugging slowly through the flooded streets.

'It's all right, Adam,' she says, 'it's going to be all right.'

Some of the people on our boat are crying quietly. But most of their faces are blank. I'm still angry and humiliated. I can't understand what just happened.

I haven't got any of my stuff. I haven't got my book. Another wave of panic sweeps over me. I'll have to get out and go back. I can't go without my book. Where did I leave it? When did I last have it? Then I feel the edge of something hard against my hip and my hand goes down to my pocket. Of course, it's there. I haven't put it anywhere – I've kept it with me, like I always do.

I relax, just a little bit. And then it hits me. We're actually leaving. We're going. I might never see the flat again.

There's a big lump in my throat. I try to swallow it, but it won't go. I can feel the tears welling up. The soldier steering the boat is watching me. I'm not going to cry, not in front of him or Nan or any of these people. I won't give them the satisfaction. I dig my fingernails into the back of my hand. The tears are still there, threatening to spill out. I dig harder, so the pain breaks through everything else. I'm not going to cry. I'm not going to. I won't.

At the transit centre, we stand in line to register. There's one queue for people who have somewhere to go, and another one for people who haven't. Nan and I aren't

5

chipped, so we have to show our ID cards and Nan fills in forms for both of us requesting transport to London. They pin a piece of paper with a number onto our coats, like we're about to run a marathon, then they herd us into a hall and tell us to wait.

People are giving out hot food and drinks. We queue up again. My mouth waters when we get nearer the front and I can see and smell the food. We're four from the front when another soldier comes into the hall and starts barking out numbers, including ours. Our coach is ready. We have to leave now.

'Nan . . . ?' I'm so hungry. I can't go without getting something to eat, just something.

''Scuse me,' I say, 'can you let me through?'

There's no reaction. Everyone's pretending they haven't heard.

I try again, as the soldier repeats the numbers. Nothing. I'm desperate. I dart forward and shove my hand through a gap between two people, and feel around blindly. My fingers find something – it feels like a piece of toast – and I pick it up. Someone grabs my wrist and holds on so tightly it hurts.

'There's a queue,' he says firmly. 'We're British. We know how to queue.'

'I'm sorry,' I say. 'It's for my nan. She's hungry and we've got to go now.'

I look up into the face of the man holding me. He's middle aged, about fifty. Grey hair and a grim face, you can see how tired he is, but that's not what shocks me – it's his number. 112027. Only six months to live. I get a flash of his death, too, and it's brutal, violent, a blow to the head, blood, brains . . .

I drop the toast back onto the plate and try to back away.

The man lets go of my wrist, he thinks he's won, but he must have seen something in me, too, because his face softens and he reaches across, picks up the toast and hands it to me.

'For your nan,' he says. 'Go on, son. Don't miss your coach.'

'Thanks,' I murmur.

I think about cramming the whole lot in there and then, but the man's watching me and so is Nan, so I carry the toast carefully outside, and when Nan and I are settled on the coach, I give it to her. She tears it in two and gives half back. We don't speak. I stuff mine in my mouth and it's gone in two bites, but Nan savours hers, making it last 'til we're out of town and heading east along the main road. The road's on a raised-up strip of land with miles and miles of flooded fields all round it. The sun's come out at last and it's turned the water into a sheet of silver so bright you can't look at it.

'Nan,' I say. 'What if the whole world floods? What will we do then?'

She wipes a smudge of butter off her chin with her finger, and licks it.

'We'll build an ark, shall we, you and me? And invite all the animals?' She chuckles and picks up my hand with the one she's just licked. There are deep red crescents on my skin where I dug my nails in on the boat.

'What you done there?' she asks.

'Nothing.'

She looks at me and frowns. Then she gives my hand a little squeeze.

'Don't worry, son. We'll be all right in London. There's flood defences there, and everything. They know how to do things properly there. We'll be fine. Good old London Town.'

She puts her head back, closes her eyes and sighs, happy

to be heading home at last. But I can't relax. I have to write down the man in the queue's number before I forget it. It's shaken me up. You get a feeling for people's numbers, when you've seen them all your life. And his number didn't seem to match him. I'm feeling edgy. I'll be better once I write it down.

I get my book out of my pocket, and record all the details I can remember: description (it's better when I know the names), today's date, the place, his number, how he's going to die. I write it carefully, and every letter, every word makes me calmer. It's all in there now, safe in my book. I can look at it later.

I put my notebook back. Nan's starting to snore gently. She's well away. I look at the other passengers. Some of them are trying to sleep, but some are like me – anxious and watchful. From where I'm sitting I can see six or seven people who are still awake. We catch each other's eyes and then we look away again, without saying anything, like strangers do.

But just one moment of eye contact is all I need to see their numbers, a different number for each one – the different dates that mark the end of their lives.

Except these numbers aren't that different. Five of them end in 12027 and two are exactly the same: 112027.

My heart's pounding in my chest now, my breathing's gone shallow and fast. I reach into my pocket 'til my fingers find my notebook again. My hands are shaking, but I manage to get the book out and open it at the right page.

These people are like the man in the food queue – they've only got six months left.

They're going to die in January next year.

They're going to die in London.

September 2026

Sarah

'You know why you're here. It's not what you're used to, but we're running out of options. They won't tolerate you playing up here – being late, or truanting, or answering back. This is a chance for you to start again, do it right this time, knuckle down. Please, Sarah, don't let us down. Don't let yourself down.'

Blah, blah, blah. Same old same old. I let it drift over me, too tired to listen. I hardly slept last night, and when I did I had the nightmare again and I had to wake myself up. I lay awake then, listening to the noises a house makes at night, until it got light.

I don't say anything back to Him, not even 'goodbye' as I get out of the Merc. I slam the car door and in my head I can see Him wince, hear Him curse me, and it makes me feel better, just for a second.

The Merc has turned people's heads, like it always does. It's not every day you see a car on the school run, never mind a gas-guzzler like Dad's. Now people are checking me out.

Great, I'll be marked out as different before I even start. Still, what do I care?

Someone whistles and purrs, 'Niiiice,' long and low at me.

A group of lads have stopped to stare, six or seven of them. They're looking me up and down, licking their lips like wolves. What am I meant to feel? Intimidated? Flattered? Screw that. I show them the finger and walk in through the gates.

It's not bad for a state school, I suppose. At least it's all new, not scruffy like I've been expecting. But it's only new because the previous one was burnt out in the 2022 riots and it's still got a bit of a reputation, Forest Green: tough regime, tough kids. My heart sank when Mum and Dad said they'd enrolled me, but then I thought, *What the hell. One school's the same as any other. School, home – they're all prisons, aren't they? All there to make you conform.* It doesn't matter where I am – my mind's my own, they can't control that.

And wherever they send me, I don't plan to stay for long. I've got other things on my mind, well, one big thing, or at least a small thing that's getting bigger. And it means that I have to start thinking for myself, planning, taking control.

I have to get my life back.

I can't wait much longer.

I have to get away.

Adam

I didn't start it. It wasn't me.

Nan told me not to get into trouble when I was setting off in the morning, and I wasn't going to. I was just going to turn up, register, do what I had to do and get back to Nan's.

I know there'll be a lot of twenty-sevens there, because there are a lot of twenty-sevens everywhere. All summer, I've been clocking them. The entries in my book show the same picture wherever I've been.

'Kilburn High Road. 84.'

'The offie, sherry for Nan. 12.'

There are so many I don't write down their details any more. I can't. I only record how many I've seen that time. I still keep proper records on people who are different, or if I know their names. And it makes me feel better, well, a bit better. At least it used to. But the longer I stay in London, the more I know we've made a mistake. We should never have come here. It's dangerous. A lot of people are going to die.

So I tell myself that for the time being I'll go through the motions, keep my head down and keep Nan happy, but only 'til I've figured out how to get out of here and where to go. I need to find a place where there are no twenty-sevens. If no one else there is going to die in January 2027, then it stands to reason I'll have a better chance of surviving, because I don't know my own number, see. I just don't know. The only way I'll find out is if there's someone else who can see the numbers – and I'm pretty sure I'm the only one.

There's a bottleneck by the door into Reception. I don't like crowds, never have – too many people, too many deaths – but I make myself walk through the gates and join the queue. In no time there's people crowding in behind me, penning me in, and I start to panic. The sweat breaks out under my arms and on my top lip. I look around for a way out. There's number after number ending in 2027 and suddenly my head is full of it – the noise, the chaos, trapped limbs, broken bones, darkness, despair.

I've got to get a grip. My mum taught me what to do.

'Breathe slowly,' she'd say. 'Make yourself do it. In through your nose and out through your mouth. Don't look at anyone else. Look at the ground. In through your nose – two, three, four – and out through your mouth – two, three, four.'

I make myself look down at the forest of legs and feet and bags. If I don't see their numbers then this feeling will go away. I'll be okay. My breath's uneven and shallow, there's not enough air getting in my lungs.

In through your nose, and out through your mouth. Come on, I can do this.

It isn't working. I'm getting worse. I'm going to be sick . . . I'm going to faint . . .

Someone behind me shoves into my back. I dig my heels in and stand my ground.

Breathe slowly. Why isn't it working?

More pressure. The boy behind me is in my space, trying to push me around. He'll have me over in a minute. I'll go down and be trampled, kicked to bits. Perhaps that's what's meant to happen, but it's not how I want to go and I'm not going down without a fight.

That's it!

I swing round and catch him with my elbow, right in the ribs.

'Fuck! Watch it!' He spits the words out, a boy a bit smaller than me, with ratty teeth and a crew cut. I've hurt him, and now the look in his eyes says he's going to hurt me back. I know that look – I've seen it too many times before. I ought to be on my toes, alert, ready for the first punch, but his number's burning into me. It's different, see, odd. He only has three months to go. 6122026. I'm getting the flash of a blade, the hot metallic smell of blood and I feel sicker than ever. I can't move – his number, his death, has me in its grip. I shut my eyes to try and get it out of my head, break the spell. I open them again the split second before his knuckles hit my face.

Someone must have jostled him, because he only catches my ear, and not very hard, but it's hard enough to snap me back to reality. I bunch up both my fists and get him in the stomach. I hurt him, but I can't have knocked the wind out of him because he comes at me again, one, two, into my ribs. People around us are screaming and cheering, but that don't matter. It's me and him that matters.

I hit him back. I want to hurt him now. I want to make him go away. I want to make all of it go away – this boy, these kids, this school, Nan, London.

'All right, lads, break it up!'

It's a security guard, the size of small mountain. He's come wading through the crowd and grabbed both of us by the scruff of the neck.

Rat-teeth tries to protest.

'I didn't do nothing! He just started laying into me! What was I s'posed to do?'

But all he gets is an extra neck-shaking and a 'Shut it'.

The crowd parts as we're hauled to the front. We're sent through the metal detector one at a time and searched on the other side. Then we're marched down the corridor to an office, where the Deputy Head is waiting.

'Based on today's performance we shouldn't even be letting you in to this school.' He's a shirt-and-tie kind of guy, the sort that can't talk to you without talking down to you. He's reading us the Riot Act now, but I'm not listening. I'm looking at the dandruff on his shoulders, the way the cuff of his jacket is frayed. 'It's a disgrace to be fighting on your first day, a disgrace. What have you got to say for yourselves?'

I guess Rat-teeth, who turns out to be called Junior, has been in offices like this before. He knows the code. We both stand in silence, and after ten seconds or so we mutter, 'Nothing, sir, sorry, sir'.

'Whatever it was between you, I want you to leave it in this room. Shake hands, boys.'

We look at each other, and again his number blots out everything else and I'm there with him as the knife goes in. I can feel his surprise, his disbelief, the searing pain.

'Take my hand, you moron,' Junior hisses at me.

I come back to myself, back to the room, the teacher and him. He's holding his hand out towards me. I take it and we shake. He squeezes so hard my knuckle bones crunch against each other. I don't show a thing, just squeeze back.

'Take them back to registration. I don't want to see either of you boys in here again. Do you understand?'

'Yes, sir.'

We're marched back down the corridor and join the end of the line. I'm in front of Junior. He leans in behind me and mutters close to my ear, 'You just made the biggest mistake of your life, Shit-brain.'

I move forwards a bit to get further away from him and nudge the girl in front.

'Sorry,' I say.

She half turns round, a girl about fifteen centimetres shorter than me with streaky blonde hair. She starts shooting me a dirty look out of the corner of her eye, but then she stops in her tracks and her eyes go wide as two dinner plates.

'Oh my God,' she whispers.

I know people think I'm weird, the way I look at them and sometimes keep looking. I try not to stare, I do, but sometimes I get kind of locked in, frozen by their numbers, the way they make me feel, like I did with Junior. But I haven't been staring at this girl. I've only just joined the queue.

'What?' I say. 'What is it?'

She's turned round properly now, and she hasn't taken her eyes off me. They're blue, the bluest blue I've ever seen, but there are dark circles underneath, and her cheeks are pale and pinched.

'You,' she says, faintly. 'It's you.' She goes even whiter and starts stumbling away from me, out of the queue, keeping her eyes fixed on mine as she walks slowly backwards, and suddenly it's as if the rest of the world has melted away.

Her number, her death, it totally blows my mind.

More than fifty years in the future, and there she is, slipping out of this life easily, bathed in love and light. I can feel it, all over me, and inside me, in my head. And she's not alone. I'm there with her – she's me and I'm her. How??

She turns away suddenly and starts running down the corridor. One of the guards spots her and shouts out, but she don't stop.

'Whoah! A runner!' Junior says behind me. 'She won't get far, not without registering,' and he's right. None of the doors will open. I watch her rattling one handle after another, desperate. The bugs in the ceiling track her movements. She's getting into a real state, banging her fist on the glass, kicking out. And then two guards grab her under the arms, one each side, and carry her back towards us, and into a side room, next to the reception desk. She's struggling and screaming, her face screwed up in a fury, but when she opens her eyes for a second and sees me again, there's something else, as clear as her number.

She's terrified.

Terrified of me.

Sarah

They want to know what's wrong with me, why I was trying to run away. What can I say? What can I tell them without sounding mad? That I've just met the boy I see in my nightmares? That night after night we're trapped together in some sort of inferno, and he grabs the baby, my baby, and takes her into the flames?

And suddenly here he is, at my new school. This devil. This person who only exists in my head – he's here.

And now I know it's not a nightmare. It's something else, something real.

Yeah, that'll go down really well. Dad's told them all about me, my record of suspensions, expulsions, exclusions. Now they'll think I'm mad as well as bad. So I say nothing. No explanation. No apology. I get the standard bollocking. They know all about my history, which schools have kicked me out, the sorts of things they've kicked me out for. I'm privileged, apparently, to be given a place here. I should treat it as a chance to start again, turn over a new leaf.

I stand there and I think, *You don't know jack shit about me*, and I feel the skin of my belly pressing against the stiff material of my skirt. *Nobody knows. Nobody knows the whole truth.*

Then they take me back to register, pair me up with some earnest-looking kid who's there to make sure I get to my tutor room and don't go AWOL again. I scan the corridors for that boy, the nightmare boy. I stand in the doorway of my tutor room checking out the kids before I go in. If he's there, in my tutor group, I'm not going to stay. But he isn't. I'm okay for a while. So I find a desk, and I sit there, eyes front, while my tutor drones on. I don't hear a word he says. All I'm thinking is, *Is he real, this boy? Who is he? Why's he here?* And after a while, I'm half-sure that I made him up, that I really am mad and my mind's starting to mess up my days as well as my nights.

Then at break-time, I see him again.

He's sitting on his own on a little wall by the science block. Where I'm standing, I can watch him without him knowing I'm there. I try to empty the madness from my mind and look at him like a normal human being would. I study him.

He's one of those people who can't sit still to save his life. All the time on that wall his leg is jiggling. Every now and again, he nods his head as if he's listening to music, but I can't see any earphones.

I'm not surprised he's on his own. There's something odd about him, something different, the way he moves, the way he is. What am I scared of? He's just an oddball, a freak, a nobody.

After a bit he pulls a notebook out of his pocket and starts writing in it, bending forward with his arm curved round.

Whatever he's writing, he doesn't want anyone else to see. So, he has secrets, this boy – I kind of like that. And I like that he's got a book, he's writing on paper, because I like drawing on paper, the feeling of holding a pencil in my hand, and hardly anyone does any more – it's all touch screens and voice recognition. He's different. Different's okay. And I really want to know what he keeps in that book.

He twists round as he writes and the left side of his face catches the light. He's actually good-looking, no, more than that, beautiful: the shape of his face, his deep-set eyes, the firmness of his jaw-line, the curve of his lips. And his skin. It's a warm brown, almost honey-coloured, and so smooth and clear . . . that's not right. The boy in my nightmare, the one I'm scared of, is scarred, his face so marked you can feel the rawness.

It's not him.

It can't be.

I snort and shake my head. I've made a fool of myself and I've got into trouble for no reason on my first day. Nice work, Sarah.

He must have seen my movement out of the corner of his eye, because he looks round and sees me. He slams his notebook shut and shoves it back in his pocket, keeping his eyes on me all the time. He looks as guilty as I feel, caught looking. And yet I don't look away, and as we hold each other's eyes my stomach flips over. There's a connection between us.

I'm not mad.

I know him and he knows me.

Oh God, what's happening?

Adam

'Get on all right?'

Nan's on her stool in the kitchen when I get home, where I expect her to be. Wherever she is – here, Weston – she finds somewhere to perch, somewhere that's hers, and sticks to it, drinking tea and chain-smoking her way through the day.

I shrug. 'S'pose.'

Even though she never seems to move, she don't miss a bloody thing, Nan, but I'm not ready to tell her everything about school. Not yet. She don't need to know I've made an enemy and met a girl.

Junior don't bother me, not his threats anyway. I've had knuckle-heads like him saying things like that to me my whole life. If he wants me to give him another pasting I will. I'm not scared of him. His number, though, that's something else. I wrote it down at break-time, but I still can't get it out of my head. It's a nasty death, and soon. And the feelings are so strong; they make me think things I don't want to. Like maybe I'm there when it happens. Maybe I'm the one holding the knife . . .

Even now, standing in the kitchen, leaning up against the bench, the sweat's breaking out on my skin, and I think I'm going to pass out. What if my number's the same as his? What if it wasn't his death I was feeling, it was mine? Not knowing my own number bothers me, more than anything. I've tried to see it. Done all the obvious things; looking in mirrors, reflections in windows, even in water. But nothing works. It has to be eye to eye and the only person in the world I can't look at . . . is me.

S'pose that's what really worries me about the twenty-sevens. There are so many of them, the chances are pretty high I'm one of them too. There are hundreds at school. There are thirteen in my tutor group.

'Wake up, Adam, I asked you a question.'

Nan's voice breaks through my thoughts and my mouth goes into action before my brain has time to stop it.

'Thirteen.'

Shit! Have I really said it out loud?

'Thirteen what, love?' Nan asks.

'Nothing. I was just thinking about something . . . from Maths.'

She narrows her eyes, and blows a plume of smoke up towards the ceiling. I've got to distract her, so I ferret in my bag and whip out the palm-net they gave me when I finally registered. I've been trying to use it in lessons, but I've never had my own computer before, Mum wouldn't let them in the house, so I'm way slower than everyone else. I could see people watching me, sniggering – a hick from the sticks.

Nan glances at it, but she don't seem interested. She's locked in on me and it'll take more than some freebie IT to knock her off target.

'You like Maths, do you?' she says. 'Like numbers?'

Do I like numbers? *Like them?* She's watching me now, and all of a sudden, I'm not sure what she's asking me. I've never told anyone about the numbers except Mum, and one teacher at school when I was little, before I knew what they were. Mum always said they were our secret, something special between me and her. And I kept it like that. I didn't tell. When she died, I thought that left just me knowing. I was on my own. Now I'm not so sure.

'I don't think I like numbers,' I say, carefully. 'I think they're important.'

'Yeah,' Nan says. 'Yeah, they are important.'

We look at each other for a minute and neither of us speaks. The radio's on – some news report about the government coming clean over the Kyoto targets being missed by miles – and next-door's dog is yapping away as usual, but the silence between us is electric.

'I know you're special, Adam,' she says, finally, and a shiver runs down my spine. 'I seen it in you, the day you were born.'

'What?'

'I saw, I see, a beautiful boy. They're there in you, your mum and your dad. Oh God, there's so much of my Terry in you. Sometimes, I swear I think he's here again . . . it's like he never . . .' She tails off. There's an extra shine to her eyes, and the rims are pink.

'What else, Nan?' I know there's something. She swallows hard, and looks deep into my eyes.

'Your aura, I've never seen nothing like it. Red and gold. My God, you're special. You're a leader. A survivor. There's courage, right through you. You're strong, you have spiritual strength. You've been put here for a reason, I swear it.'

I take a risk. I have to know.

'What about my number?'

She frowns.

'I don't see numbers, son. I'm not like you and your mum.'

So she does know.

'How do you know about them?'

'Your mum told me. I knew about her years ago, and then when she found out about you, she rang me up.'

Suddenly, I've got to tell her, tell her the thing I've been bottling up all summer.

'Nan – half the people in London are going to die next year. I'm not making it up. I've seen their numbers.'

She nods.

'I know.'

'You know?'

'Yeah, Jem told me about 2027. Warned me.'

My hands go up to the sides of my head. Nan knew! Mum knew! I'm shaking, but I'm not scared, I'm angry. How dare they keep this from me? Why leave me on my own with it?

'Why didn't you tell me? Why didn't she?'

The anger's fizzing through me now, in my arms and legs. I kick at the board under the kitchen cupboards.

'Don't do that!'

I want to smash something. I kick out again, and this time the board thunks down onto the floor.

'Adam! Stop it!'

Nan's on her feet now, coming towards me. She makes a grab for my arms. I try to shrug her off, but she's strong, much stronger than you'd think to look at her. We stand wrestling with each other for a few seconds. Then, quick as a flash, she lets go one of my arms and slaps me across the face.

'Not here!' she shouts. 'Not in my house! I won't have it!'

I come back to myself then, I see things like they're happening to someone else, a teenage boy grappling with an old woman in her kitchen, and I feel the shame spreading through me like a blush.

'I'm sorry, Nan,' I say. I rub my cheek where she got me. I don't know where to look, what to do with myself.

'Should think so,' she says, and she turns to put the kettle on. 'If you've calmed down, if you'll *listen*, then we can talk about it.'

'Okay,' I say.

'In fact you make the tea. I need a fag.'

She sits down and reaches for her packet, and her hand is shaking, just a little, as she draws a cigarette out and lights it.

When the tea's ready I sit down opposite her.

'Tell me, Nan,' I say. 'Tell me everything you know. About me and Mum and Dad. I've got a right . . .'

She's studying the table top or pretending to. She brushes a little bit of ash onto the floor, and then she looks up at me, blows a long trail of smoke out of the corner of her mouth and says, 'Yeah, you do have a right, and I s'pose now's the time.'

And she tells me.

Sarah

He's trying the door.
I hold my breath.

In the darkness, I can hear the handle turn, the scraping of metal on wood as the door pushes against the chair I left tipped up against it. There's a scuffling sound as He moves the door backwards and forwards, gently at first, then with more force. I can picture His face – confusion turning to anger – and I shift up further on the bed, sitting upright, knees up to my chin and I cross both sets of fingers.

The room falls quiet for a few seconds, and then He's there again. He can't believe it. He needs to check.

Then footsteps, and silence.

It worked! It fucking worked!

I hug my knees in closer and rock from side to side. I want to shout out, scream, dance, but I can't break the silence. I can't wake the others; Marty and Luke in the room next door, my mum further down the landing.

I should sleep now. It's safe to sleep. I uncurl my legs and slide them down under the duvet. I'm tired, but not sleepy, and I lie there for ages, triumphant and scared at the same time. I've won a battle, but the war's not over yet. Rain starts battering against the window.

I ache for sleep, eight hours of blankness, but when I do drift off there's no rest. I'm back in the nightmare that waits for me every night.

The flames are orange.

I'm being burnt alive. I'm trapped, penned in by rubble.

The flames are yellow.

The baby's screaming. We'll die here, me and her. The boy with the scarred face is here too. He's fire and flame himself, scarred, burnt, a dark shape in the thundering, crackling, spitting heat.

The flames are white.

And he grabs the baby, my baby, and he walks away and is consumed.

The room's still dark when I force myself awake. The back of my tee-shirt and my sheets are drenched. There's a date in my head, neon-bright, dazzling my eyes from the inside. The first of January 2027. I've never dreamt that before. It's new. He's brought it to me. The boy.

The boy at school *is* the boy in my nightmare. It's him. I know it is. He's found his way out of my head and into my life. How? How has he done that? It's bullshit. It's not real. Stuff like that doesn't happen.

I reach out next to me and switch on the light. I screw up my eyes until they adjust and then I see the chair wedged up against the door handle.

Of course stuff happens, I think, dully. Stuff happens all the time.

Adam

They were famous! My mum and dad. I never knew they were famous. For a couple of weeks in 2009 everyone in the country knew about them, was looking for them. 'Most wanted.' For something they didn't do – just wrong place, wrong time. And all because Mum could see the numbers, like me.

Nan's kept some of the cuttings from the papers – gives me chills looking at them. My mum and dad, so young, younger than me now, staring out of the front page. They were only kids when they had me. Well, Dad never even knew about me. He died before Mum knew she was pregnant.

If only I'd known about all this. I could've asked Mum, we could've talked about it . . . all she ever said to me about the numbers was that they were secret. I could never tell anyone their number. And the only person I ever did tell was her in that picture at school.

What the hell did that do to her? What must her last few years have been like, knowing? I've got part of the answer now. Next to my notebook, there's an envelope folded in half. When she's finished telling me Mum and Dad's story, Nan gives it me.

'She wanted you to have this. When the time was right. I reckon that's now.'

My name's written on the front in Mum's writing – I'd know it anywhere. I swear my heart stops for a second when I see it. I can't believe it's real. Something from Mum. Something for me.

And Nan's been holding on to it. What right had she . . .? The anger sparks up again.

'How long have you had this?' I say.

'She gave it to me a few weeks before she went.'

'Why didn't you give it to me? It's mine. It's got my name on it.'

'I told you,' she says slowly, like she's explaining something to an idiot, 'she asked me to keep it for you. For when you was ready.'

'And you'd know, would you? You'd know what was best?'

She looks me straight in the eye. She can feel the tension as much as I can and she's not backing down.

'Yeah, at least your mum thought so. She trusted me.'

I snort.

'I'm sixteen. I don't need you making decisions for me. You don't know nothing about me.'

'I know more than you think, son. Now, why don't you calm down for a minute and open that envelope?'

The envelope. I've almost forgotten that's what we're arguing about.

'I'm gonna read it on my own,' I say and I hold it up to my chest. Mine, not hers. She's disappointed, I can see that – she wants to know what's in it, nosy old cow. Then she sniffs loudly and reaches for another fag.

'Course,' she says. 'Course you do. Come and talk to me when you've done. I'll be right here.'

I take it up to my room and sit on the bed. My private space, a room of my own, except that it's not mine. I've only got a handful of my things with me. Everything else here is my dad's: a boy younger than me, a boy I never knew and who never knew about me. I'm inside a shrine, surrounded by his stuff. Nan never moved a thing when he died, and you could tell it hurt her to put me in here, but there was nowhere else I could go.

I put the envelope on my lap and stare at it. Mum's writing. Her hand held this envelope. Is there any of her left on it? I smooth my fingers across it. I want to read whatever's inside, but I also know that once I've read it, that'll be it. There'll be nothing else from her. It'll be like saying goodbye all over again.

I don't want it to end. I know it has already. I know she's gone, but I've got a little bit of her back now.

'Mum,' I say. My voice sounds strange, like it belongs to someone else.

I want her to be here, with me, so much.

And I open the envelope, and she is.

The instant I start reading, I can hear her voice, see her sitting propped up in bed, writing. Her hair's gone, and there's no weight on her at all any more. She's so thin you can't hardly recognise her face. But it's still her. It's still Mum.

'Dear Adam,
I'm writing this knowing you won't read it until after I've gone. I want to tell you so much, but it all comes down

to the same thing. I love you. Always have, always will.

I hope you remember me, but if you start to forget what I looked like, or sounded like, or anything, don't worry. Just remember the love. That's what matters.

I wish I was there to see you grow up, but I can't be, so I've asked Nan to look after you. She's a diamond, your Nan, so you be good for her, don't cheek her or nothing.

Adam, I need you to do something. I can't be there to keep you safe, so I'm telling you this now. Stay in Weston, or somewhere like that. Don't go to London, Adam. I seen the numbers when I was growing up. We're the same you and me – we see things that no-one should ever know. I told people, I broke my own rule and it was nothing but trouble. You mustn't tell. Not anyone. Not ever. It's trouble, Adam, trust me, I know.

London isn't safe. 112027. I seen it in tons of people when I was growing up. Find somewhere where the people have good numbers, Adam, and stay there. Don't go to London. Don't let Nan take you there, and keep her out too. Keep her safe.

I'm going to go now. I can't hardly bear to stop writing, to say goodbye. There aren't enough words in the world to tell you how much I love you. You're the best thing that ever happened to me. The best. Don't forget,
Love always,
Mum
xxxxxx'

A tear drips off the end of my chin and splashes onto the paper. The ink spreads out like a firework turning her kisses all blurry.

'No!'

I wipe the paper with my thumb, but that just makes it worse. I find an old tissue in my pocket and dab it dry, and all the time the tears keep pouring down my face. Then I put the letter on the end of the bed, out of harm's way and I let go.

I haven't cried for a long time, not since before she died. Now I can't stop. It's like a dam bursting – something bigger than me sweeping me away. My whole body's crying, out of control; great heaving sobs; tears and snot; noises I never knew I had in me. And then I curl up in a ball and I rock backwards and forwards, backwards and forwards, for I don't know how long 'til I slowly come to a stop. And there's nothing left. No more tears.

I look around me like I'm seeing the room for the first time, and I feel the anger back again, tingling in the tips of my fingers, pulsing right through me.

Don't go to London. Don't let Nan take you there.

I knew this was a bad place. I knew we shouldn't have come.

I slam out of the room and down the stairs. Nan's still in the kitchen. Cup of tea in front of her and a fag on.

'She never wanted us to come to London! She wanted us to stay in Weston! Did you know that? Did you? Did you?'

I'm leaning on the other side of the table, gripping it with both hands, gripping so hard my knuckles are white.

Nan puts her hand up across her forehead and rubs it. She shuts her eyes for a second, but when she opens them, they're defiant.

'She said something, yes.'

'She said something, and you still brought us here?'

'I did, but . . .' She thinks she can argue with me, justify herself. She's got to be kidding. Nothing she can say will make this better. She's been found out for the lying, selfish cow she is.

'When I said I didn't want to go! When Mum had said not to come!'

'Adam . . .'

'She trusted you!'

'I know, but . . .' She reaches her hand out towards the ashtray. Her fingers are trembling as she stubs out her fag. The dish is overflowing – stale, disgusting, like her. I reach forward too, pick the vile thing up and hurl it against the wall. It smashes when it hits the floor. Glass and ash spray out.

'Adam!' she screams. 'That's enough!'

But it's not enough. Not nearly enough.

I tighten my grip on the table and heave it over, sending it crashing down on its side by the sink, broken china and tea mixing with ash and glass.

'Jesus Christ! Stop it, Adam!'

'Shut up. Shut the fuck up!'

'Don't you dare . . .'

The ashtray's not enough. The table's not enough. It's not their fault anyway. It's hers.

And now I've got to get out of here. 'Cause I know what I want to do next and that's crossing a line. It's wrong. And I want to so much, but if I start . . . if I start, I might not stop.

'I hate you! I hate you!'

I'm out of the kitchen and through the lounge and out the front door before I can change my mind. The cold air hits me, and I stop for a minute to suck it in. But standing still's no good. There's too much energy charging through me, I'm too wound up, so I walk and then I run. And as I run it starts raining, icy drops stinging my face.

I'm not running away from her. I'm running away from what I might have done to her. It's better this way. Better for both of us if I keep on running and never go back.

Sarah

I won't be able to take much. He always gives me a lift to school, and He'll notice any extra bags. So it's only what I can get in my normal bag, and money. If I've got enough money with me, I can buy anything else I need.

They'll look at my account when I go. Ask the police or someone to see what I've been spending, where I've been. So cash is the thing. As much cash as I can find.

I've been pinching tenners out of my mum's purse for weeks now. One at a time, so she won't notice. I know Dad keeps cash in His study. I haven't had the nerve to go in there – it's His room, it smells of Him. Even when I know He's not in the house, won't be back for ages, I can't bring myself to do it.

Now, it's different. I'm going to go tomorrow. I take all the books out of my schoolbag – I'll manage without them – then I carefully fold up some underwear, my favourite tee-shirts, some trackie bottoms. I look at my jeans in the drawer. I really want to take a pair – they're all I wear normally, but even my favourites, the ones I've worn and washed 'til they've gone soft and floppy, won't do up now. No point taking things I can't wear.

I count up the cash I've got stashed away: eighty-five Euros, not enough. I know Marty and Luke have got some money. Can I steal from my brothers? I could – if they weren't in their rooms right now. I need more. It's going to have to be Dad's money.

He's out for the evening, entertaining some clients at dinner. Mum's watching TV in the sitting room. I pass by the doorway, and hesitate. There's another way, isn't there? I don't have to leave. I could go in there now, sit down next to her and tell her. She'd have to do something then, wouldn't she? Ring the police? Throw Him out? Or gather all our things up and take us somewhere, me and the boys?

Or would she tell me to shut up? Send me to my room for telling such wicked lies? Or shrug her shoulders, say that's just the way things are, the way He is?

At the back of my mind, I know that she already knows. How can she not know? But she doesn't know about the baby. Nobody does. And that's why I'm getting out. This baby's mine. He's never going to see it. He's never going to get His hands on it. It's mine, growing inside me. I'm going to keep it safe.

I'm not sure how far gone I am. My periods had been up the creek for ages, so I didn't notice that they'd stopped altogether. But all my clothes are so tight now I won't be able to go on hiding it for much longer. It's time to go.

I'm expecting the door to His study to be locked, but it isn't. The handle turns and the door opens smoothly. I take a step into the room and start to gag. Everything about the room speaks of Him: golfing prints on the wall, mahogany desk and chair. I almost lose my nerve, but I make myself go over to the desk. I try the drawers. They're all locked. Shit! He's probably got the key on Him, so that's that. If I tried to break the locks, He'd notice and the game would be up.

There's a fireplace in the study with a mantelpiece over the top. He's got family photos in frames arranged along it; happy smiling faces, the perfect family. The camera never lies. Does it?

There's one of me on my own, taken on holiday somewhere. The beach in Cornwall. I'm in a stripy swimming costume, blonde hair tumbling down onto my shoulders. I'm squinting at the camera because the sun's so bright, smiling straight at the lens. I loved my dad. He was my hero – a big man, strong, funny. He knew everything, could do everything. And I was His princess. I was seven in that picture, and I was twelve when He started visiting me at night.

What happened? Why did He start? Why couldn't life stay like it was in the picture – golden, sunny, innocent?

I reach forward and pick up the picture. It's a long time since I felt like the girl in the photo: we could be different people. I look into her eyes for a few seconds then hold her close, hugging the frame into my chest. I want to mother her. I want to keep her safe. It's too late for me, I think to myself, but not too late for the child inside me. We can start again – we can live life how it's meant to be.

Ahead of me, at eye level on the mantelpiece, there's a key. He keeps it behind my picture. I pick it up and put my photo back. I want to hang on to that picture desperately, want to take it with me, but if anything is different, if anything's out of place, He'll notice and He'll start asking questions. I can't risk it. I've got to be careful.

The key fits the desk drawers. His money's in the top one.

There are three rolls of notes, done up with rubber bands. Do I take them all and hope He doesn't look there later tonight or in the morning? My hand hovers over the open drawer. In the end, I just take one, the one at the back, so if He opens it, everything'll look just as it should be. He'll only find out something's wrong if He pulls the whole thing out.

I put the roll in my pocket, close the drawer, lock it and replace the key behind my photo.

'Goodbye,' I say to the girl in the photo. I close the study door behind me, and go upstairs. I put the money in the zipped pocket in my bag, and check through my things again.

Yes, it's all there. I'm ready.

Adam

'Find a partner and sit either side of a desk, facing each other. We're doing sixty-minute portraits. Come on, partner up!'

I'm back at school, of course. When I don't come home, Nan rings the police and reports me missing. I never thought she'd do that, but she does. They find me the next morning, take me down the station, fingerprint me, photograph me, take a DNA swab from my mouth and then chip me, a quick injection in the side of my neck. It's done before I even know it's happening.

'What the fuck? Fucking get off me!' But it's too late. It's there inside me now, a tiny microchip that will tell whoever wants to know everything about me.

'You can't do that! I haven't done nothing!'

'You've been reported missing. You're under eighteen. Not so easy to run away now. We can always find you.'

When Nan comes to pick me up, I don't speak to her. I can't even look at her. She tries to make the peace in the bus

38

on the way home.

'We both lost our tempers, and said things we shouldn't, but that's no reason to go off. I was worried about you. I didn't know where you was. We need to stick together, Adam. We've only got each other now . . .'

Only got each other. It's true, but I don't want her. She's not my mum. I hardly know her, and what I do know I don't like.

'Shall I tell you what they did to me?'

'Who?'

'The police. Shall I tell you what they did? They took my DNA, Nan. They chipped me. Just because they picked me up. Because you reported me missing.'

'Did they? I'm sorry, Adam, I didn't know they'd do that. Still, it won't matter if you keep your nose clean, will it?'

'It's what they do to dogs, Nan.'

'They're doing it to everyone, aren't they? Working their way through. It would have been your turn eventually, you just got yours early.'

I press my lips together to stop any more words coming out, and turn my head towards the window. There's no point talking to her, no point at all. She don't understand.

I come back to school because it's better than being at home with her.

There's a racket of scraping chairs as people swap places and get themselves organised. I stand up, ready to move, but nobody's trying to catch my eye. No one wants to be my partner. On the other side of the room, a girl is standing on her own: it's her – the girl with the dirty blonde hair. Sarah.

'Okay, you two, find a desk.'

Sarah looks up at me and it's like she's throwing knives

across the room. The look in her eyes is so hostile, pure hatred, well not pure 'cause it's mixed up with what I saw before – fear. Whatever she knows about me, or thinks she knows, it's something bad. Really bad.

'Not him, Miss,' she says. 'Don't make me sit with him.'

Some of the others turn round, sensing something's up, or about to be.

The teacher sighs.

'We haven't got time for this. Unless anyone else wants to swap, you need to work together. Anyone?'

They all shakes their heads, shuffle their chairs further in.

'Sit down, then.'

'I don't want to sit with him.'

'You'll either sit with him or I'm putting you on report.' That means a phone call home. It means detention. Sarah takes a moment to consider her options, then sits down at an empty desk. She's got a face like thunder. I pick up my bag, walk over and sit down opposite her. *Keep cool,* I'm thinking, *don't say anything stupid. Don't do anything weird. Just act nice and normal.*

'Hi,' I say, 'I'm Adam.'

'I know who you are,' she says, talking to the desk, but then her eyes flick up to me briefly, and I catch her number again.

And, again, it stops me in my tracks.

In an instant, the world has disappeared and it's only me and the moment of her death.

I can feel it in every nerve ending, every cell, in my mind as well as my body – there's this overwhelming sense of warmth, a peaceful journey out of this life and into another. I'm there with her, I know I am. My arms are around her, the scent of her hair's in my nostrils. I'm lying there, just being there – with her, for her. Suddenly I don't know if it's Sarah or my mum next to me. And I don't know if she's leaving or joining me. Which side am I on?

'Stop that. Stop staring.'

With a jolt I land back in Forest Green School.

'I've got to look at you to draw you,' I say.

'I don't see any drawing.'

I glance down at the desk. She's already drawn an oval outline and put soft marks where my eyes, nose and mouth are going to go.

'Right,' I say. 'Yes.' I fish in my bag for my pencil case, slide a piece of paper over the desk towards me and start to sketch the shape of her face. She has shoulder-length hair with a slight wave in it. Her eyes aren't large, but they are piercing, beautiful, fringed with stubby lashes. Her nose is straight, quite strong-looking, not a little turned-up button like some girls, but it don't spoil her face. The more I look at it, nothing could spoil it for me.

I try my best to draw what I see. I want her to like it. But it don't do her justice – you can see it's a girl, but it's not her. I keep rubbing bits out, trying again, but it just isn't happening. And when I look across at her picture, I stop altogether. She works like a real artist, with shading and lines to give her picture a shape. Somehow she's switched off her feelings. She's looking at me like I was an object.

The face she's drawn is a young man, not a boy. It's strong around the jaw and the cheekbones, and soft around the mouth. But it's the eyes that strike me most. They look out of the paper straight at me and nowhere else. She's done something so you can see the light reflected in them, and that gives them a spark, brings them to life. There's a person in there, someone who laughs and hurts and hopes. She's drawn what I look like, but, it's more than that – she's drawn who I am.

'Wow,' I say. 'That's amazing.'

She stops, only she don't look at me but at my drawing of her. I put my hand over the paper, trying to cover it up.

'Mine's rubbish,' I say. 'I wish I could draw you, your face, properly. I wish I could do it justice.'

Her eyes flick up then, but instead smiling or blushing even, she scowls.

'I just meant . . . I was just trying to . . .' I struggle to find the right words. 'I only meant that you've got a lovely face . . .'

I should have kept my mouth shut. It's like I've insulted her. She looks away and presses her lips together like she's stopping herself from saying something.

'. . . and you've done a brilliant job with me. You've made me look . . . well, you've made me look . . .'

'. . . beautiful,' she says. She's looking back at me now, and even though she's frowning, she's holding my eyes with hers and suddenly I'm full of her number again, the warmth and the peace of it. It's me and her, only me and her.

Then she does something amazing.

'I don't understand,' she says and her voice is quiet and upset, like she's talking to herself, and she reaches across the table and gently holds her hand up to my right cheek. My mouth falls open with shock and when I breathe out spit gathers at one corner and catches the edge of her thumb.

'Sarah,' I whisper.

She looks deeper into me, and she opens her mouth to say something back . . . and then someone at the back of the class wolf-whistles and she jerks her hand away. I look round and the whole class is watching.

I look back to Sarah for some help, but she's switched off again. She's putting her pencils away in a pencil case, gathering up her bag, blushing furiously. The bell rings for the end of the lesson and everyone starts to move.

'Finish your pictures at home for this week's homework!' the teacher shouts over the noise.

I put my things in my bag and scrape back my chair.

'Sarah,' I say again, but when I look up there's only an empty chair. She's left her pencil case and her paper behind, and she's gone.

Sarah

There are 20,000 CCTV scanners in London, unblinking eyes watching the streets twenty-four hours a day. They'll follow you, photograph you, read your chip, log you: who, where, when. I used to think it would be easy to disappear, just walk away and get lost in the crowd, but when you try it, you find out it's almost impossible. Almost.

I'm feeling confident when I walk out of school at the end of the day. I've got clothes, money. I told Mum and Dad I'd be going to camera club after school. They were pleased – a sign that I was joining in. I bought myself an extra hour.

I go straight to the Learning Resource Centre and into the public toilet there. I lock myself in a cubicle, take off my school uniform and change into my own clothes. I was going to leave the uniform – I'll never need it again – but at the last minute I stuff it back in my bag. I've got so few clothes with me, I can use them as extra layers. Two minutes later, I'm out on the street again. A bus is coming down the road. I run to the stop and get on, find a seat at the back and sit there, looking out of the window.

I'm not too bothered where the bus is going, only that it's taking me away and faster than I could walk. My heart's beating hard in my chest, so I close my eyes for a minute and try to calm down. I've done it! I've got away! *We've* got away. We aren't safe yet, but every minute, every second we're moving further away – from home, from school, from *Him*, from Adam.

Adam.

Sitting so close to him, drawing him, looking at him, really looking, I was more certain than ever that he was my nightmare boy. But close to, he isn't frightening. He's weird, yes, he's twitchy and he can't sit still, and he has this way of looking at you, as though he's seeing right into you. But instead of freaking me out, I wanted to look back.

In my nightmare, I'm terrified. He's there with me, in the middle of the flames, and he takes my most precious thing, my baby, takes her out of my arms and walks with her into the fire. But Nightmare Adam is scarred, one side of his face is disfigured and hideous. The Adam at school has the most beautiful skin – smooth, warm, cappuccino skin. When I touched it, when I reached across and touched his face, it felt just the way it looked. Perfect. He has the perfect face, and for a crazy moment I imagine my face near to his, his eyes looking into my eyes, his lips brushing my lips . . .

The bus jolts and I open my eyes. I'm looking directly at a scanner on the ceiling. Shit! Of course! They all have scanners. I've got to get off. Now. I ring the bell and go and stand by the door. *Come on, come on.* The next stop seems like miles. Finally, we grind to a halt and I'm out through the gap in the doors and walking as fast as I can. I'm trying not to run – people will notice that and remember. There are scanners every hundred metres or so along this road, and a big public information screen on the corner. They put up photos of missing people on those screens. I've seen them before. I never thought they could be people like me – people who didn't want to be found. Will my face be up there tomorrow? As soon as I can, I duck down a side-street.

As I'm walking, I'm thinking. *How am I going to do this?* If I go to a hotel or a B&B, they're going to ask for ID. I need a false one, or I need to go where no-one asks for ID. I need to slip under the radar, disappear.

It's not the sort of thing you can do on your own, without contacts.

I'm suddenly aware of my situation; a sixteen-year-old girl, from a gated community, pregnant, alone in a strange part of London carrying two thousand Euros in cash. What the hell was I thinking? How did I think I was going to manage?

I glance at my watch. 16.40. In about ten minutes, my mum will start wondering where I am. I've got no time! At the end of the street, a train rattles past. I could go further on a train. If I could get on one without being seen, I could be fifty, a hundred, two hundred miles away this evening, anywhere in the UK. I've got the money. I could do it.

That's it. I need to get to Paddington.

Not knowing exactly where I am doesn't help. I'll have to risk it – go back to the main road and get another bus. Mum won't call the police until at least six, will she? And by then, I could be away.

Yes, Paddington's the place.

Back on the main road I don't have to wait long for a bus. I pull my collar up even though I know it won't make a difference, and keep my face turned to the floor. I make it to

Paddington station, buy a bottle of Coke and try and suss out where the scanners are, find a place where I can look at the departure board, work out where to go, but not be seen. But of course I am seen. As I check it all out, I notice that I'm being watched.

A bloke comes up to me.

'You new round here? Need somewhere to stay?'

'No,' I say, 'I'm fine. I'm waiting for a friend.'

He looks me up and down and smiles.

'I can be your friend.'

He's standing too close to me now. He's in my face.

'No,' I say again. 'I'm all right.'

'Come on,' he says, 'it's not a nice place to be on your own.' I can smell him now, cheap aftershave fighting with the booze on his breath.

'Fuck off and leave me alone,' I say, the words braver than I feel. I walk across the concourse, not thinking about the scanners any more, just wanting to get away from him.

I need to buy a ticket, get on a train, get away from here. I'm not sure where, that's all. Where I should go. There's a girl standing near the ticket office. She's not much older than me. Leather jacket, studs all round the edge of her ear. She's watched me walking over, making my getaway from the sleaze that was chatting me up.

I stop and take a swig of Coke.

'They're sick, aren't they?' the girl says.

'Who?'

'The blokes here. Think they can hit on you just 'cause you're on your own. Wankers.'

'Yeah,' I say. I hold the bottle out towards her.

'Ta,' she says, and takes a swig.

'You on your way somewhere?'

'Yeah, out of London.'

'Somewhere good?'

'Anywhere.'

'They'll ask for ID when you buy a ticket, you know.'

'Oh.' I didn't know.

'If you need somewhere to go, I've got a flat. You could stay for a couple of days, 'til you get sorted. There's the sofa . . .'

'Really?'

She nods.

'Yeah, course. Been where you are myself. Know what it's like. You need somewhere to get started. Somewhere safe.'

I don't know her. I don't know where her flat is. But I like her, her attitude. She's the same as me, she said it herself.

'Well, just for a couple of days . . .'

'Just for a couple of days.'

She hands the Coke bottle back to me.

'Meg, by the way,' she says.

'Sarah.'

'Come on,' she says. 'Let's get out of this meat market.'

And I follow her through the station. We're swallowed up in the crowd, hundreds, thousands of people around us, but it's okay because I'm not on my own any more.

I've got a contact, someone who knows the ropes, and I've got somewhere to go.

Adam

She's disappeared.

I go to school the next day really psyched. I'm going to find her and talk to her. I can't wait. But she don't turn up, not that day or the next one. I start asking people about her – other kids in her tutor group, but no one knows where she is. No one knows much about her at all.

It's doing my head in. The connection between us – that electricity – it's all I can think about. Lying in bed at night, I feel her hand on my face and I break out into a sweat. I didn't dream it. It was real, just like the ache in my balls is real when I think about seeing her, holding her, touching her . . .

It's so unfair. The only person in that school to get me, to see me for who I am, and now she's gone.

'Where's your girlfriend gone?'

'One look was enough, then she fucked off!'

'Aah, he's all on his own.'

I don't like what they're saying, their stupid, ignorant

comments, but I try to ignore them. They're not important. Nothing here is important.

I sit in lessons and it just feels like I'm wasting time – the teachers don't know squat. They spend their days wittering on about history and geography, literature and science, when I know everything's going to come crashing round our ears in a few months' time. It's all words, just words – plate tectonics, global warming, peak oil, peak water – I can't see how it connects with what's happening outside, in London, now. Something's already started out there, something that's going to change everything, kill half the people in this room. School's got nothing to say about it.

I need to find Sarah. She knows something, I'm sure of it. She's out there somewhere, and I'm not going to find her sitting here. The teacher's put up a map of the world on the front screen, telling us to copy the shapes of the earth's plates onto the base map she's sent to our palm-nets.

I reach down into my bag to get my palm-net out, and I pull out Sarah's pencil case instead. I picked it up after she ran out of the art room, thought I'd keep it for her, give it back to her the next day with her picture of me. I unzip it and look inside. There's only pencils and pens and rubbers, but it feels like I'm looking at something private. I go to zip it up again and something catches my eye – there's writing on the inside, her name and address printed clearly in black biro. I run my thumb across it, like I did with my mum's letter, hoping to pick up something of her. I read it a couple of times, and the words stick in my head. All the rest of the lesson, I'm running over and over them, until by the time the bell rings, I know what I'm going to do.

Instead of going home, I check out Sarah's address on my palm-net, and it sat-navs me there. It's more than six kilometres to Hampstead and it takes me just over an hour, but I don't mind the walk. It feels like the right thing to do. It feels right to be doing something.

I start to get second thoughts when I reach her neighbourhood. It's all detached houses, big ones, with electric gates. Is this really where Sarah lives? I know she comes to school in a posh car, I've heard people talking about it, but this is something else. I can understand why she'd want to stay here instead of coming to school. If I lived somewhere like this, I'd never leave.

Number six is hidden behind a high brick wall with two scanners perched on the top. The gate is metal, solid, so you haven't got a clue what's behind there. There's an intercom grill with a button under it. It's the only way I'm going to get in, so I press the button. A woman's voice comes through almost straight away.

'Yes?'

I clear my throat.

'I'm here to see Sarah. I'm a friend from school.'

'Which school?'

'Forest Green.'

There's a long pause. Then the gate starts swinging open. I take it that's an invitation to go in and start crunching up the gravel drive. The house takes my breath away. It's painted white, with big pillars propping up a porch at the front. There's a black Mercedes parked by the door, next to a red Porsche. Jesus! Her family isn't just loaded, they're super-rich!

The front door opens as I get close, but it's not the woman who spoke to me on the intercom, there's a man standing there. He's a big bloke, tall, looks taller because he's standing in the doorway, and I'm at the bottom of the steps. His shoes are black slip-ons, shiny and expensive. He's wearing dark suit trousers and a crisp white shirt, with the sleeves rolled up. He's yanked his tie loose around his neck. He looks at me like I'm something his cat's just dragged in and I clock his number. 112027. Another one. Sarah's dad.

He don't ask me in.

'You know something about Sarah?' he says. 'Have you seen her?'

So she's not here either. She's run off.

'No,' I say, 'I haven't seen her for days. I thought she might be here. I wanted to talk to her.'

'Talk to her?'

'Yeah, we're . . . we're friends.' It sounds lame as I say it.

'She's friends with *you*?' He don't believe me or he don't want to. I don't like him, don't like his tone.

'Yeah,' I say, 'we sit together in Art.'

'And you like her, do you?' What's he getting at?

'Yeah. Like I said, we're friends.'

He steps out of the doorway and starts down the steps towards me.

'She was only there a few days,' he says, 'and now she's run away. What did you do to her? At school. What did you say?'

'Nothing. I didn't say nothing. We were just friends. That's all.'

I'm picking up on his body language and I know I should get out of here. I start backing off, but I'm not quick enough. A hand shoots round my neck and pins me up against one of the pillars. He leans in so his face is close to mine, puts his weight into his hand so I start to choke.

'You touched her, didn't you? You got your filthy hands on her, my daughter.'

'No.' I force the words out. 'No, I never.'

'You couldn't keep your hands off her, could you? You're disgusting. Disgusting.'

His number's in my face now. He's a twenty-seven, but not like the others, there's something different about his death – it comes from inside him, pain radiating through his body, shooting down his arm, crushing him.

'Gary? What is it?'

Over his shoulder, I can see a woman just inside the door-way. Must be Sarah's mum. She's in her dressing gown, with bare feet.

'What is it? Have they found something?'

Her dad loosens his grip.

'No,' he calls back to her. 'It's nothing.'

I twist away from him, holding my hands up to my neck, my chest heaving as I try to get some air.

'Nothing,' he says. He watches me stumble down the drive and break in to a run. The gates are still open, thank God, and I'm out of there and running down the road. I don't stop until I'm shot of that whole hateful estate and back to a place where there are shops and cafes and houses that open onto the street.

I go into the first paper shop I find and buy a Coke, open-ing it as soon as I've paid.

''Ere, not in the shop! Take it outside,' the guy behind the till shouts at me. I take no notice. The sugar in the drink is hitting my bloodstream, and my shakes are starting to go. God, I need this. I thought he was going to kill me. What a wanker! Okay, he's worried about his daughter, but that's not normal, going off on one like that, nearly choking the breath out of me.

I drain the can and hold it out to the shop-guy. He tips his head towards the recycling bin and hands over my five cents, like it was killing him to do it.

'Thanks, mate,' I say and I wander out of the shop and start heading for home. My legs are tired and slow, but my mind's still racing. She's not at home. She's not at school. Where the hell is she?

Sarah

It's a two-bedroom flat, and six girls sharing, including me. It's okay. They're friendly enough, show me a corner in one of the bedrooms where I can put my bag.

Meg introduces me to the others, then takes me into the kitchen and cooks us both egg and oven chips. I'm starving. I can't eat in the mornings, but by the afternoon, I'm ravenous.

'One good meal a day,' she says. 'Other than that, it's the rock-chick diet – fags, vodka and . . . well, you know.' The thought turns my stomach. I've never drunk alcohol, never smoked, and I'm even less likely to now.

I must have pulled a face because Meg says, 'You'll have to have a drink. Everyone drinks. It's the only way to survive here. Not today, though, not on your first night.'

'Survive? It doesn't look that bad . . .'

Her face doesn't move a muscle, but there's something, a flicker behind her eyes. What's going on here? The front door opens as a man lets himself into the flat and breezes into the kitchen. He's not very tall, a few centimetres taller than me, but he's thick-set, with muscular arms bulging under the cloth of his denim jacket. He's got a cigarette in one hand and car keys in the other.

'All right?' he says to Meg, and leans forward to kiss her on the lips. At the last minute, she tilts her head and gives him her cheek instead. 'Don't be like that, you silly bitch,' he says, and the coldness in his voice makes the hairs on the back of my neck stand up. Then he notices me and his body language changes. 'Who's this?' he says, and now his whole focus is on me.

'This is Sarah. She needs a place to stay.'

'Right, right.' He looks me up and down, then holds out his hand. 'Shayne. Welcome to our humble home.'

I take his hand – it would be rude not to, and I'm not sure enough of myself to be rude to him, yet – and we shake. He holds on just a little bit too long for comfort.

'Bet there are people looking for you,' he says.

I shrug.

'Don't worry. You'll be quite safe here. No one's going to rat on you. I'll need a contribution to the rent though. Not tonight. First night's free. Tomorrow.'

'Oh,' I say. 'Okay.' I've got my money – he hasn't said how much, but I'm only going to stay for a day or two and it's not going to be more than fifty Euros, is it. Or a hundred?

The girls are getting ready to go out, doing their hair and make-up. Shayne's in and out of the bedrooms. I'd tell him to get lost if I was them, but none of them do. Meg settles down on the sofa and pats it, inviting me to sit next to her.

'Not going out?' I ask.

'No, not tonight. I'll stay in with you.'

'Thanks,' I say.

She gets out a tin of weed and some papers and starts rolling a joint. We watch the telly, and when Shayne comes back into the lounge, she passes the joint to him and he stands at the side, smoking. He's looking at us, not at the telly. Then he looks at his watch, a big, flashy gold thing.

'Come on, girls!' he shouts. 'Time to go.'

The others all start filing out of the flat. Shayne's the last to leave.

'Vinny will be round in a bit. You're all right to see to him, aren't you?' he asks Meg.

'Sure.'

He steps forward, hands her a wad of cash. She stuffs it into her bra.

'Okay, see you later, girls,' he says, and then he winks at Meg and gives her the thumbs up.

The door closes behind him.

'He seems . . . nice,' I say. 'Taking everyone out.'

She snorts, reaches down to the floor beside her, grabs a bottle of vodka and takes a swig.

'He's a dick. But he's less of a dick than some of them. Here . . .' she holds the bottle out to me.

'No thanks,' I say.

'Go on.'

'No, it's all right, I don't drink.'

'Some of this? It's the good stuff.' She wafts the joint under my nose.

'No. Thanks.'

Meg looks at me, and her face goes softer. She reaches out and smoothes my hair around my face.

'How old are you?' she asks.

'Eighteen,' I say. She smiles.

'How old are you really?'

'Sixteen.'

'Go home, Sarah. Go home before it's too late.'

'I left home for a reason.'

'Yeah, we all did, but this isn't any better, trust me. I'll help you. I'll give you some money to get a taxi or whatever.'

'It's all right. I've got money . . .' Her eyes go a little bit wider. She holds her finger up to her lips.

'Don't tell anyone. Don't even tell me. I hope it's hidden, because they're a bunch of thieving cows here.'

'It's in my . . . I'd better check.' I left the bag in one of the bedrooms. I jump up and go and fetch it. The zip's open. Someone's been through it. The money's gone, of course. All of it. Every last note.

'Shit! Someone's had it. Will you help me get it back?'

She shakes her head.

'It's gone. You won't see that again. If you get money, keep it on you.' She pats her chest, where she stashed the money Shayne gave her.

'But it's one of the girls, or Shayne. He was in and out of the bedrooms, wasn't he? People can't just take stuff. It's mine!'

'It's gone. There's your first lesson. Hard, innit? Let's hope it wasn't Shayne, 'cause he'll have seen this.' She pulls my school shirt and tie out of the bag.

'Why?'

'He'll make you wear it tomorrow. He can charge double for a kid in a school uniform.'

Tomorrow. Shayne wants some rent money, but some bitch has stolen mine. How am I going to get money? How the hell am I . . . then Meg's words register.

They're going to charge for me. Tomorrow.

'The girls,' I say, 'they've not just gone out on the town,

have they?'

She has another swig out of the bottle.

'No,' she says, 'they're out working. I should be too, but Shayne's given me the night off. Wants me to keep an eye on you.'

Keep an eye on me. Make sure I don't run away. Keep me there until tomorrow. Tomorrow. Oh God.

'Meg,' I say, 'I can't . . . I can't do what the other girls are doing.'

I feel sick at the thought of it. It's what I'm running away from. I'm never going to let anyone do that to me again. I'm not going to let it happen. I'm not . . .

She reaches out to me again. Her hand's on my hair, stroking, reassuring.

'Sure you can. Everyone gets nervous the first time, but it's okay. Have some vodka, have some weed or whatever, you'll be fine.'

'No, I mean, I *can't* . . . I'm pregnant.'

She sits up in the chair, starts to frown, then tips her head back and laughs.

'Oh, Jesus! I'm losing my touch. I never even noticed. How far gone are you?'

'I dunno.' I sit up and smooth my top over my swollen belly.

'Oh Christ, look at you! Five months? Six? That's it, I'm gonna get you out of here.'

'Won't you get in trouble?'

'Yeah, there'll be trouble, but I don't care. Even I can't send a lamb like you to the slaughter.'

'But no one would want to . . . with me . . . would they?'

She unwinds her legs and gets up off the sofa.

'Oh yeah, they'd want to, all right. There are some sick

fucks out there, and Shayne knows them all. Are you sure you can't go home?'

I shake my head. Whatever happens, however bad it gets, I'm not going back there. She comes over to me then, crouches down and puts her arms round me.

'We'll find you somewhere. Somewhere safe,' she murmurs into my ear.

The doorbell rings. Meg pulls away from me, and the make-up round her eyes is smudged. She drags her finger under each eye, blinks and sniffs hard.

'Look at me. Soft, aren't I? This'll be Vin. Stay here.'

She goes to the door. I hear two voices talking, hers and a man's, for quite a long time, but I can't hear what they're saying. Then Meg comes back into the room.

'This is Vinny,' she says. 'He says you can go with him.'

The man behind her steps forward. He's tall and gangly, eyes bulging in his skull-like head.

I don't know what to say, what to do. I don't know who to trust. I thought Meg was okay. Turns out she was recruiting for a pimp. Now, who's this?

'It's all right,' Meg says, 'he won't hurt you. I'd trust him with my life. I *do* trust him with my life. Every day.' They exchange a quick smile, and then she puts her arm through his and leans her head on his shoulder. 'Sarah, he won't hurt you. I wouldn't do that to you.' *Wouldn't you?*

Vinny ruffles Meg's hair, then disentangles himself from her.

'You can stay in our squat,' he says. 'No strings. Nothing. Shayne won't touch you there. No police. Nothing like that.'

'Why? Why would you do that?'

He looks down at the floor, shuffles his feet a bit.

'Meg told me. About the baby. You need somewhere to

go – I've got somewhere. It's simple.'

I'm pretty sure it's not that simple, but I know what will happen if I stay here. Let's face it, my options are limited. So I take a chance.

'Okay,' I say.

'Are you having a drink, Vin?' Meg asks. 'Stay and have a drink with me.'

He looks at his watch, shakes his head.

'Better get off, darlin'. If we're going, we'd better go. Okay?' he says to me.

'Okay,' I say.

Meg gives me another hug on the way out.

'Take care,' she says, and she pats my stomach. It's the first time anyone's done that, apart from me, patted the baby. It makes everything seem real. There's someone growing inside me, a new person. The reality of it, what it means, makes me almost dizzy.

'You all right?' asks Vinny, as I stand still, swaying a little.

'Yeah,' I say. I take a deep breath. 'Yeah, I'm all right. Let's go.'

Adam

Sometimes I think I made her up. Sarah. In my head, she's so perfect – her face, her eyes. I close my eyes and I can feel that moment when her fingers touched my face. It's like a dream, but it's real. I know it's real, because I wrote it all down as soon as I got home that day.

It's here in my book, her number and everything else I can remember about her. She's got a whole page to herself. I look at it every day, but it don't help. It don't bring her back.

It's been weeks now since she disappeared. Nearly a month.

I go out on the streets looking for her. She's got to be somewhere. I ought to have a picture of her, so I can show people, ask around, but I haven't. All I've got is a memory.

I don't like being where there's lots happening. Normally I try to steer clear of people, keep my head down, avoid eye contact, but this is different. I make myself go into crowds. I move through them or I stand and watch, scanning the faces that go past. Everywhere I go, I'm being watched too.

It don't usually take the police long to find me and move me on. And all the watching and waiting and hassle don't bring me any closer to Sarah. They just bring me more numbers.

Everyone has a number. Everyone has a death.

Gasping, shrieking, shocks and pain; pain in my legs and arms; pain gripping my head; pain through my whole body. Metal slicing through me; a weight on my chest that's so heavy I can't fight it; blood flooding out of me, unstoppable; lungs that won't work, battling for breath that won't come. I feel all the deaths. They flash through me, leaving traces behind. Each one batters me. Each one shocks and weakens me.

I write them down, trying to let every single death or group of deaths disappear out of my mind and into my book. That used to work, but it don't any more, and I can't take more than a couple of hours at a time. After that, my head's too full. I need to get away, away from other people, their stories, their ends.

'Bloody hell, Adam, you look rough. Where've you been?'

As soon as I walk through the door Nan starts pecking away at me.

'Where've you been? Where do you go? Who've you been with?'

I wish I had somewhere else to go, but this is it now. Home. Or what passes for it. A little box with two people in it who shouldn't be together. I brush past her, head up the stairs to my room and close the door. It's what I want, what I need – a closed door, no more faces, no more eyes, no more deaths.

I lie on my bed or I sit on the floor, but my mind's buzzing and I'm drumming a rhythm on the bed-frame with my fingertips or my leg's twitching, twitching, twitching. I can't just sit here and wait. I need to do something.

I get my book out and flick through the pages. Places and numbers and deaths. I go over and over them. And twenty-sevens everywhere. What's going to happen here? What's going to happen to London that's going to kill so many people? Some places the twenty-sevens are one in every four, others one in three. How many people are there in London? Nine million? Can three million people only have ten weeks to live? Am I one of them?

The deaths are violent; broken bones and backs, heads caved in. The sorts of deaths that happen when buildings collapse, or blow up, or get hit by something.

It's got to be something like that, 'cause if it was an illness – flu or plague or something – the deaths would be spread out, wouldn't they? It wouldn't all just be in a few days. And I wouldn't feel what I feel when I see the numbers – I'd be hot and weak and exhausted. Wouldn't I?

I get it into my head there's a pattern, if I could just see it. A pattern in the numbers. They're trying to tell me something. Then I get to thinking that my notebook is just the start – I could be doing things with this information. I've got places. I've got dates. I've got ways of dying. Maybe I could plot them on a map. I fetch Nan's A-Z from the lounge. She pokes her head round the kitchen door when she hears me, starts to say something, but I blank her, grab the book and crash back up the stairs.

It's only small, the A-Z, and it's difficult to see the middle of the pages. I start with the maps showing the roads round here and tear them out. They don't come cleanly, so when I put the pages together on my desk there are bits missing in the middle. I get my pencil case out of my bag and start working through my notebook. I start off by doing a dot for each person, but the map's so small that by the time I've put ten dots on it, it's just a blobby mess. I know it's rubbish, but I carry on for a bit longer, then I sit back, look at what I've done, put both hands on the pages, crumple them up and chuck them across the room. It's hopeless.

My palm-net's on the desk. That's only small too, but I've used it in lessons and for homework, and it's got tons of apps. There must be one that would help me with this. If only Mum had let me have a computer . . . She didn't want the internet in the flat, see. She always said it was 'full of lies.' Now I realise it must have been 'cause she wanted to keep the truth from me. If I'd known about her and Dad, I could have asked so many questions. Coulda, shoulda, woulda . . . no point going over it now.

I pick up the palm-net, fire it up, and go and sit on the bed, propped up against my pillows. The front page comes up: 'Welcome, Adam, to the Forest Green network. You have four assignments outstanding – for details of tasks and dead-lines, click here.' I ignore the message and start exploring the apps. There's loads of functions, including databases. I'm sure that's what I need. And the only way to find out is to try.

When you play around with it, it's pretty easy. To start with, you just make a big list, with different categories. Once you've got that you can search or put them in a different order. I start inputting the stuff from my book. And then I stop.

'Welcome, Adam, to the Forest Green network.'

If I'm on the school network, does that mean that every-thing I do on here can be seen? I can hear Mum's voice again, 'You mustn't tell. Not anyone. Not ever.'

Shit!

'Delete all.'

Enter.

'Are you sure you want to delete this database?'

Yes. Enter.

It's gone.

I switch the palm-net off and throw it to the end of the bed. Bloody thing. They only want us kids all connected up so they can keep tabs on us. Maybe Mum was right: better to have nothing to do with it. But I was on the right track with a database, I'm sure of it.

There's a laptop sitting on the desk the other side of the room. Retro-looking, it must have been Dad's. Would a six-teen-year-old computer still work? I lever myself off the bed and go over to it, wipe my sleeve across the top to get rid of the dust, open it up and press the button.

The last person to press it was Dad. Nan called him Terry. Mum called him Spider. He was fifteen the last time he did this. Had he met Mum by then? Perhaps she was here, with him, in this room.

The screen lights up and music starts blasting out of the speakers either side of it on the desk.

'You are not alone. I am here with you . . .' It's a high, pure voice that sends a chill through me. Michael Jackson. He died the same year as my dad. Is this what he was listening to, the last time he was here? I thought he was tough, my dad, a bad boy. This is sentimental stuff, it gets to you. I close my eyes and listen to the end of the track. What would my life be like now if he was here? I wish he was here, or Mum, or someone.

I wish I wasn't in this on my own.

Sarah

There's a man in my room. He's kneeling down by my mattress – he's got his hand on my shoulder. It's Him, He's here. I don't want this any more.

I lash out and my fist makes contact with his chin.

'Ouf! Christ, what are you doing?'

It's not the voice I was expecting. It's younger, higher pitched. It sounds familiar.

'Sarah, it's me. It's Vinny.'

I can't be at home because the bed's on the floor, the window's in the wrong place. And suddenly I remember Vinny leading me through the back streets and into this place, this squat, and up some stairs to the top of the house. He showed me this room; there was a mattress on the floor, nothing else, and said, 'This can be yours, if you want it.' I looked at the empty room – floorboards, sheet pinned up against the window – and in spite of everything, my heart lifted. My room, my space, mine.

'Vinny,' I say out loud. 'What are you doing here?'

'You were shouting out, screaming. I thought you were being murdered in your bed.'

My eyes are getting used to the light now, soft yellow streetlight coming through the gaps at the edge of the window sheet. I sit up. Vinny moves off his knees and sits with his back against the wall next to the bed.

'You all right, then?' he asks.

'Nightmare,' I say. 'Sorry I made a noise.'

''S all right,' he says. 'I wasn't asleep, but some of the others are. What's it about, your nightmare?'

'Fire,' I say.

'Fire and brimstone?'

'I dunno, what's brimstone?'

'Not sure, the stuff you find in hell.'

'That's about right then, but it's not hell, it's here.'

'Here?'

'London. The city's going to burn, and I'm in it, and the baby . . .'

'That's heavy.'

'Mmm . . . there's someone else too. He takes her away from me. He takes her into the fire.'

'Shit.'

We sit in silence for a minute. I'm still in that zone – half-asleep, half-awake – when your dreams feel real.

'I've met him,' I say. 'The devil in my nightmare. He's real.'

'Bloody 'ell.'

Vinny shuffles a bit closer and puts his arm round me. Makes me think, *Here we go; this is what he really wants. No strings? There are always strings.* I must have reacted, frozen up or something, because he moves his arm away again.

'It's all right,' he says, 'I'm not after anything.'

'Why are you letting me stay here then? I can't pay you.'

He sighs then, a long breath out into the soft, quiet air of the room and I wonder if he's just buying some time, thinking of a good line. But when he speaks, it's not like that. He doesn't look at me, just stares ahead.

'I had a sister, few years ago,' he says. 'She got pregnant, like you, left home. She asked for help, went to a doctor, but they turned her away. They turn everyone away now, don't they? Unless there's something wrong with the baby. Doesn't matter if the girl can't cope. Doesn't matter if she's desperate, like Shelley was. So she got an abortion in some back-street dive, died a few days afterwards. We never knew until the hospital rang us.'

His words hang there in the room, with us. I wonder how many people he's ever told. I wonder if I'm the only one.

'Vinny, I'm sorry.'

'Not your fault.'

'No, but . . .'

'It's not your fault, and it's not my fault. But I miss her. So you've got a place to stay as long as you like. And when we've got food, you've got food, and when I've got a bit of spare cash, you can have some, for the baby.'

I'm glad it's so dark in here. He won't be able to see the tears welling up.

'Thanks, that'd be . . . that'd be great.'

'I might be able to get some stuff, baby things, anyway. If you're not fussy where it comes from.'

'Why? What are you talking about?'

'Better if you don't know. But that's what I'm good at, see. Supplying. I'll get you some things.'

The baby's awake inside me, moving around, stretching her arms and legs trying to get more space.

'Do you want to feel her? The baby? Here . . .'

I take his hand and place it on my stomach. For a couple of seconds there's nothing and then she kicks.

'Oh, man . . . that is awesome.'

'I know. When it started it was just a little fluttering feeling, but it's way more than that now.'

'Is it a boy or a girl? In your nightmare, you said "her".'

'Did I?' It dawns on me then that he's right. 'I suppose I did.'

'So it's a girl, is it?'

'I've not had any tests, but, yeah, I do know. I do know – it's a little girl.' I hold my stomach with both hands, imagine holding her in my arms.

'That's it, then. I'll get pink stuff.'

'Vinny, that's so old. Blue for a boy, pink for a girl.'

'Oh.' He sounds disappointed, crushed.

'It's all right,' I say, 'you can get pink. I don't mind.'

Adam

There's no answer in the numbers. They are what they are. The only thing they tell me is a lot of people are going to die in London next January. Something happens on the first that kills people and they keep dying for days afterwards.

I type everything in my book into Dad's computer when the electricity's there to let me. The supply in London is shit, seems it's normal to lose it for a couple of hours and be sitting in the cold and the dark. But all I end up with is a list. It'd take someone a lot cleverer than me to sort this out, a university professor, a teacher. A teacher. Could I go to someone at school? What about a bright kid – there are people who love this stuff, computers, figures, statistics, aren't there?

The next few days I look round school for someone who could help. But to get them to help, I'd have to tell them what it was all about. I'd have to break the rules: *You mustn't tell. Not anyone. Not ever.*

I print out the database, but only the places and the dates, nothing else.

I decide to go where the nerds hang out. I've seen on the noticeboard there's a Maths club in the lunchbreak, so I head there. When I walk in the classroom, it's like walking into a saloon in the Wild West. They all stop what they're doing and look up, even the teacher. She's quite young. She's got a shirt on and a long, hippyish skirt.

'Hello?' she says. She smiles and I smile back without thinking and catch her eye. She's a twenty-seven. I start to lose my nerve. I must remember not to look at people. This is going to be hard enough.

'Hi,' I say.

'Are you coming in?'

'Um . . . dunno. S'pose.'

'We're doing calculus today.'

Calcu-what?

'Right. Um . . . come to the wrong place, actually. Sorry.' I back out of the room. Damn, damn, damn. There was enough brain-power in there to fuel the National Grid.

I go back the next day.

'Yes?' the teacher says.

'I need help with a problem.' Some of them start to snigger. 'A problem with Maths.'

'You should talk to your own Maths teacher,' she says. 'Who teaches you?'

'No,' I say, 'it's not schoolwork, it's something else.'

I put the printout on a desk.

'I've got lots of dates and places and I want to see them, see where they are.'

Everyone starts to gather round.

'What are they? The dates.'

72

I've tried to think of a good lie, something they'd believe.

'It's birthdays, people's birthdays. I've been collecting them.'

'Why? Why would you do that?' a kid with metal-rimmed glasses asks. I'm feeling defensive now, expecting everyone to start doing that thing, you know when you hold a finger up to the side of your head and loop it round. But they don't.

'I'm just interested in them, that's all.'

They seem to accept it, and I twig I'm in a room where collecting things like facts and figures is okay. They probably all do it.

'Have you got postcodes for them?' the glasses kid asks. He's got this nervous twitch on the side of his mouth, keeps going into a sort of half a smile.

I shake my head and hand him my printout.

'You've only got street names, and place names. Ideally we need postcodes. I can get them from the online directory if you can give me house numbers and then it's really easy to map it. I'd say we use different colours for the different dates instead of numbers. That way any patterns will show up.'

The others are drifting away, but Glasses-boy seems signed up.

'Is this where people live? Their home addresses?'

'No,' I say, 'it's where I . . . saw them.'

'On the street? You interviewed them?'

'Yeah . . . something like that.'

'Mm, pity you didn't ask the postcode . . .'

He's starting to get on my nerves a bit now. Okay, so I didn't do it right, so I'm not a market researcher. But I keep a lid on it. I need him, don't I?

'So, will you help me?'

'I will, but I need better data.'

I can feel my heart sinking at the thought of going out there again, watching people. I don't know if I can do it any more.

'I could see what I could do with this,' he flaps the paper at me, 'if I can take it home.'

'Course,' I say. 'Thanks . . . er . . .'

'Nelson.'

'Nelson. Thanks. I'm Adam.'

'That's okay. I'll be interested, too.' I can't help it, I look at him then, and my heart sinks. His number. 112027. He'll be mapping his own death.

I want to snatch the paper back from him, take it away. It's too close to home, but instead I hear myself asking, 'Where do you live?'

'Churchill House.'

I look at him again, and I'm falling, the floor's disappeared and I'm tumbling down and down in the dark. There's nothing to hold on to and I'm getting battered from all sides — bricks, ceilings, walls, all mixed up.

'Adam?'

'Yeah.'

'Are you all right? You were . . . staring at me.'

'Yeah, I'm fine. Sorry, I do that sometimes. Can't seem to help it.'

His half-smile blinks on and off. Twitch, twitch, twitch. He puts his hand up to his face.

'I'll see you tomorrow, then,' he says, 'unless you're staying. It's still calculus today.'

'No, that's okay. See you tomorrow.' I swing my bag onto my back and go out of the classroom, but there's part of me, a big part, that wishes I could stay. If I was bright enough, if I could stay and not feel stupid, it'd be good to be somewhere where it's all right to be different. Just for an hour.

Outside, everyone's in groups and gangs. Twos and threes having a chat, bigger groups playing football, or basketball. Out here being different don't cut it.

I find a quieter corner, check no one's looking and get my notebook out. I write Nelson's details down. I want it to calm me down, but it don't. I can feel the panic rising inside me – I can't stop it. He's a decent guy, the kind of kid that's never done anyone any harm. Why should he die so young? It's not fair. It's not right. He's got less than three months to live, that's all. And maybe I have too.

When I look at my book it's like the deaths in there are crying out to me, shouting out to be heard. The future of this city's there in my hands – a terrible, terrible, violent future. All those feelings, those voices, those last cries of agony, they're inside me, in my ears, behind my eyes, in my lungs. It's too much. I'm going to burst. Still clutching my book, I bring my hands up to my head, gripping hard, eyes tight shut. I try and do that breathing thing – *in through your nose, and out through your mouth* – but my throat's so tight there's nothing getting through and the noise in my head is so loud I can't hear myself think. I can't hear the words.

'What are you doing, weirdo?'

I know that voice. I open my eyes, just a bit. There's four pairs of feet in front of me, four people close up. I don't need to look up to know who it is. I don't need to see his number to feel the violence, smell the blood. Junior and his mates.

'What are you doing here, spaz? What's in your book?'

Sarah

I'm living in the past here. This is what it must have been like in the old days, the 1970s, before mobile phones and computers and MP5 players. I've still got my phone, and that crappy net-palm thing they give you at school, but I can't use them because they're traceable, and I don't want to be traced.

Vinny and his mates don't bother with technology, except one antique CD player (CDs?) and an old telly. I don't even bother with the TV. Whenever you switch it on, it's always freak shows or re-runs of sad sitcoms which weren't funny the first time, or the news. And who wants to see the news? Wars all over the world, half the world flooded, the other half dying of thirst. I can't do anything about any of it, so what's the point of knowing? Last time I watched, they'd closed the Channel Tunnel, trying to stop all the migrants from Africa. Why would they want to come here? We've got problems of our own, floods, power cuts, riots . . . if they want to come here, let them come, I say. They'll soon find out it's not all it's cracked up to be.

Maybe more people should live like us. You'd think I'd miss what I used to have, wouldn't you? Plush house, home cinema and gym. The only thing I miss is the pool, because my bump's getting huge now. It drags down on me when I'm walking around and the only time I feel really human again is in the bath. So swimming would be lovely. But everything else here is fine.

There's two other guys apart from Vinny: Tom and Frank. They're all smack-heads. You'd think I'd be scared, living here, wouldn't you? But I'm not. No one's interested in me, not in screwing me anyway. All they're looking for is the next fix. And Vinny funds his habit by dealing. He's got his regulars, like Meg and her thieving mates, and he goes out and about. None of them come here. He keeps them away. There's a couple of baseball bats in the kitchen downstairs for when there's trouble, but there hasn't been any in the few weeks I've been living here.

I pay my way by cooking for them. I never knew I could cook, never needed to before. The first day I wander down to the kitchen. It's a mess. Like, really bad. So I start clearing up. I don't have anything better to do. That evening I cook everyone pasta and grate some cheese on top. It's all I can find in the fridge.

The next day, Vinny comes home with an armful of fresh stuff.

'You need to eat vegetables, and fruit,' he says. 'Lots of green things.'

'Since when were you an expert?'

He shrugs.

'I dunno, you do though, don't you? Need to eat this stuff when you're pregnant?'

'Yes, I s'pose, but I haven't got a clue what to do with it.'

'Soup,' he says. 'Chop it all up and bung it in a pan.'

So I do. And it's beautiful. Everyone has some. They're not big eaters, my housemates. Sometimes they don't eat anything all day. But I am. It's not just eating for two. When you've cooked something yourself, you really appreciate it.

It tickles me as well, pottering around in the kitchen, keeping things straight, cooking for three blokes. I hate all that stuff, women staying at home and looking after men. It's what my mum's done all her life. Skivvying for other people. Running round, making everything perfect; clean house, clean clothes, dinner on the table. It makes me sick. Now I'm doing the same, but it's different. We're a different sort of family. The sort where half the time everyone else is too wasted to eat. The sort where you don't ask where the food came from. The sort where people vomit in the yard and don't even mention it.

But it's also the sort of family where no one judges you, where no one's trying to get into your knickers, where, despite it all, you feel safe. I feel safer in this squat in Giles Street than I have for years.

When I'm not cooking, or clearing up, I'm drawing. One day I find some old wallpaper and start doodling. Vinny sees me.

'These are amazing, man,' he says, and he brings me some tape, so I can stick them up on my wall. I draw all sorts – things from real life, things I remember. I catch Vinny and the boys all asleep one day, lying about in the lounge downstairs, and I draw them. I think they'll like it, and they do. They put it up on the wall. But it makes Vinny sad as well.

'This is my life, Sarah. You've drawn my life.'

'You look so happy when you're asleep. Peaceful.'

'I'm not asleep, I'm high. And I'm not happy, not any more. Just relieved I've made it.'

'Still, I wish I could get that sort of peace.'

His face darkens, as if a cloud just went overhead.

'You don't need that. If I thought you'd go down that road one day, I'd kick you out of here, Sarah. It's not for you. You're going to have a baby.'

'I didn't mean . . .' Or did I? When you think about it, reality stinks. There's not much to recommend it. So if there's some way – a smoke, a pill, a pinprick – of making things better, why not?

'The best way to get clean is not to get dirty in the first place. Don't start. Don't ever take the first step.'

'Just say no?'

'You're laughing at me – it's not funny. All my friends, all of them, are on something. Most of us will never get off, get clean. Some of us will die from it. You're different. You're the least fucked-up person I know. Don't change.'

'I'm not going to. I'm not going to take anything. I'd just like to be able to sleep, that's all. A proper night's sleep, without dreaming.'

'Why don't you draw it?'

'What?'

'Your nightmare. If you draw it, get it out of your system, it might go away.'

I'm scared. It feels as though I'm bringing it into the light. It will take up my day as well as my night. But who am I kidding? I think about it anyway, so Vinny's right, I might as well draw it.

I find a fresh roll of wallpaper and I start to draw. But pencil's no good. I ask Vinny to fetch me some charcoal. It needs dark lines. It feels right to be drawing with something already blackened by fire. My hand's shaking as I start to sketch. I can't do it. I close my eyes and I'm back there again. It's in my head, filling me up, and then it spreads through me – the light and dark, the faces, the fire, the fear. I start drawing with my eyes still closed, and when I open them, there's a face looking back at me from the paper.

A man is holding a child in his arms.

It's him.

It's Adam.

Adam

They take it – my book. They take it and they won't give it back. Junior starts looking through, flicking the pages.

'What's this? Your little black book? You've not had all of these, have you? Dirty bastard.'

'Shut up. Give it back.'

'It's boys *and* girls. I knew there was something sick about you. You've not had all these, not in a million years. But maybe you want to . . .'

I try to grab the book back, but he whisks it up above my head and dances away with it.

'Junior, it's private. Give it back. Don't you have anything private?'

'I have now. I've got your book.'

'Give it back, you moron. It's nothing to do with you.'

I'm desperate. He mustn't look at it. I'd rather it was torn up, destroyed. The adrenalin surges through me. There's four of them and one of me, but it don't matter. I've got to get the book back and I will. Junior's twenty metres away now, and his mates are blocking me in. I shove them as hard as I can, get my elbows in there. I take one of them out, but the others are in my way. Beyond them, I can see Junior's stopped. He's leafing through more slowly now. If I don't get to him in the next couple of seconds, I'm stuffed. He'll see the column headings, he'll read the descriptions. He'll find names he knows. He'll find himself.

I head-butt the tallest guy and knee the other one in the balls, then barge past them and run straight at Junior, tackling him round the stomach, taking him down. We hit the tarmac together.

'Get off, you mental bastard!'

He's still got the book. I get hold of his fingers and bend them back one by one. He starts screaming like a girl, not such a big man without his mates. Three fingers in and he lets go of the book. It falls next to us, and I scoop it up and scramble away from him. Back on my feet, I stuff the book down my trousers. He's still on the ground, holding his fingers with the other hand.

'You've fucking broken them, you dickhead. You've broken my fingers!'

Someone must have called security, because all of a sudden we're surrounded by them. One kneels down next to Junior and starts looking at his hand, while two guards grab me under the arms and frogmarch me into school. My feet hardly touch the ground. As we head towards the door I can hear one of Junior's mates doing a number on me.

'He just attacked us. He went mad. Like an animal. Like he's on something.'

I'm put in the interview room and the first thing they do is search me. I'm thinking they won't feel the book – it's so flat, I should get away with it – but, of course, they do. They ask me to take it out. I don't want to. Then they tell me if I don't, they will. So I reach down my trousers and pull out the book. It's a bit crumpled and it's moulded to the shape of my bum.

'Put it down on the desk.'

I'll put it down, but I won't let them look in it. It's not theirs. It's private.

'That's not a schoolbook. What is it?'

'A notebook.'

'A notebook, *what?*'

'A notebook, sir.'

The guy reaches forward to pick it up, and I'm there before him, snatching the book up.

'Put the book down, Dawson.'

'No, sir.'

He starts quoting from the school rules.

'Pupils shall not bring any personal property into school that is not required as part of their studies. If such property is . . .'

I hear the door open behind me. Someone else is coming into the room. I don't even need to think – I lurch round and make a break for it. Seconds later alarm bells start screaming, and my ears are rattling. The whole place is on red alert. How the hell am I going to get out of here? The interview room is near the main entrance, but the doors are tight shut, and there's no way they'll open with my ID card. The receptionist is watching open-mouthed as I throw myself down the corridor towards her. She screams when I vault over her desk.

'Which one?' I shout in her face. 'Which button does the doors?'

She don't answer, but when I look, it's pretty obvious.

There's a square, black button on the left. I press it and the doors slide open. At the same time, she presses another one – her panic button – and another alarm kicks in. But I don't care. I'm out. I'm away.

I run full pelt down the road. The school'll get the police looking for me, and it won't take them long to find me. I'm chipped, aren't I? So all it'll take is a check on their satellite or a call to one of the drones buzzing around the skies over London all the time. They'll pick me up all right. But I don't want anyone getting their noses into my book any more. It's getting too hot to handle. I've got to destroy it or hide it.

I'm still running when I get to Nan's. I swing round the gatepost and up the path. She's standing in the doorway, with her coat on. She holds her hands out in front to stop me crashing into her.

'I was just coming to see you. Got a phone call from the school.'

I can't speak yet, need a minute to catch my breath, but I'm thinking we might only have a minute before the cops get here. So I push her indoors, and close the door behind us.

'All right, all right, no need to shove. Fighting again, was it?' says Nan. 'I told you about that, didn't I?'

I'm still out of breath, but I can't wait.

'I've got to hide something,' I gasp.

'What is it?'

I pull the book out of my pocket.

'Aah, your book.'

'You know about it?'

'I might be old and daft, but I'm not blind. Give it here.'

I hesitate.

'You can trust me, Adam. I'm on your side. I know you

don't think I am, but I am.'

There's a knock on the door and a shout.

'Police! Open up!'

She holds her hand out towards me.

'Trust me, Adam.'

I hand her the book. She turns away from me and stuffs it down her top.

'No one's been down there for thirty years. Safe as bloody houses, that is.'

Then she walks past me and goes to the door.

'Mrs Dawson?'

'Yes.'

'We're looking for Adam Dawson. Is he here?'

'Yes, he's here.'

'We need to take him down to the station.'

'That's fine. He'll come. And I'll come with him. I'm not letting him out of my sight.'

We spend five hours there. Lots of questions, about me and Junior and the book. I don't say a thing. Not a thing. And I don't look at anyone, neither. They want me to 'fess up, say I'm sorry, but I'm not sorry and I'm not crawling to anyone. And through it all Nan plays a blinder.

'He's sixteen,' she keeps saying. 'Sixteen. He got in a ruck at school, that's all. I daresay you did an' all, once or twice.'

They're talking about charging me with assault, but instead they make Nan agree to bring me back to the station in a week's time. Let me stew for a bit, see if I change my mind about talking. She signs the papers and we make our way home.

It's after ten when we get back and there are two envelopes on the mat inside the front door; one addressed to Nan and one to me. Nan's is from the school. I'm excluded for six weeks. At the end of that, I'm to go in for an interview with the Head to see if they'll let me back in. Screw that. As far as I'm concerned, I'm out of there now.

I open the letter to me in my room. I don't recognise the writing and, just for a moment, I think it might be from Sarah. I hold my breath as I open it. *Let it be from her. Let her be all right.* It's not signed, but it don't need to be.

'Dear Loser, I know whats in yur book you sick bastard you got my name an you got a date for me but its not me you need to worry about fuckface its you 6122026 C U then.'

It's there again, the smell of sweat, the searing pain, my eyes flooding red, the taste of blood. Is it my blood? Is it?

Sarah

I take off my clothes and look at my reflection in the mirror. From the front, I still look like me, pretty much. My stomach hasn't spread sideways, so my outline is still the same. My boobs have swollen up, though, and they're sort of wider. My ankles are getting thicker too.

I turn to the side. My belly's huge. It hardly changed when I was at home – it was easy to hide it under my clothes – but since I've been here you can almost see it grow. The skin's stretched so tight, I can't believe I can get any bigger.

Vinny brought me a book. It's full of pictures, what a baby looks like as it grows from a few cells to a sort of tadpole and then into a tiny thing that starts to look like a person. I've read it from cover to cover. I read the birth bit twice. I never really thought before about how this baby is going to get out. I can't go to the hospital, because they'll need ID and then they'll tell my family and I'll be trapped. And I don't want my daughter chipped either. That's what they do these days, inject a microchip soon after they're born. They used to do it to dogs – ours was chipped – but now they do it to people. Gives me the creeps.

So I'll have to do the birth here, on my own. I look down at my stomach. The baby's moving – I can see a knee or an elbow moving under the surface. She'll be here soon. How the hell is that going to happen? It's like getting a ship out of a bottle. It's impossible.

I've got goosebumps all over me. It's too cold in this room to be naked, but I'm not ready to get dressed yet.

Look at me, the state of me. How did I get like this? Of course, I know how. I never fought Him off – I should have. Kicked Him, hit Him, bitten Him. I never even said, 'No'. He's a big man, so I could say I was frightened of Him, and I was when He was like that, at night, in the dark – switched off, impersonal, not like my dad at all – but it wasn't fear that stopped me from crying out. It was love. He was my dad and I loved Him. And He loved me.

Only I never asked for that sort of love.

Now here I am. Pregnant. Alone. He did this to me. He's a twisted, sick man and I hate Him. People should know what He's like. He should go to court, be named and shamed. He should rot in prison. And yet . . . and yet . . . I know I would never do that to Him, because He's still my dad.

Maybe I'm as sick as He is.

I look back at my reflection. The body has changed, but the face in the mirror is the face He saw when He was with me. The hair is the hair that He touched. Suddenly I don't want to be that person any more. I don't want to look like her.

I'm shivering now, and I reach for my clothes. When I'm dressed again, I go into the bathroom, find some scissors and hack at my hair. It falls onto the sink, the floor, all around me. I turn on the tap and swish the hair down the plughole, then I put the plug in, and put a towel round my shoulders. When the sink is full I lean forward and dunk my head. Then I rub shampoo in to what's left of my hair, pick up a disposable razor and I start to shave my scalp. I leave a stripe in the middle, a Mohican. I'll ask Vinny to get hold of some dye tomorrow; pink, green, black, I don't mind. Something different.

So when I look in the mirror, I won't see the old Sarah. I'll surprise myself, do a double-take.

I'll be a new person tomorrow.

Adam

How do people sleep at night? How do they close their eyes, relax and give in to it? When I close my eyes, I see numbers, deaths, chaos. I see buildings falling around me, feel water forcing its way into my lungs, see flames all around me. I hear screams, people crying out for help. I see the flash of a blade, feel it slip between my ribs, know that this is it, the end.

I can't bear it, being alone, in the dark, with just the things in my head for company. Everything's bigger in the dark, louder, more urgent. I lie here and I can't get away from it all. My legs twitch, ready to run, but I've got nowhere to go. My heart's thudding in my chest; my breathing's fast and shallow. My hand gropes around, finds the light switch and I sit up, rubbing my eyes until they can cope with the brightness.

I look round the room. This is my world now. I don't go to school. I don't go out. I stay here, day and night, night and day, listening to next door's dog yapping away, twenty-four seven.

I tried to get some better information for Nelson. He was right, I needed addresses, postcodes. I needed to know where people lived, not just where I saw them out on the street. You can do it two ways; start somewhere busy and follow people home or wait outside flats, houses, whatever, and write down the numbers when they come out. Either way you get picked up by the police.

I start off thinking this is something I can do – I can treat it like a job, going to work in the morning. After three days and three arrests, Nan grounds me and I don't want to go out anyway. The local filth has me on their radar, programmed into their searches. As soon as I'm out of the door, they know about it and they're tracking me. Only takes half an hour on the third day before I hear the whine of the drone over my head.

I'm not doing anything wrong, and they don't charge me with nothing, but in London just hanging around and being sixteen and black is enough to get you picked up and taken down the station. Searched, left in a cell, questioned and left again. They find my book on the first search.

'What's this?'

'Nothing.'

'It's a notebook. What are you writing?'

'Nothing.'

They start to flick through.

'There are names in here, dates, descriptions. You some sort of stalker, are you? That your nasty little game?'

I clam up then. Better to say nothing. Let them think what they like. I haven't hurt anyone or picked on anyone – they've got nothing against me. They video me, and write notes directly onto the laptop in the interview room.

On the third day, it's not the police asking questions, it's a couple of guys in suits. There's a young one with ginger hair and a ridiculous bootlace tie and an older one, belly spilling over the top of his trousers. They ask me pretty much the same things as the coppers: why am I hanging around? What am I writing down? I don't say a thing. Not a word. Then the older one throws me a curveball.

'I knew your mum,' he says. 'Jem. Met her sixteen years ago. I was sorry to hear about her . . . well, you know.'

He's got me now. Got my attention. Got me wanting more. I look him in the eye and he's a survivor. His date gives him another thirty years.

'I interviewed her in the Abbey, when she was holed up in there. She said she could see numbers, people's death dates. Caused a bit of a fuss at the time. Then she denied it all, said she'd made it up.'

He picks at his teeth with his fingernail.

'The thing is,' he says, 'it's always bothered me, because I don't think she did make it up. I think she saw those people at the London Eye, saw their deaths. Is that what you see, Adam? Are you like her?'

I want to say 'yes'. I want to tell him. He'll believe me. He might help me; help me deal with this thing.

''Cause if you are,' he carries on, 'you've got my sympathy. I mean, it's a terrible thing to live with.' I'm looking at him, trying to suss him out, trying not to show my excitement. 'It can't be easy. Thing is, you could be damn useful to people like me. You could cause a lot of trouble as well.'

And all of a sudden, a chill goes through me. It wasn't a threat exactly, but I know we're not on the same side. And I'm wondering who this guy is. MI5? MI6?

'I've seen what you wrote on your palm-net, seen some copies from your notebook. There's a lot of numbers around the start of January. What's going to happen, Adam? What's going on in your head?'

I say nothing. I'd been thinking of telling him about New Year, but he's seen it anyway, it's been flagged up with him, noted, that's why he's here. In any case, I haven't got any answers. I don't know what's going to happen.

I look away from him and as his voice goes on and on, I try to picture him asking the same questions to Mum.

'What was she like? My mum. What was she like when you met her?'

He smiles.

'Stroppy. Manipulative. Rude. I liked her.'

'I am like her,' I say. 'We're the same.'

He sighs, and it's like air escaping from a balloon, and it's then I realise he's as tense as I am, however laid-back and cool he's pretending to be. He leans forward.

'It's a dangerous thing, what you've got. Dangerous. It shouldn't be shared around, blabbed about. It's easy to upset people, frighten them. Do you understand what I'm saying?'

'Yeah.'

'So you have to keep quiet about it. Only it's okay to tell people like me. In fact, we want you to tell us. Tell us everything you know. Here . . .' He reaches in his jacket pocket and slides a little card across the table: name, mobile number, email address. 'You can call me,' he says, 'anytime.'

But when Nan comes to collect me, they take her to one side and talk to her like I'm not in the room.

'Exhibiting disturbing behaviour . . . recommend psychiatric assessment . . . out of the house unsupervised . . .'

She makes a show of listening to them. I keep my head down and my eyes on the floor until it's all over and we're heading back to Carlton Villas on the bus.

'What are you up to, Adam? What are you trying to do?'

She's the one person I could talk to, not those spooks in suits, but I can't. There's a brick wall between us, and I can't get through it. It's partly the sort of person she is, her attitudes, the things she says, and it's partly the sort of person she isn't. It's not her fault she's not Mum, but I can't forgive her for it. Not yet.

So I stay in my room, awake twenty-four hours a day, and I search the internet for clues and I listen for post coming through the letterbox. As soon as I hear it rattle, I'm down those stairs. I need to beat Nan to it, because I don't want her to know. I don't want her to see the stream of notes that's coming from Junior. I know what they'll say, or pretty much. You get the idea from the first few: '6122026. Your numbers up. R u redy?' 'Say goodbye to yr nan, loser. Yur finished.'

Nan gets to the door first sometimes. She keeps funny hours too.

'It's for you,' she says. She's got the envelope in her hands and now she's examining it.

'Give it here,' I say, holding my hand out.

'Friend?' she says. 'Girlfriend? You can have people here, you know. If you want to.'

I don't say nothing, just keep holding my hand out until she gets the hint.

'Adam,' she says as I turn away and head up the stairs. 'Stay here a minute. We need to . . .'

Her voice is lost as I shut my door behind me. *Talk*. We need to talk. If only I could.

I put the envelope with the others and switch on Dad's computer. It's ancient but it connects to the web, though it takes forever, and even I know how to use Google. I normally type '2027' or 'the end of the world' but tonight's different. Tonight I'm going to ask about the thing that keeps me awake.

My fingers pick out the letters haltingly, until the search box says, 'When will I die?'

And I press enter.

Eight hundred and thirty one million hits. I click on the first one. It asks me questions. How old am I? Do I smoke? What do I weigh? How much exercise do I take?

I don't even bother going to the end. Sites like this don't know about the unexpected. They don't know about the bomb or the fire or the flood. They don't know what's going to happen to London in a few weeks' time. They don't know if a nutter with a knife is going to get me before all that.

And neither do I.

Sarah

I feel a bit sick all day, a bit uncomfortable. Then sometime, I don't know when, I realise that this odd feeling is coming in waves, every ten minutes or so, and it's more than a twinge, it's pain. Each time, my stomach goes rigid, the muscles clench like a fist.

There's no one else in the house.

Shit! Shit! This can't be it. I don't know exactly how far gone I am, but I'm nowhere near nine months, am I? I'm not ready. I get the book, scrabbling through the pages. 'Labour and Delivery.' Oh God, why didn't I read this properly? There's stuff about breathing and keeping moving and then positions. The words dance in front of my eyes and another contraction starts.

Keep moving. Keep moving. I try to pace around the top floor of the house, but when a new contraction comes it paralyses me. I hold on to the wall and try to breathe.

In between I can't keep a lid on the panic. I'm crying and whimpering, noises coming out of me that I have no control over.

It wasn't meant to be like this. I didn't want doctors and hospitals, but I thought there'd be other people around. I thought Vinny would be here. I'm on the landing when my waters go. Not a gush, just a trickle down my leg. *I've pissed myself*, I think. *Great.* But when I try to stop the flow, nothing happens, the liquid just keeps on coming, and coming. There's blood mixed up in it. That can't be good, can it?

I get myself into the bathroom. The noise, my noise, is louder in there, echoing off the tiled walls. I sit on the toilet, letting the rest of the stuff drain out. I could sit there for ever, but I make myself stand up. I can't let the baby be born in a toilet.

I hold on to the sink, bracing my body against the pain. It's taking over, there's no time to rest. I want to get away from it, but there's nowhere to go. I lean sideways and vomit into the pan, two, three times, then I sink down onto the floor.

The noises are like an animal now – low, grunts and groans.

I could die here.

If the pain doesn't stop soon, I will die and I don't even care. I just want it to stop. Make it all go away. The pain's in my stomach and my back, pressing down into my arse. I'm going to split in half and bleed to death.

I'll die on the bathroom floor, like a junkie, but it's okay. It'll be better than this, this torture, this hell. I'm ready to go.

Vinny finds us. We're still on the bathroom floor. I managed to reach some towels, put them over us like blankets. I was worried she'd get cold, see, my daughter. I held her close to me, skin to skin, so she'd get my warmth. She cried a little bit, but she soon stopped, and then she looked at me, with her beautiful cornflower-blue eyes, and I kissed her, kissed her little face, her little hands.

My daughter.

My little girl.

Mia.

Adam

'It's truth or dare, simple as that.'

'I don't want to play games.'

'What are you here for, then?'

'I want you off my back. I want you to leave me and my nan alone.'

'Your nan, she spends a lot of time at home, doesn't she? Sitting on that chair in the kitchen. She don't move much, does she? Sitting target, you could say.'

There's a window at the back of the house. The estate starts the other side of the wall. Hundreds of windows all facing our direction. And there's been a note through our door every day.

'That's what I want to stop. These stupid threats. She's got nothing to do with it. It's between you and me. So let's do it, fight fair and square.'

My words sound braver than I feel, but that's what you've got to do with people like Junior. You've got to talk the talk.

'I'll fight you, if you like, but I want some answers first. I want to know why you stare at people. I want to know what you write in your book. I want to know why you wrote that stuff about me.'

'Truth?'

'Truth.'

'So what will I get in return?'

'I'll call the boys off. Stop watching the house.'

'Why would I believe you? You obviously get off on it.'

'Get off on it? Watching your nan smoke herself to death? I'd rather watch paint dry, man.'

'So I'd have your word?'

'Yeah, man. You'd have my word.' The others are watching us. There's a buzz in the air, they're wondering how this is going to play out, ready to jump on me if I make the first move.

'Let's sit down,' I say, 'talk like men, you and me.'

We're in an old warehouse. They've got a fire going in one corner, with crates pulled up around it. We sit down, a metre apart. The flames are reflected in his eyes, as he leans forward.

'So, tell me. What are these lies that you're writing?'

You mustn't tell. Not anyone. Not ever. But maybe I can tell Junior. He won't believe it anyway, and it won't make any difference to him now, he won't have months of agony, not like Mum, because today's his last day.

I take a deep breath.

'When I look at people, I see a number. It's the date of their death. Sounds freaky, I know, but it's true. I've always seen them. There's nothing I can do about it.'

'So you can see my number?' He's playing me along, trying to make me think he believes me.

'Yeah.'

'And you wrote it down, in your book. That's the number I saw?'

'Yeah.'

'Today.'

I fall silent. It's half-past nine, dark and cold. The rain's battering down on the corrugated roof. He's got three and a half hours left, tops. It don't seem likely. All his mates are here. There's four of them, and one of me.

He looks around him and spreads his arms out wide.

'So, where is it, man? How's it going to happen?'

This is creepy. It's sick.

'How's it going to happen, Adam? I read it, read what you said. There's a knife, blood. Who's it going to be? There's no one else here except us. There's no one here who wants to fight me, except you. Is it you? Are you going to kill me?'

He's mocking me to start with, but then his voice turns serious. His tongue flicks over his lips, and there's something in his eyes apart from his number. He's scared. Maybe he's as scared as I am.

I don't want it to be me. I don't like the guy. He's a maggot and I want him off my case, but I don't want to kill him: I don't want to kill anyone.

I want the clocks to stop ticking. I want time to stand still. I want the numbers to go away.

The heat from the fire is toasting my face. Someone throws a plank into the middle. Red-hot ash flies up around it, making a million sparks in the darkness.

'I'm going,' I say, getting to my feet. 'Junior, I came here to fight you, but I don't want to fight. I told you the truth, my truth, so now you can leave me alone. It was our deal. Yeah?'

He signals to the others, and they home in on me,

grabbing me from behind, pinning my arms behind my back.

'I'm a man of my word. I'll lay off your nan. But don't think you can just walk away. You said you came here for a fight, so I'll fight you fair and square. Search him.'

I kick out with my feet, but it don't keep them away. They're on me with their hands, slapping me all over, delving into my pockets. They find my blade, of course. I didn't hide it – I had it handy, tucked into my belt, so it would be there if I needed it.

'You brought a blade.'

'Self defence, man.'

'I'm not armed.' He holds his empty hands up.

'I don't believe you.'

I can't be the only one who's brought a knife. He turns out his pockets, opens his jacket to show me there's nothing there. Shit, the only knife here is mine. And now I'm defenceless, wide open.

'You came here to use it on me. You came here to kill me.' He comes up close, jabbing his finger into my chest. 'Well, I'm not going down. You're not having me. Tomorrow you'll have to find your book and cross my number out, 'cause I'm not going anywhere today. You got it wrong.'

He punches me hard in the stomach.

'The only one in trouble tonight is you, loser.'

He gives me another punch, in the bottom of my ribs. And another. And another. I try and stand up to him, but with my arms pinned back, I've got nothing. He's hitting my head now. My lip's split and there's blood pouring down. The smell of it sends me further into my nightmare.

'That's enough, Junior, you said it was going to be fair.' Someone's talking, the guy who searched me.

'Shut up.'

'He's had it, look at him.'

'I said shut the fuck up!'

'Who's gonna make me?'

I only half-hear what they're saying. My head has flopped forward, and my legs have gone. If the guys weren't holding me up, I'd be on the floor now.

Junior's not stopping. He's got into his stride now. More punches to the stomach, and I vomit up blood. He's killing me. He don't need a knife – his fists'll do the job.

'Leave him.'

Another punch.

'I said leave him.'

I can't see anything any more. The space behind my eyes has gone red. I'm hanging forward, and then suddenly I'm falling. There's a cry, a great wail of rage, and someone buts my shoulder and I'm falling to one side. Then grunting, feet scuffling, shouts, voices but not words, and the space behind my eyes turning from red to black.

The fire sighs as I fall into it. My arms and legs aren't working. I can't push myself away. I force my eyes open and see the pinpricks of ash showering upwards, points of light travelling up, up, up around me. Through the flames I see the flash of a blade, the look of surprise in Junior's eyes, and his number flickering like a fluorescent light on the blink.

On, off. On, off, on. Off.

Someone's screaming.

The flames lick my face, fill my nostrils with the smell of cooking flesh.

Someone's screaming.

It's me.

Sarah

The first few days pass in a calm, milky haze. If she cries, I feed her. I have to steel myself to do it, because it hurts like hell when she starts sucking, but after a few seconds the pain eases and the milk works its magic – on her and on me. She gets drunk on it; warm and woozy and happy. Her whole body relaxes, her arms flop down by her sides, and the only movement is her ear wiggling as her jaw moves rhythmically – suck, suck, suck, pause . . . suck, suck, suck, pause. And I'm drawn down into a place where it's only me and her, nothing else, a soft, warm, milky world.

I didn't know it would be like this. How could I possibly know? That you can love someone so completely from the very first moment you see them.

Because I do. I love her. She was part of me and now she's separate – her own person, and I love her. I hated my life, every bit of it. I hated being me. But that's gone now, my past is gone, how I got here, who I was. I wanted to be a new 'me' and I am. I'm Mia's Mum.

Adam

I'm like a snowman left out in the sun. Everything on one side of my face has melted. The edges have gone. I've lost my detail. The first time I see myself in the mirror I don't cry, I just stare and stare, trying to find myself in that face. I look away and back again, hoping it'll be different when I look again, hoping some miracle will have happened and I'll be back to 'normal'.

But there's no miracles. I'm scarred from the fire. I always will be.

The police come calling, asking all sorts of questions, but I won't talk. I close my eyes. I keep my mouth shut. And they go away. I keep the curtains round my bed closed. I don't want to see anyone and I don't want anyone to see me. When the nurses come in, I don't look at them. I don't need to see anyone's number right now. For a couple of weeks, that works, but one day the nurse don't draw the curtain properly and now the boy in the bed next to me is watching me through the gap when I hold the mirror up to my face. He's younger than me, about eleven, a pale little kid with no hair. I recognise that look. He's on chemo, like my mum was.

I catch him watching, but instead of being embarrassed and looking away, his eyes lock onto mine and he says, 'What happened to you?'

I don't want to talk to him. I don't want to talk to anyone, but especially not another twenty-seven. Because that's what he is. He's in here, up to his eyeballs in chemo, when his number's telling me he's going to be wiped out in a few weeks with all the rest of them. I pretend I haven't heard him, but he just says it louder.

'What happened? Looks like a burn.' He's not giving up.

'Fell in a fire,' I say eventually. *There, I've told you. Now shut up and leave me alone.* He nods.

'I'm Wesley,' he says. 'Cancer, like Jake over there, but he's kidneys and I'm leukaemia. In my blood.'

When I don't say nothing, he takes it as some sort of invitation, and before I know it he's moving his sheets out of the way, slipping out of bed, pushing back my curtain and perching on the side of my mattress.

'That's Carl,' he says quietly, tipping his head towards the kid in the opposite bed with both legs in plaster, feet raised up. 'Car crash,' he whispers, 'lost his dad and his brother.'

'Shit,' I say.

'Yeah.' Carl is looking over our way, but he's not really seeing us. His eyes are glazed over, but I still clock his number. He's going tomorrow.

'He's sick, man. Really sick,' I whisper to Wesley.

'No,' he says. 'He looks bad, but he's way better than he was. It's just the fractures in his legs now. The rest of him's okay.' Wesley's obviously listened to the doctors but they're

106

wrong. The numbers don't change. They don't lie. I should know.

Nan comes to see me in the afternoon.

'Nan, you gotta get me out of here.'

'Goin' a bit stir crazy? Don't blame you.' She's brought me a bag of mint humbugs and is chewing her way through them.

'It's doing my head in.' I lower my voice and beckon to her, and she leans in nearer. 'The numbers, Nan. The numbers. Some people in here, they ain't got long to go.'

She stops chewing then, and looks me straight in the eye.

'That boy over there, with the legs up. He's checking out tomorrow, but nobody else sees it. They think he's okay. They hardly bother with him.'

'Are you sure?'

'Yeah, course I am. I wouldn't say it if I didn't know.'

'You should tell someone.'

'Should I?'

'Maybe . . .'

'It wouldn't make no difference, Nan. It didn't make no difference with Mum or Junior.'

'Maybe it would this time.'

'Nan, I've seen it my whole life. The numbers don't change. I could've died in that fire, but I didn't, because it wasn't my day. Junior could've just been nicked by that knife, but he wasn't. It killed him, straight out. I seen his number. It was fixed. No one could change it.'

'But that shouldn't stop us trying . . . I'll have a word with the staff. We need to get you out of here anyway. I don't think it's a good place for you.'

She gets up and goes off to find someone to talk to, taking the bag of mints with her.

That evening, when the duty nurse makes her last round before lights out, I stop her.

'Can you check on Carl?' I say.

'Of course,' she says. 'I check on everyone.'

'But can you keep checking him. Tonight.'

She looks at me like I've lost my marbles, then smoothes the sheet over my legs.

'Don't worry about him. He's doing fine.'

I keep my bedside light on when the ward lights go off, and I sit up. I promise myself I'll watch over him, raise the alarm if I hear or see anything. When I feel myself starting to drift off, I give myself a good pinch. It wakes me up for a minute or so, but then I feel myself going and I can't stop. The next thing I know the overhead lights are on and there's a team of staff crowding round the bed opposite and someone's yanking the curtains across.

'What is it? What's happening?' I call out, but no one's listening to me. Wesley and Jake are still asleep, even with all the frantic activity a few metres away from them, and everyone else is focussing on Carl.

Later, all the staff are tight-lipped about what happened. Even Wesley can't find out what's gone on.

'It's something bad,' he says to me. 'Someone slipped up, made a mistake, otherwise they'd tell us.'

What he don't know is what I saw when they was working on Carl, trying to save him: the pool of blood spreading out from under the curtain, the scissors kicked along the floor in the confusion. I reckon Carl found his own way out.

I think about it all day. I can't think about nothing else. If I'd stayed awake, I could've raised the alarm earlier. They might have saved him. I knew something was going to happen – I should have made them listen. It was my fault.

There's an empty space where his bed used to be. I get out of mine and walk over to it.

'I'm sorry, man,' I murmur. 'I let you down.'

I'm thinking Nan was right. *If you try hard enough, you might be able to change the numbers.* If I'd stayed awake, if I'd seen him make his move, it could all have been different. Now I'm thinking about all the twenty-sevens. They're still out there.

If I warn people, make myself heard, perhaps it won't be thousands or millions dead. Maybe I can save them, or some of them. Even if I only save a few, it will be worth something, won't it?

There's not long to go now, I'd better start telling people.

But how do I get people to listen?

And what am I going to tell them?

Sarah

She won't stop crying. She just won't stop.

It starts out of the blue, one evening, she just starts to cry. Feeding doesn't help. Changing her doesn't make any difference. I pick her up, hold her to my shoulder and walk her backwards and forwards across the room. After what seems like hours she falls asleep from sheer exhaustion.

I put her into the drawer I'm using as a cot and flop onto the bed. The sound of crying is still ringing in my ears, bouncing off the walls in an everlasting echo. I curl up and put my hands over my ears to try to stop it. I suppose I drop off to sleep, but I don't know how long for. All I do know is that her cries reach into my dreams and drag me to the surface. Automatically I reach down to her. Her skin is red hot and sticky with sweat.

I try the things that I know; feeding, changing, singing, pacing. And she cries and cries and cries.

Vinny knocks on the door and comes in.

'You all right? I saw your light on. Well, I heard you.

Brought you a cup of tea.'

'What time is it?'

'Fiveish.'

'In the morning?'

'Yeah.'

'I can't stop her, Vin. I can't stop her crying.' My voice is high and wobbly.

'Give her here. I'll have her while you have your tea. Let's see what we can do.'

He takes her from me.

'Jesus, Sarah, she's boiling.'

'I know. What do I do, Vin? What do I do?'

'We'd better take her to the walk-in, at the hospital.'

'I can't. They'll want ID, an address, everything.'

'We'll have to take her somewhere. We can't leave her like this. Just pretend you've forgotten your ID, give them a false name. It'll be all right. They'll take one look at her and treat her – she's tiny, she needs their help, they'll see that. Come on. Get some clothes on. I'll find the car keys.'

There's no car seat for Mia, so I sit in the back and cuddle her.

'Drive slowly,' I say.

'Course.'

The hospital is a bright, white place. I've hardly left the house in weeks, and it's overwhelming being there. It's so busy, so big, so clean. I look down at myself; stained sweatshirt pulled over my tee-shirt and jogging bottoms. No socks, feet stuffed into slippers. I look like I've been sleeping rough.

'Name?'

'Sally Harrison.'

'ID, please.'

'Oh God, I left it at home. We were just in such a rush . . .'

The receptionist looks at me and raises an eyebrow.

'You're not chipped?'

'No.'

'And your baby?'

'No.'

They can refuse treatment without ID. I look at her, wondering which way she's going to jump.

'Please,' I say.

The eyebrows shoot higher, but then she just sighs and asks me for more details. I give a false address and phone number and tell her as much about Mia's symptoms as I can.

We only have to wait for twenty minutes, and then a nurse takes us to an assessment room. A doctor joins us there – she's young, but she's got grey rings under her eyes and her blonde hair is escaping from a messy ponytail.

'Let's have a look at her.'

They lie her on a white mattress in a plastic tank, like a fishtank, and gently take her clothes off.

'How long has she been running a temperature?'

''Bout twelve hours. She's been crying for twelve hours, too, on and off.'

'Feeding okay?'

'Not since she started crying.'

They look at every inch of her, examine her eyes and ears and mouth, move her arms and legs gently.

'She's got a bit of an infection around the umbilical stump. Can you see how it's red and swollen here?'

When the doctor points it out, it's obvious. The skin is puffed and angry-looking on her belly where the remains of her cord are. Oh God, why didn't I see it? What sort of mother am I? She's crying because she's in pain.

'We'll give her some antibiotics straight away.' Before I know it they're injecting something into her leg. And then they've got another syringe out of its cellophane wrapper.

'She's not chipped, is she?'

'No, but . . .'

'It's compulsory.' Her eyes flick up to mine, and I know it's no use arguing. Even if I wanted to, it's too late. The needle is in, the plunger is pressed.

'We can register all her details on the ward.'

'The ward?'

'We have to be careful with infection in this part of the body. Occasionally it can lead to tetanus, so we'll keep her in today, while we see how she responds to treatment.'

Keep her?

'Can't you just give her some medicine? We don't want to stay. We need to be somewhere . . .'

'We need to observe her. Tetanus could be extremely dangerous for such a young baby. We can't take that risk. You look like you could do with a rest. You can both go on the maternity ward for the day – I'll request a single room if you like.'

It feels like things are spinning out of my control. Now they've got her here, they won't let her go. They've got her. They've chipped her. The thought of a microchip settling into her body makes me feel sick. I didn't want that for her. I didn't want her tagged and labelled and tracked for life.

But if I stick to my story – forgotten ID, false name, false address – we'll be safe here, won't we? I look back at Mia's tummy, at the infected skin taut and shiny, and I know I've got no choice.

Adam

They refuse to discharge me, but I'm going anyway. I can't stay here no longer. I'll go mad. Nan brings some clean clothes in and I get dressed while the nurse tells her how to look after my face. Then it's time to go.

Wesley has his head over a bucket when I go over to say goodbye. He raises a hand up, but he don't speak.

'Hang in there, Wes,' I say. I want to tell him to stop the chemo, enjoy what time he has left. He's a twenty-seven after all, so he's only got just over a week to go. But then I start thinking how I'm going to try and change all that, change things for the twenty-sevens, so maybe he will need the chemo – it might buy him some extra time.

I'm choked up as I walk down the ward. I can't help glancing at the bed where Carl was. There's someone else there now, and there'll be someone else in my spot soon. It's a never-ending production line of the sick and wounded, and some of them will get better and some of them won't, but a dark cloud settles over me when I think about Carl. It still feels like my fault. All I had to do was stay awake. And I let him down.

'What's eating you? I thought you wanted to leave?'

'Nothing. Just . . . this place.'

She's looking where I'm looking.

'You tried your best,' she says, reading my mind, 'and so did I.'

'Didn't try hard enough.'

'Stop beating yourself up. Let's get out of here.'

It's surprisingly difficult to walk. I've been in here seventeen days and my legs have switched off. The corridors go on for ever.

'There's a bus stop just to the left here. Adam? Adam . . .'

Her voice fades away until I can't hear anything at all. There's a girl getting into a beaten-up old car in the car park. She's got a coat slung round her shoulders so you can't see her arms. A tall skinny bloke is helping her. He's standing my side of her so she's mostly hidden from view, but all I need is a glimpse to know.

It's Sarah.

She's changed her hair, shaved half of it off, but it's her, oh God, it's her.

I stand there like an idiot, watching her get settled in the back of the car. The bloke closes the door for her and goes round to the driver's seat and then it's like I'm waking up. She's going! In less than a minute she'll be out of here. What am I doing?

'Adam? Where the hell . . .?'

I start to walk over to the car park, then break into a run. He's already started the engine, they're moving. I make to cut them off at the barrier. They'll have to stop there to be let out. The car moves slowly and I'm there just before it. I wave at the driver, to flag him down. He looks alarmed, but he has to stop anyway. He pulls to a halt, winds down the passenger window and leans across.

'All right, mate?' he says.

I peer in the back. The headrest of the passenger seat is in the way.

'I just wanted to . . . I just wanted . . . Sarah?'

She moves to one side and I see her face. It's definitely her, the face I've had in my head all this time, the face I've gone to sleep thinking about. She gasps, and her mouth falls open, and then I remember my own face, what a shock it must be to see it.

I put my hand up to shield it.

'It's not as bad as it looks . . .' I start to say, but she's looking away and screaming.

'Get out of here, Vinny! Get out of here! Drive! Drive!'

'Sarah!'

The wheels squeal on the tarmac as Vinny stamps on the accelerator and the car lurches forward a couple of metres. The barrier is taking its sweet time. I put my hands on the car and lean towards the back passenger window. Sarah's still shouting, but when she sees me, she stops and shrinks away from me.

The moment the barrier starts to rise, Vinny's out of there. The metal of the car spins away from under my fingers and I'm left standing, shell-shocked. It was like the first time she saw me, only worse. Why is she so scared of me? Who is she really, and who does she think I am?

'Adam!'

I look behind me. Nan's standing on the pavement, watching. I walk back slowly to join her.

'Who the hell was that?'

'A girl I know.'

'What's up with her?'

'She hates me. She's scared of me.'

Her face darkens.

'Scared? What you done to her?'

'I haven't done nothing. She knows something about me, or she thinks she does.'

'People been gossiping? Telling tales?'

'No, nothing like that. She was like it the very first time we met, on the first day at school.' And then the penny drops, and when I say it out loud it sounds true. 'She's different. Different like you and me. You've got your auras, I've got the numbers. She's got something. She knows something.'

Nan don't laugh. She don't think I'm nuts.

She reaches into her bag and fishes out a cigarette, then she lights it, inhales deeply and blows a stream of smoke out towards a sign saying, 'No smoking on hospital grounds. Penalty €200.'

'You'd better find her then, son,' she says. 'You need to find this girl and she needs to tell you what she knows.'

Sarah

It was him.

And his face was the face in my nightmares. Scarred on one side, melted.

How could I possibly have known his perfect face would be burnt? How do I know that I'll see him again in another fire?

I thought the nightmares might stop when the baby was born. They started when she did, the first ones weeks before I even knew I'd fallen pregnant. She brought them to me somehow, and I thought that they might be hers, that once we were separate she might keep them. But she's left them with me. The night we get home from the hospital, I have the nightmare again. This time I see the whole city wrecked; buildings crumbled to heaps, cracks in the road too wide to jump over; people dead in the streets; bodies carried out of rubble. And all I can think about is Mia. She's not with me. I need to get to her.

I make myself wake up. Where is she? Oh my God,

where's my baby? My hands reach blindly out. They find the top of her head, soft and warm. She's there, asleep in her drawer.

It was just a dream. It's not real.

The nightmare is full of lies. I would never let Mia out of my sight. It's just some cruel trick my mind's playing on me. Taking my deepest fears, twisting and running with them.

Except. Except . . . one by one the pieces in the nightmare are fitting into place, like a jigsaw. Mia. Adam. Me.

There's something inevitable about it.

I can't bear it. It's too lonely dealing with this on my own in the dark. I reach down again and scoop her up, bringing her into bed with me. I've woken her. I don't think I've ever done that before, I've always let her find her own rhythm of sleep. But she's awake now and she doesn't cry. I prop her up on my legs. I hold her hands gently and she grips on, and we look at each other, eye to eye, silent for a long time.

'I won't leave you,' I say to her eventually. 'I'll never leave you.'

I wait for her to say the same thing back to me. Sometimes I think giving birth has sent me over the edge. It's softened my brain, blurred all the edges. If she spoke to me now, *I'll never leave you, Mum,* I wouldn't even be surprised. It would be okay in a world washed through with milk and sleepless-ness.

She doesn't talk to me. She just looks and looks and looks. And gradually her eyelids get too heavy for her. For a few minutes they flutter open and shut, and then finally they stay closed. She's breathing through her mouth, each breath in is deliciously heavy, almost a snore. I move her onto the mattress next to me.

Whatever's going to happen, whatever the future holds,

we've got now, Mia and I, faces so close we're breathing air from each other's lungs, and I've the comfort of sharing her sleep. We've got now. And for the moment, that's enough.

I drift off to sleep again and now the baby's crying and I'm crying too. We're trapped by a wall of flame. We'll die here, burnt alive. I don't care about me, but I can't bear it for Mia. I fold my body round her, trying to shield her. The flames are getting nearer. It's so hot my clothes are melting into me.

'Sarah! Sarah!'

Someone's shaking my shoulder. It's him. Adam. He's trying to tell me something, but the place is falling down round our ears. I can't hear.

'Sarah, wake up! Wake up!'

I open my eyes. I'm screaming and the baby's screaming, but the air's cool against my hot face. I'm in my room at the squat, and it's not Adam waking me up, it's Vinny.

'You woke the baby,' he says. I pick her up. My little girl. I frightened her. I get out of bed and walk up and down, rocking her, but it's no good, so we get back into bed and I try a feed. She clamps on, her hands holding on for dear life, digging in. I wipe the tears from the eye that I can see, and gradually she calms down, and her steady suckling calms me too.

'You need to do something. Talk to someone.'

'A shrink?'

'Maybe.'

'Tell them about my childhood, talk it out?'

'Why not? It might help.'

'It's not my past in my nightmares. It's the future.'

'What?'

'It's what's going to happen, to Mia and me. Not just us, it's bigger than that. Something big.'

'Can I see the pictures? You drew it, didn't you?'

I'd drawn it on the wallpaper I found, but I'd rolled it up again, couldn't stand to sit and look at it.

'Over there,' I say, nodding towards the roll of paper leaning in the corner of the room. Vinny starts to uncurl it, holding it up in front of him, then realises how big it is and puts it down on the floor, weighting down the ends with my shoes.

'Jesus,' he says. 'Jesus Christ al-fucking-mighty. That's the guy, the kid in the car park. And the buildings and the fire. Jesus, Sarah, you know what you've drawn?'

I shake my head and when I look back at him, he's scared.

'The date, there, 1st January 2027. That's it, is it?'

'That's the date in my nightmare.'

'Jesus.'

He rubs his hands over his face and when he looks up again there's that same haunted look.

'You can't keep this to yourself, girl. Not if it's real. Is it real?'

'I don't know, Vin. It feels real to me. The boy, Adam, I saw him in my nightmare before I met him. He never had that scar either, but I saw it, I knew it was going to happen to him.'

'Shit. This is some weird stuff. This is heavy. You gotta tell people. I know just the place. Come on, I'll show you.'

'It's five in the morning, Vin. I'm feeding the baby.'

He's never worked on the same clock as everyone else.

'When she's stopped feeding. We'll go then. I'll show you. And I'll get you some spray cans – I know someone who'll have some. You need to show the world.'

'Vinny, do you mean paint it on a wall?'

'Yeah, man.'

'No. No way.'

He turns serious then.

'You've got to. You haven't got a choice. You've got to tell people.'

'Shut up, I don't have to . . .'

'Yes, yes, you do, 'cause you know what this is, don't you?'

I shake my head.

He looks back at the picture.

'It's Judgement Day, Sarah. You've drawn fucking Judgement Day.'

Adam

I don't want to go out. I don't want to see nobody. Nan leaves her perch ten times a day to check on me but all I want is to be left alone.

One day she comes in holding something behind her back.

'I've got something for you,' she says. She produces a little square package, a parcel wrapped up in paper with robins on it.

'What's this?'

'It's nothing really. Just something for Christmas. It's Christmas Day.'

Is it? 25122026? One week to go.

'You going to open it then?' she says, nodding encouragingly.

My fingers fumble with the tape, but I get there in the end. It's a chocolate orange.

'Thanks,' I manage. 'I didn't get . . .'

'Don't matter. Don't s'pose you know what day it is, do

you? I'm doing a dinner, roast and everything, if you want to come downstairs.'

'Nah, it's okay. I'll stay here.'

'I'll bring it up then, shall I? It's a nice one, bit of everything on it, turkey and sausage and that, roast potatoes, stuffing . . . I never knew you could microwave all that. Amazing really . . .'

'No, it's okay. I'm not hungry.'

'You should eat something, Adam. Have a go. Just today.'

'I said I'm okay.'

'Just today, Adam. It is Christmas . . .'

'Nan, if I want something, I'll come and get it.'

It's like I've slapped her in the face.

'I just want you to be all right,' she says.

'Take a look,' I say. 'Do you think I'm ever going to be all right again? Take a look at my face.'

I can hear myself doing it, I hate myself for it, but who else have I got to take it out on?

'I've seen your face,' she says quietly. 'It'll get better, better than it is now.'

'It's not going to get better, you silly cow. This is it. This is what I look like.'

She reaches in her pocket for a cigarette. She puts the end in her mouth and holds her lighter to the other end. She flicks the flame into life, and the smell of the paper catching, the tobacco starting to burn, hits me like an express train. The smoke is in my eyes, behind my eyes, all around me, and I'm burning, the hair sizzling off my head, my skin crinkling in the flames.

'Stop it! Get the fuck out of here! Get out!' My voice rises to a scream.

She looks up, puzzled, and then horrified as I snatch the

cigarette out of her hands, drop it the floor and stamp on it.

'Adam!'

'Get out! Just leave me alone!'

She leaves, and I've got what I wanted. Except it isn't really – I'm on my own again, alone with my reflection and a head full of flames and fists, knives and the last look on Junior's face. There's another face too. Sarah's, with that terror of hers, and her body squirming to get away from me in the car.

Sarah

I can't get on with the spray-cans. It's too different, not my style, but once I've got some brushes, I'm away. I thought Vinny was mad, but there's something in this. Each sweep of my arm is liberating. It feels like I'm getting the nightmare out there and maybe that's where it will stay. Out of me.

I'm in a tunnel where the road cuts under the railway. Hardly any cars use it, but there are some pedestrians, walking from the estate through to the High Street. Even so, I can paint here during the day. It's amazing – people look as they walk by, but no one's tried to stop me. Perhaps because I'm doing something big, they think it's official, or maybe they can see it's going to be better than a blank wall.

I come here whenever I can, even Christmas Day. It's a funny sort of Christmas. No decorations, no tree, but there are presents. There's a little plastic bag on the kitchen table when I go downstairs in the morning. Inside, there's a box of chocs for me and a little woolly hat for Mia, with a note:

'Happy Christmas, from Vin xx'

I feel ashamed 'cause I've not got him anything and I've got no money, so before I go out I make him a cup of tea and some toast and I take it up to his room. Breakfast in bed, that's something, isn't it? He's out for the count. I want to wake him up, so he can see what I've done, but I haven't got the heart, so I just leave the mug and plate next to his mattress.

I bring Mia with me. She lies in the old buggy Vinny got out of a skip. I don't leave her at the house, ever. They're all nice guys, don't get me wrong, and they'd never do her any harm, but, at the end of the day, they're junkies. I'm not judging them – who the hell am I to judge anyone? It's just that Mia's too precious. I can't take any risks with her.

So I paint for as long as she lets me, sometimes two or three hours at a time. It starts to come together and I love it. I almost forget what it's all about and get lost in the physical thing of painting, of creating something. Then when I step back and look, I'm taken by surprise. The violence in it, the chaos, the horror. It's come from me, it's part of me.

When I paint Adam, that's when I start to get emotional. It's so obviously him: it feels like naming and shaming. I start to lose my nerve. Can I put real people up there? Is it right? But then I think, I've got to stay true to myself. This isn't just a dream, it isn't a fantasy, it's real. I'm warning people. So I do Adam, exactly as I see him – beautiful eyes full of flame, scarred face, and I do Mia and I do the date.

And suddenly there it all is. It's big, you can't really see the whole thing at once. You have to walk along and take it in bit by bit. But it's there. The thing I've lived with for so long. It's out there. I did it.

I walk up and down, looking. There are bits I would

change, bits that could be better, but I'm not going to start tinkering with it now. It's starting to get dark. I cuddle Mia closer.

'Let's go home, Mia. Let's get some sleep.'

Adam

I lie on my bed for hours. When I drift off to sleep, the same thoughts morph into nightmares so bad I have to wake myself up. I don't know where I am. The window's on the wrong side, the bedside table's the wrong height. This isn't Weston. Where the hell am I? Where's Mum?

Reality creeps back into my head, but it don't bring any comfort. Because as well as the fire, the fight, Junior, Sarah, there's something else. 112027. I'm another day nearer. Time's running out. If I'm going to do something about it, it'll have to be soon, but I can't do anything. Not a damn thing. All I can do is lie here, and listen to the clock ticking, and listen to my heart beating and wish I was a million miles away, and wish I was someone else.

The police come for me early. Six o'clock on Boxing Day morning. I hear them battering at the door and, in an instant, I'm back in Weston and I feel sick in the pit of my stomach. I can hear voices – Nan's and theirs – and then Nan is in my room.

'They want to question you, down the station. You better get dressed. I'm coming too. They're going to search the house while we're there, got a warrant and everything.'

'Shit!'

'Don't kick up, Adam. Not this time.'

'I didn't do nothing.'

'I know. You're the victim, that's what I said to them, but you were there, and a kid's dead, so they're bound to ask you questions.'

I look round the room. It's all I've got, my space, the weird mixture of my things and Dad's. I don't want anyone poking about, looking at stuff that isn't theirs.

'Get up, son. We've got a couple of minutes to get ready, that's all. Oh, and your notebook.'

'What?'

'Give it here. Wouldn't help if they found that, would it?'

My notebook! With Junior's death right there in black and white. Predicted. Premeditated. Planned. My notebook could make me into a murderer.

'Have you read it?'

She could've, last time she looked after it for me.

She shakes her head.

'Don't need to. I know what's in it. It's your dates, innit, your numbers.'

'There's the computer as well. Dad's PC, and all the stuff I put on it.'

She shrugs.

'Can't do nothing about that one.'

We look at each other, and suddenly, at last, I feel like I could talk to her.

'He was making threats, Nan. But I didn't kill him. It wasn't me.'

She puts her finger up to her mouth.

'Don't say a word to them,' she whispers. 'Not a bloody word.' Then she takes the book and scuttles off to her room to get dressed.

The questions go on all day.

I don't say a thing.

'Who else was there?' *Do you think I'd tell you that?*

'How did you end up in the fire?' *What do you think?*

'Did you see anyone with a knife?'

It starts to become obvious they haven't found the knife. It's still out there somewhere; dumped, hidden or being carried about.

They haven't got the knife. They've got names but no evidence.

I'm waiting for it to play out like a TV cop show, for someone to come in and whisper in the ear of the guy asking all the questions – the killer clue that'll seal the deal for them. *It was planned. The kid was ambushed, he didn't stand a chance.* There'll be that look of triumph on their faces – we've got him. But it don't come.

Nan has a word with the solicitor sitting in with us, a young woman, dark and intense, making notes on her laptop the whole time. She shuts the laptop lid and starts asking her own questions.

'Are you going to charge him?'

'If you want to keep him any longer, I'm going to insist on a doctor being present – he's only just come out of hospital. Are you going to keep him?'

'You're putting undue pressure on him. He's sixteen. Are you familiar with the contents of the Children and Criminal Justice Act 2012?'

They're not happy but they finally agree I won't be

charged today, and I'm allowed to go. Outside, Nan shakes hands with the solicitor and nudges me to do the same.

'Thanks,' I say. The solicitor breaks into a smile.

'You can speak, then,' she says. She hands Nan her business card. 'Ring me if you need to, day or night.'

We make our own way home, not knowing what we'll find when we get there, but it's just as we left it. I check my room, all okay, nothing missing, not even the computer.

Back downstairs, with the kettle on and a fag sparked up, Nan fishes down her top and produces the notebook.

'You'd better have this back.'

'Nan,' I say, 'you know I never wanted to come to London?'

She narrows her eyes, looking at me through a cloud of smoke.

'Yeah.'

'I reckon we should get out now. London's a bad place for me. My mum said it, didn't she? It's not safe here.'

'Well, that's where she and I disagreed, see, 'cause I think you're here for a purpose. Times like these need people like you, people that show other people the way. You're a prophet.'

'Like Jesus or something.'

'Maybe.'

I feel like the ground shifting under my feet. I knew Nan was weird, but I reckon she's really losing her marbles now.

'Shut up. Don't be so fucking stupid.'

'There's that language again. You're right, you're not Jesus – Jesus would never have sworn at his Nan.'

'Nan, I'm not Jesus. I'm not anything like that. I'm just . . . ordinary.'

'Well, we both know that's not true.'

There's a pause, while we look at each other – we both know she's right.

'Okay, I'm different. I can see things, but that don't mean I can change the world.'

'Can't you? Can't you really?'

'No, Nan!'

'I think you can. I think you will.'

'And I think if I don't get out of London, I'm going to die in a prison cell.'

Her hands go up to her face then.

'Don't say that! Don't ever say that.'

'Nan, I don't know what my number is. But a fuck-load of people are going to die here, and maybe I'm one of them.'

She slumps down in the chair and runs her hands through her hair. It's a while since she's dyed it and the grey roots are showing through. For once, she's speechless. I think at last I've got through to her. I know I've got to get out of here, and maybe she'll come with me.

'Let's pack some bags now, leave tonight.'

She looks up from the chair.

'What about that girl . . .?'

Sarah. And her number. The number that tells me I won't die in a cell. Or does it?

Nan's question's still hanging in the air when the doorbell rings. We both freeze. My first thought is that it's Sarah. The old witch has summoned her up. My heart starts pounding in my chest. What if it is? What'll I do? What'll I say? My second thought is that it's the police. They've found the knife. My heart won't let up pounding.

'You gonna get that?' Nan asks.

'Dunno,' I say, and I bite the edge of my lip.

'Don't sound like they're going to go away. Go on, Adam.

Save my old legs.'

I go to the front door. It's dark outside, so I flick on the light as I open the door.

There's a boy on the doorstep, a little kid with glasses. For a minute I can't remember where I've seen him before. He clocks my face and looks away, but then he looks back again, at my eyes, not my skin.

'I'm . . . I'm sorry . . .' he stammers. His face twitches and the penny drops – Nelson, the boy from Maths Club.

'What are you sorry for?' I ask.

'For your accident, for coming here. I just thought you should have this . . .' He holds out a sheet of paper, rolled up with a rubber band round the middle.

'What is it?' I ask.

'It's those birthdays. I plotted them. Only . . .'

'What?'

'Only . . . they're not birthdays, are they?' The twitch in his face is going mad. All I can think of is, *More evidence, printed, plotted, mapped.*

'You better come in.'

We flatten out the printout on the coffee table in the lounge. It's a map of West London covered in dots. There are so many dots you can't hardly see the map underneath.

'I worked with the data you gave me, although I don't think it stands up to scrutiny. Anyway, it was what I had so I had a go. I looked up postcodes, had to make a best guess for some of them, and plotted them. Different colours for the different dates – there's a key by the side there. The bigger the circle, the more people. I've done it in bands, the smallest dot for up to five, then five to ten, ten to twenty, and the biggest one for over twenty.'

He's done black for the first of January, blue for the

second, red for the third, and so on.

'So where are we?'

Nelson points to an area with a massive black dot on.

'Where do you live, Nelson?'

He points again. Black.

We sit and look at it for a minute in silence. Nelson keeps looking at me and back at the map. His face is going mad – twitch, twitch, twitch. Finally, he pushes his glasses further up his nose, and says what he's been screwing himself up to say.

'I don't think it's birthdays, Adam. There are too many in some places and the distribution is so uneven. What is it? What are these dates?'

I look at him blinking nervously at me, face dancing on its own. It's there in his eyes. His number. 112027. If I can't save the world, perhaps I can save him. Perhaps the best place to start is the truth. There's a voice in my head, Mum's voice, but I push it to the back of my mind.

Then another voice cuts in.

'Tell 'im. Tell 'im the truth.' Nan's standing in the kitchen doorway.

'They're death dates,' I say. 'I can see them. Do you believe me?'

Nelson blinks and swallows. I can't help looking at him, and his number makes me scared. Scared for him, scared for me.

'I do believe you,' he says. 'I don't understand, but I do believe you, 'cause it's all over the internet, Adam. Here, let me show you.'

He leans down next to the sofa and fetches up a laptop case. He unzips it, puts the machine on his lap and switches it on.

'I did some research around the first date, New Year's Day. There are sites all over Western Europe with hints about it. Weird things on forums and blogs. There's a cult up in Scotland, predicting the apocalypse on the first. They've moved to an island, and holed up there. Their leader's quoted on a ton of sites saying, "We have all sinned. God's retribution is coming and those without God will die on New Year's Day. I have seen the truth in their eyes."'

He calls up a site.

'Good,' he says, 'it's still here.'

There's a blurry photo of a man in the middle of a circle of people.

'Who is he? This guy?'

'None of the sites give his full name. He's known as Micah.'

A chill runs down my spine and I shiver.

'He can see the numbers too,' I say. 'That's what he's saying. That's what he means.'

'There's a lot of nutters out there. There always have been. There's a whole history of people saying the end of the world is about to happen and it never has.'

'Do you think I'm a nutter?'

Nelson hesitates for a second. His face twitches unhappily.

'It's all right,' I say. 'You don't have to answer.'

'No, no,' he says, 'I don't think you are. It's just . . . I just can't explain what you're seeing. I can't think of a scientific explanation. What *do* you see?'

'I don't know if I even see the numbers or if I just think them. When I look in someone's eyes, the number's just there. It's there and I know it. I've always been able to see them.'

'And they're the date when the person dies?'

'Yeah. My mum, other people. I've seen their numbers. I've seen their deaths.'

Nelson don't know what to do with himself, where to look. He's not the kind of guy who can come right out and ask me his number. But he's thinking it, and I'm seeing it, and I'm cursing this thing, this gift, this burden. I wish I could say something, tell him he's going to be okay, but his number's screaming at me, tearing through my head.

'Nelson . . . mate . . .' I start to say, but he gets agitated 'cause he don't know what's coming next.

He clears his throat and his fingers tap across the keyboard.

'The Government knows something, too,' he blurts out. 'Look. They're blocking public events. All licence applications across London from 30th December onwards have been refused. It's coming up to New Year's Eve, Adam, they've got to be worried to cancel parties on New Year's Eve.'

'The Government knows . . .?'

'Looks like it. As soon as 01 01 pops up on a site, they close it down. That's why I was surprised that image of Micah was still there.'

I should be pleased, shouldn't I? Pleased I'm not mad. Pleased other people know something about the first. That I'm not on my own. But all I feel is a wave of panic. Every nerve end's vibrating, my whole body's on red alert. *It's real. It's happening.*

'There's something closer to home too. If it's still there. I bookmarked it . . . here.' He brings up another web-page and slides the laptop over to me. At first I don't get what it is he's trying to show me. The screen's full of a picture, something painted.

'You have to scroll left and right to see the whole thing.'

It looks like a war zone: darkness, chaos, a sky full of smoke, hands reaching out of rubble, gaping holes where there should be houses.

I scroll right. There's a date, like a banner across the top: 1st January 2027. And then the blacks and greys and browns turn into reds and yellows and oranges, as flames lick across the screen. Nelson isn't looking at the laptop; he's watching me to see my reaction. I scroll across again, and now there's faces, twisted with pain and terror. There's a baby with its eyes screwed up, tears flying off its face and a man holding it, a black guy. The flames are reflected in his eyes, but it's not his eyes that turn my guts to water, it's his face. The skin is scarred and bumpy.

It's me.

I'm the guy in the picture.

I'm the one with flames in his eyes.

I'm fighting the urge to gag. I'm trying not to smell the smoke, hear the angry crackling of the flames.

'What is it?' Nan comes and looks over my shoulder. The smoke from the end of her fag curls into my face and I start choking. She wafts it away from me, but it's too late. I'm back there, helpless as the fire eats into me. I'm coughing my guts up, I can't breathe.

I stagger over to the front door. Outside, I bend over, coughing and retching over Nan's collection of gnomes, until finally I'm sick.

'Adam! Adam! Are you all right? Mind Norris. He's my favourite. Oh God, you got 'im.'

Nan's beside me, watching while I spew up everything in my stomach. Then, after one last spasm, my whole body starts to relax. Cool night air surges into my lungs, and bit by bit, I unpeel and stand up again. We stay there for a while, me breathing in and out, remembering what it's like to feel human again, Nan tutting about her garden ornaments.

When we go back in Nelson is packing up his laptop.

'Where was it, that painting?' I ask him.

'Paddington, under the railway, just off Westbourne Park Road.'

'I'll have to go there, have a look.' Even thinking about it gives me the jitters.

'Nelson?'

'Yeah?'

'You should get out of London. You should get away from here.'

'What? With my mum and my brothers? Where we gonna go?'

'I dunno, somewhere. Take them off that map anyway.'

He shakes his head.

'I could try. But what do I tell them? How do I get them to go?'

'I dunno. That's the million dollar question and if I knew the answer, I'd broadcast it to the nation. Get everyone out. Everyone out of London.'

Nan's looking at me now, and there's a gleam in her eye.

'That's more like it,' she says. 'That's the spirit!'

'Na-an . . .' She's looking at me like I'm the Messiah again.

'You can do it, Adam. You can save people.'

Nelson looks quickly from me to her and back again. If I was him, I'd make a quick exit and not look back. But I'm not him, and instead of making a bolt for the door, he says, 'It's the internet. That's where you can do it. They control the main servers and search engines, but there's a whole parallel web they haven't got to yet, a million blogs and forums and tweets. It can be out there before anyone can stop it.'

'You're a genius,' I say.

He shakes his head, but you can tell he's pleased.

'Technically, I'd need an IQ of over 140 for that, and I'm only 138.'

'What's a couple of points between friends? Listen, I don't know squat about the internet. Can you do it?'

He frowns.

'Not straight away. I don't know much about the paraweb. I'd need to create a hidden identity and find a way to stop them tracing me.'

'Will you try?'

'Sure.' He gives me his address and mobile number.

Nan closes the door behind him and grins at me.

'We're doing it, Adam. We're going to change history.'

I want to get caught up in it like her. I want to believe we can make a difference. But I keep coming back to the numbers and how I've never been able to change them before. Mum, Junior, Carl. Are we just kidding ourselves?

And in the middle of it all, the mass of numbers, all those deaths coming to London, there's me. Someone's painted me at the heart of it, swallowed up in flames. They must know me, or have seen me, to get my number, to picture my death like that.

So I won't be packing my bags tonight, because I know what I've got to do next. I've got to find the person who painted me. I've got to find them and look them in the eye.

I set off early the next day, catch a couple of buses and then walk. I need to follow the railway line and it don't take me long to find it. The street that leads to the subway is empty. Some rubbish blows up in the air towards me. I dodge it and jog on.

It's a dark place even in the daytime. The walls either side are covered with graffiti. When I get close I slow down. I stop at the entrance, suddenly scared. I make myself take a few deep breaths, and then I go in. What I notice first is the cold on my fingers and my face, and the way sounds from outside are muffled in here while sounds inside are bigger, so even my shoes scraping on the rough surface make a loud noise. It smells wet and dark and mouldy, and then, suddenly, there's something else.

A whiff of smoke catching in my nose, at the back of my throat. The crackle of flames. A woman screaming.

And it's there in front of me.

The picture from the web – the face. My face. And now I can see how big the painting is, it's massive, floor to ceiling and five metres long.

'Oh my God,' I say and my voice echoes off the walls.

It was a shock just seeing it on screen in sections, but this is something else.

I want to step back and take the whole thing in, but there's nowhere to step back to – the tunnel's only a few metres wide.

So I reach towards it instead. My arm's shaking, my whole body is. My skin's red hot, there's sweat soaking into my hat, trickling down between my shoulder blades. I put my hand on the wall. The writing's huge. My fingers are flat against the paint, stretched out, but they don't even cover the bottom half of the 7. The wall's so cold and my skin's so hot. I take my hood down, peel off my hat and go right up close. I put both hands to the wall and lean my head in too, so my forehead's against the brick.

It's like some kind of religious experience. I've held the numbers inside for so long and here's proof I'm not alone.

Someone else knows. 2027 has haunted me. But here – in a cold, dark tunnel in West London, with that picture of death and destruction over me and round me – I know there's someone else sharing that pain. It feels like coming home.

The brick under my skin is alive. I can feel it through my fingers; it's humming in my ears and coming up through the soles of my feet. I can hear noises again, the screaming, the flames licking up, a deep rumbling sound getting louder and louder. It's filling my head now. I stand my ground but I close my eyes tight shut. The vibration and the noise are the same thing, building up around me, inside me. There's flames and faces, twisted, distorted, terrified.

I open my mouth and scream. It's the sound I made when I fell in the fire, an animal noise coming out of the middle of me. The tunnel's not bricks and stones any more, it's a wild, living, roaring beast, a living nightmare. My scream goes on until there's no breath in me.

Then I breathe and scream again.

The rumbling and clattering dies down, and I'm left with my voice echoing off the walls and the thunder of an express train dwindling away to a background hum, and then nothing.

I step back from the wall and open my eyes. I don't know what just happened to me: how much of it was real. My hands are freezing. I rub them together, then hold them up to my mouth and blow on them. The discs of light either end of the tunnel are grey and there's rain slanting across them. My eyes are playing tricks on me, confused by the painting in front of me, up close in the dark, and the light outside, so it takes me a while to grasp someone's standing at the other end of the tunnel, not walking, just standing.

I can only see an outline: baggy trousers, some sort of

jacket and a spike of hair. And all of sudden I realise how lonely and isolated this place is.

Shit, I'm going to get battered.

I don't need any aggro, so I start walking the other way. *Keep cool. Don't show you're rattled.* Out in the open, I turn round for a second to see if I'm being followed. He's still there, watching me. I stop walking and make myself stand and look back at him. Both of us standing in the rain, both of us looking. And then the hairs on the back of my neck go up. We're a long way from each other but our eyes meet and I get a warm rush.

It's not a boy, it's a girl. The girl who hates me, the girl whose last breath surrounds me as she slips away in fifty years' time.

Sarah.

Sarah

I see him before he sees me. The weird thing is I kind of know he's going to be there even before I turn the corner. It's not a complete surprise. And I ask myself, why did I walk this way? It's raining, it's quicker to go through the estate to get to the shop, not round the back, but I walked this way. Why?

Seeing him in the flesh – the real thing, not the picture in my head, on the wall – brings me out in goosebumps. I'm scared of him. I'm thrilled as well. What the fuck is wrong with me?

I should turn around before he notices me. Turn around and walk away. No, I should run. He's the boy in my nightmare. The boy in my future, who takes my baby and walks into the fire. He's evil, so why am I still standing here?

Adam

'Sarah!'

She don't move, so I start walking towards her. I get ten metres away, and then she reacts.

'Stop there. Don't get any nearer.'

She sounds unsure.

'I just want to talk to you.'

'I've got nothing to say.'

'It was you, wasn't it? You put me up there. Why have you put me up on that wall?'

'You know. You know what you do.' Her voice is low and quiet, but I can hear the poison in it. She hates me. She thinks I'm disgusting.

'I don't! I don't know!'

I take a step towards her. She steps back and bends down to pick up a stone.

'Don't come any nearer.'

'Sarah, I don't know what I've done. I haven't done nothing to you. I don't understand. But I do know about New

Year's Day.'

She's listening now, really listening.

'What do you know?'

'I see them too, people's numbers. There's hundreds and thousands of people with the first or second or third. It's big, Sarah, something big is going to happen.'

'Numbers?'

'The numbers you see when you look at someone. You know.' And then I realise she's been looking at me; she's looking at me now. My number must be staring her in the face.

'Numbers?' she says again. 'What are you talking about?'

'Death dates. You know. You see them too.'

'Shut up. I don't see any numbers. You don't know me. You don't know anything about me.'

And I think, *Yes, yes, I do. I can see your years stretching out ahead. I can feel you with me, feel how we love each other, you and me.*

She glares at me, but it's not just hate in her eyes. There's fear there, too. Even in the cold she's sweating.

'Shut up,' she says. 'Don't talk. Just leave.'

'Please, you're the only other person who understands. Please can we talk.'

She raises her arm and hurls the stone at me. I put my hands up to protect myself. Too late – it clips the top of my head.

'Jesus!' I yelp. I bend over, trying to breathe through the pain as the world turns red and black in front of me. I look up to see Sarah disappearing into a side road.

I try to straighten up, but the pain in my head's like a weight keeping me down. So I stumble after her, lurching about like a drunk.

There are rows and rows of terraced houses, with alleyways running down the back between them. No sign of her, though, and I'm ready to give up when I see a load of paint tins in a skip by one of the alleyways. I look down the backs of the houses, and think I see a gate swinging.

It's half off its hinges. The yard behind is in a state and the back of the house is even worse; windows broken or boarded up, slates missing from the roof. Surely, no one lives in here?

I lean on the wall opposite and stare at the house. If I stand still, my head don't hurt so much. There's an itch on my face. I put my fingers up to touch it, and they come away red.

Something moves at one of the windows. I can't see what, or who, but there's definitely someone there. Should I knock on the back door? Go round to the front? Or wait?

I'm stood there wondering what to do when the back door opens. A bloke comes out. He's tall and skinny, the bloke from the car. He's heading my way and he's carrying a baseball bat.

Sarah

I stay out of sight, at the window upstairs. It's open a few centimetres, so I can hear what's going on. I had to wake Vinny up, but he didn't need much persuading to go out there – he could see how terrified I was.

'What you doing here?' he says. 'Fuck off.'

'There's someone in there I want to talk to.' The sound of Adam's voice twists at my guts.

'Yeah? Well she doesn't want to talk to you.'

'I'm not going,' he says. 'I'll wait.'

I move a fraction so I can see. Vinny's stopped a little way away from Adam. He's gangly, but he looks like he means business.

Come on, Vinny. Get rid of him. Frighten him if you have to, just get rid.

'Listen,' he says, 'I don't want to get violent, but you shouldn't go chasing girls through the streets. It's not right.'

'Well, perhaps she shouldn't chuck things at people and hurt them. I only wanted to talk to her.'

I lean a little further forward. There's blood all down his face, on the bit that was burnt.

'Did she do that to you?'

'Yeah.'

'You're the kid from the hospital, aren't you? Look,' says Vinny, 'I dunno what's going on, but you should just go, before there's any more damage done.'

'I'm not going. It's important. It's about her graffiti, in the tunnel. Did you know about that?'

Vinny shifts position. He's backing off, damn him.

'Yeah, I know.'

'She's put me in it. I'm up there, on the wall.'

'You're the one in her nightmare.'

Shut up, Vinny. Shut the fuck up.

'What?'

'The painting. It's a dream she has, over and over. You're in it. Why are you in it?'

'I dunno, mate. That's what I want to find out.'

The bat's hanging down by Vinny's side now. This is no good.

'Wait here,' he says, and walks back into the house. He yells up from the hallway.

'Sarah! It's all right. It's just a kid.'

'I don't want him here. I told you to get rid of him! For God's sake, Vinny, use the fucking baseball bat on him. Get him out of here!'

'He just wants to talk to you . . . I'm not battering anyone. He's a kid. Anyway, you got him good and proper yourself. Come down . . . he's not going 'til you talk to him. Are you coming?'

He's too soft, Vinny. I'll have to do it myself.

I unzip my jacket and gently take Mia out of the sling and

lay her down in the drawer. She's asleep, thank God. Then I make my way downstairs. In the kitchen I grab a knife.

Vinny's in the doorway. Beyond him, I can see Adam, he's come into the yard. I push past Vinny.

'I don't want you here,' I tell Adam. 'Can't you take a hint?'

He puts his hand up to his face and I'm back in a classroom, a million years ago, when I reached across the desk. His skin was perfect then: smooth, clear, warm. Half his face still is – the other half is changed utterly. You could say disfigured. I'd say different. In my mind's eye, I see myself touching it again, and my fingers tingle at the thought. Why am I drawn to him when he's one of the two people on earth I'm scared of?

He stands there now, with blood on his fingers. I've got to get rid of him before I crumble.

'Come on, Sarah,' Vinny says. 'He might be able to help you.'

It jolts me back to reality, my version of reality.

'Help me? Help me?' I can hear my own voice becoming shrill. 'You don't know him, Vin. You don't know what he does. He's the Devil, Vin, the Devil. I don't want him here. Please get him away. Please!'

The words coming out of my mouth sound wrong, even to me. I suddenly see myself as they do: wide-eyed, wild, mad, wielding a knife in my hands. Who am I kidding? I'm not going to stab him. I don't want to hurt him – I just want him to go away.

'Sarah?' he says quietly.

I can't deal with him. I can't be here with him. I back away and stagger into the kitchen. I drop the knife on the floor and then drop down next to it, drawing my legs in towards me, curling up. Tears are coming now. I hate this. I hate me for doing it. I don't cry. I'm tougher than that. But I am crying and now I've started, I can't stop.

I know they've followed me in, but I don't look up. Neither of them comes over to me. Typical men, they don't know what to do with a crying woman. I should have known that all along, stones and knives won't scare a man away, but tears will.

'I'm sorry.' It's Adam. 'I'm so sorry. I never meant to upset you.'

I unwind a little, and glance up at him. He looks stricken.

'Just go,' I say.

'Okay,' he says, 'I will. I'll leave you alone.' But as he turns to go, he stops again. 'Sarah?'

'What?'

'My number. Is it the same? Is it New Year's Day?'

He can hardly look at me. He's scared too. I get the feeling he's holding his breath.

'I don't know what you're talking about,' I say and the tears well up again and I bury my head in my arms. He leaves then. I hear him blunder against the door frame, hear his steps in the yard outside.

Up above me, Mia's woken up, her kitten's cry building to a full-throttle scream. It cuts through my self-pity, and I unwind and get to my feet.

'All right now?' Vinny asks.

I can't even begin to answer that. Adam's gone – thank Christ he's gone – but inside me, I know this isn't the end. He's found me now. My safe house isn't safe any more.

Adam

I stumble out of the house in a daze. She don't see numbers, but she has a nightmare, a recurring nightmare, and I'm in it. It's unreal. It can't happen. She must have dreamt about me before we met, that's why she reacted how she did that first day at school. She'd already seen me in her dreams. But how?

I accept the numbers, because they've always been with me. I've grown up with them – they're 'normal' to me. But she's got some other kind of gift, a different curse, and it's set my mind reeling. I don't get it. It don't make any sense.

Without thinking I head back to the tunnel. It's still raining, and it's dry in there. I lean against the wall opposite Sarah's painting, then I realise how tired my legs are and sink down to the ground. I look at the wall in front of me, and my own face looks back. If this is how she's seen me, night after night, no wonder she's scared.

I close my eyes, but the picture stays with me. It's there in my head, crowding in on me, and it's not just paint – it's sound and taste and touch and smell. I can hear a baby crying, high-pitched and desperate. Sarah's crying too, in a different way, she's given up hope. All around us are the sounds of a building being destroyed, consumed by fire. The flames aren't touching us yet, but the air is hot, unbearable. We're trapped.

I open my eyes, scoop up a handful of gravel and throw it at the wall.

'It's a painting, just a fucking painting!'

I know it's more than that, but I don't want it to be. I don't want any of this – the numbers, the nightmares: a terrible future getting closer every day, unstoppable. No-one should have to live like this.

I grab another handful of stones, get to my feet and go over to the painting. I grind the stones into the face, my face.

'It's not me. I'm not there. Fuck you! Fuck you! Fucking go away!' The stones make no difference. The image is still there. I smash my fist into it tearing the skin off my knuckles. It's so stupid, but what else can I do? You can't fight the future, can you? Can you? I want to. I want to kick the future right up the arse. I want to jab my fingers in both its eyes, knee it right in the balls, slam my fist into its guts so it folds over and coughs up blood.

But all I'm doing right now is making my own hand hurt. Shit!

'That won't make it go away. Nothing does.'

I spin round.

She's there, in the entrance to the tunnel, in the rain. How long has she been standing there? How much has she seen?

'I don't know what to do,' I say, and it's the truth. I don't know what to do, what to say, where to go.

'Come back with me. We should talk.'

Something terrible happens then. My mouth wobbles, and my whole face crumples and I start to cry.

I turn away. I don't want to let her see me like this, but I can't hide what I'm doing because it rips right through me, takes over my whole body. I crouch down with my back to her as the tears stream down my face and the snot pours out of my nose. I'm sobbing, out of control, and the noise of it fills the tunnel. I know what I look like, what I sound like, but I can't help it. I wish I was dead. Oh God, that's why I'm crying. I wish I was dead.

She touches my shoulder, trying to help I suppose, but I'm so ashamed. I twitch away from her, shout, 'No!'

I hear her step away.

'Come back to the house. When you're ready. I'll be there,' she says and she leaves. I try to stop crying, so that I can listen to the sound of her footsteps, but by the time I've calmed down, all I can hear is the rain spattering on the ground outside.

I wipe my face with my hands and my sleeve and stand up slowly, so the blood can flow back into my legs. I feel empty, emptied out, blank.

I see the painting out of the corner of my eye and I remember how angry I was. It was minutes ago, but it feels like years. I wanted to smash the future. I still want to, but not the next minute, the next two minutes, not even the next ten minutes.

Because I'm going to walk to Sarah's house.

She's waiting for me.

Sarah

Why do I ask him back? Because while I'm calming Mia down, I can't shake off the look in his eyes when he was standing in the kitchen. He's scared, too, see. Like me.

And besides, he knows where I live now, so he can come back any time he likes. I don't want him just turning up. I'd rather he was here on my terms.

So I go after him, and find him where I expect, in the tunnel. But I didn't think he'd be like that. He crumples in front of me. It tugs at my heart – this beautiful boy, cocky, aggressive, now burnt, terrified, in despair. He's crying like a baby, like my Mia. I've changed since I had her – I can't stand to hear people crying now. I know that tears can be soothed away. And part of me wants to put my arms round him, rock him till he calms down, tell him everything's going to be all right. I put my hand on his shoulder, but he shrugs me off. Don't blame him; I'd probably do the same. Pride, isn't it? It's okay. Best to let him come out of it himself.

I tell him I'll be here waiting for him, and now I am. I

know he'll come. I'd bet my life on it. And he does. Five minutes after I get back, he turns up at the back gate. I can see him through the kitchen window, so I go to the door.

He's soaking wet. The rain's washed most the blood off his face, but there's still a bit on his forehead. You can't really tell he's been crying, but he feels it, the embarrassment, he can hardly look me in the eye.

'Come in,' I say. He walks in to the kitchen, dripping everywhere. I hand him a tea towel. 'You can get dry with that.'

He dabs at his face, then rubs his head.

'Ta,' he says.

I look back at him. Standing there, soaked to the skin, he's shivering.

'Do you wanna drink? Water? Coke? Cup of tea?'

'Cup of tea. Yeah. Please.'

I potter about with the kettle and tea pot and tea bags. It's odd doing something so normal with the two of us there.

'Where's your friend?' he asks.

'In the next room,' I lie. Vinny's out, delivering.

'He's left his bat here.' Adam looks at the baseball bat leaning against the wall.

'I can use that, if I have to,' I say, then I realise how pathetic that sounds – who's a tough little girl, then – and I smile, in spite of myself.

Adam doesn't know if he's allowed to smile too. The corner of his mouth twitches.

Then he says seriously, 'You won't need to. I'm not here to hurt you, Sarah. I'll never hurt you.'

I hear my dad's voice then, 'It won't hurt if you keep still.' Lies, lies, lies.

I must have shown something on my face because Adam

frowns and says, 'Did I say the wrong thing? I mean it, Sarah, I won't hurt you. I just want to talk.'

I snap out of it.

'No, it's fine. I believe you. I want to talk too. Let's sit down.' I lead him through to the empty front room.

He looks around. 'I thought . . .'

'What?'

'Nothing. Never mind.' He thought Vinny was here. I told him Vinny was here.

We sip our tea, me sitting on one broken-down, filthy sofa, him on the other. There's so much to say, but it's difficult to know where to start. It's awkward, the silence between us. The longer it goes on, the worse it gets. Eventually, Adam dives in.

'Sarah, you were calling me things – the Devil. I don't understand why. I've only met you a couple of times. I've never done anything to you.'

I take a deep breath.

'Okay, we've only met a couple of times, but I've seen you. I've seen you every night for the last year. You're in my nightmares. You were there before I ever met you. I knew about your scar before it happened.'

He puts his hand up to his face.

'Shit,' he says. 'You saw my accident, the fire.'

'No, I don't think so. I do see fire, buildings collapsing, flames all around but the thing is . . . the thing is, the dream, my nightmare. I think it's the future. It's not what's happened. It's what's going to.'

Most people would think I was mad if I said that to them. Adam doesn't.

'New Year's Day,' he says.

'Yeah, that's the date, the date in my nightmare. I didn't

dream it until I met you. It came into my dream the night after I saw you at school.'

'I brought you a number,' he says. 'That's what I see, numbers. Death dates. When I look in someone's eyes,' – he's looking straight at me – 'I see a number, the date they're going to die, and I feel it too. Sometimes I can see it, or hear it, just a flash. I can tell if it's violent or peaceful, if something inside does it or something from outside.'

The fire hasn't changed his eyes. They're beautiful: crystal-clear whites, dark, dark-brown irises, fringed with thick lashes. I could lose myself in his eyes, if I let myself . . . except now I know he sees more than other people, and I wonder, can't help wondering, what he sees when he looks at me.

'Can you see my death?'

He doesn't look away, and neither do I. I don't know if he's heard me. He's looking so intently, it's like he's somewhere else.

'Can you see my death, Adam?'

He takes a huge breath in, and he's back in the room with me.

'Yeah,' he says. His whole face softens. He's still looking, but now it's not just my eyes he's taking in. His eyes sweep down and up, over my body, my face. It's like he's shining a spotlight on me. It's intense and it's uncomfortable.

'You know when I'm going to die,' I say, and my words break the spell.

He looks away and says quietly, 'I can't tell you, Sarah. I don't tell people their numbers. It'd be wrong.'

'I don't want to know,' I say. 'I'm not scared,' (which is a lie), 'I just don't want to know. Don't ever tell me.'

Ever. Why did I say that? Like we're going to be friends.

Like we're going to know each other for a long time. Like we've got a future together.

'I won't tell you,' he says. Then, 'Are you really not scared?'

'I'm not scared of me dying. I'm scared of . . .' I stop. *Scared of losing Mia. Scared of Mia losing me.*

'Scared of what?'

'My nightmare,' I say slowly. It's true, after all. 'It's driving me mad. The same dream, the date. I can't live with it. I can't do anything about it.'

'It's the same for me,' he says. 'There's hundreds, thousands of people with numbers on the first or second or third. Violent deaths. It's getting nearer and nearer. Five days to go now. I feel like it's crushing me sometimes. Like there's nothing I can do, except I do want to do something. I want to fight it. Warn people. Get them out. Get them out of London.'

He's getting agitated now, clenching his fists, moving his body where he sits, almost rocking. The energy in him, it's kind of frightening. It's kind of exciting too.

'I think we can do it,' he says. 'I think we can beat the numbers, save people. Only I'm not sure how . . .'

'Is it just London?'

'I dunno, there's more of them here than there was in Weston.'

'Weston?'

'Where I come from. Weston-super-Mare. By the sea. I lived there with my mum.'

'What happened?'

'She died. When I was eight. Cancer. I saw her number and I didn't know what it was. So I told her, well, wrote it down and she saw it. She understood, because she'd seen them too. She was the girl at the London Eye in 2009, the one who knew it was going to be blown up. She saw people's numbers in the queue. Then she had to live with it. With knowing her number. I did that to her . . .'

He trails off, and I can see he's trying not to cry again.

'It's all right,' I say, 'it's all right being upset about your mum. I've got some tissues somewhere.'

He sniffs loudly and wipes his nose on his sleeve.

'No,' he says, 'I'm all right. I don't need any. I'm all right.' He sits up in his chair, rearranges his restless arms and legs. 'I'm sorry.'

'What for?'

'For everything. For being embarrassing. For being in your nightmare.'

I shrug. 'Not your fault. You didn't ask to be there, did you?'

He leans forward and clasps his hands, twisting his fingers together.

'Sarah, what if your nightmare don't have to come true? What if we can change it?'

It doesn't have to come true. If only he was right . . . if only.

'I've tried to warn people,' I say. 'It's out there, in the painting.'

'Is that why you did it?'

'I don't know. Vin suggested it. He heard me screaming every night. He said I should draw it. I've got piles of paper upstairs with my drawings. It's so real, Adam. I wanted to let people know. I wanted to make it go away.'

'Has it gone away? The nightmare?'

'No.'

I sag back into the sofa, suddenly exhausted. All at once, the months of broken nights are weighing down on me.

'You look knackered,' he says. 'I'll go.'

He's got up now. I start to get up too.

'It's all right,' he says, 'stay there. I'll let myself out . . . only . . . is it all right if I come back again sometime?'

I sink back down, all the energy completely drained out of me. I was so ready to fight him, to defend myself against the demon in the nightmare. But Vinny was right. He's just a boy, a boy who's as messed up as I am. I'm exhausted and I do want him to go.

But I want him to come back too.

'Yeah,' I say. 'You can come back.'

He smiles then, a lopsided sort of smile, because where it's burnt the skin is stiff. There's something about that skin that makes me feel soft inside. He passes close to me and hesitates for a second.

'Bye, Sarah,' he says.

'Bye.'

My eyes close before he's out of the door, and I'm sucked down into a deep, dreamless sleep.

Adam

She closes her eyes. She looks softer like that, younger. Her skin's very pale, almost white. When I walk past her, we're so close I smell her musky scent, and all I want to do is put my arms round her, hold her close, put my face in her hair and breathe her in.

I stand in the doorway for a while, watching her. I could stand here for ever.

Somewhere in the rooms above me, a noise starts up. Deep in her sleep, Sarah must hear it too, because she shifts around a bit, before settling down again. It's weak, like a kitten, some sort of animal, but something about it bothers me. I ease myself out of my sofa and tiptoe past Sarah and out into the hall. At the bottom of the stairs I look up. There's no sign of anyone else around, only this cry. Standing there, I think I know what it is.

I'm torn – I want to find it and I want to run away. Perhaps curiosity gets the better of me, perhaps it's more than that. This house and Sarah, I was meant to find them.

I'm meant to be here, now. I'm meant to hear this noise. If I run away now, I'll only have to come back some other time and face it. I pick my way carefully up the bare stairs. On the first floor, the noise is still above me. By now, my heart's banging away in my chest. I can hear my breath sighing in and out of my open mouth.

Up again to the top floor. The sound's louder now and getting more desperate. There are four doors off the landing. I push each door in turn, standing back, like I was expecting a man with a gun to be taking aim the other side. Bathroom first – mould on the walls, a tap dripping onto a rusty stain in the sink. Then a bedroom with clothes all over the floor, a mattress on the bare boards, a guitar propped up against the wall. A second bedroom with an old sofa used as a bed and piles of books and magazines and newspapers everywhere. All empty.

One more room to go.

The door's half-open. The noise is filling my ears now, and it's definitely not an animal. I stop outside. I can't do it. *Come on,* I say to myself, *come on, you've got this far.*

I push the door further open and stand there. Compared to the other rooms it's surprisingly neat. There's a mattress on the floor in one corner with a duvet smoothed flat across it, and piles of clothes and blankets and towels folded all neat on some shelves – someone's made an effort, you can see that.

Next to the bed, on the floor, is a large drawer. From the doorway all I can see is two little pink hands thrashing backwards and forwards in the air.

I walk over and look down. The baby's red in the face from crying. Her eyes are tight shut and her eyelashes are wet with tears. She's waving her arms above her and her feet are going too – left, right, left, right, rubbing against the sheet. I crouch down.

'What's all that noise, then?' I say.

All of a sudden her arms and legs go still and she opens her eyes. They're bright blue. Like her mum's. I gasp, 'No. Oh please God, no.'

Like a bullet to my brain, her number shoots through me. 112027.

Sarah

'What the hell are you doing? Get away from her.'
He's there, in my room, kneeling down next to the
cot. He was after her the whole time. All that little-boy-lost
stuff was bullshit. He knew the baby was here – he wanted
to get at her.

He looks round over his shoulder. Guilty. Caught in the
act. And I see his face, her face and I know the nightmare
will come true.

'She was crying. I just came up to see if . . .'

'Get away from her!'

I barge past him, shoving him with my shoulder, and
scoop up Mia. I take her away from him, to the other side of
the room and pace up and down, trying to calm her down,
but it's not easy to soothe someone when you're furious
inside, boiling up.

'You shouldn't have come up here. You should have woken
me up.'

Of course he wouldn't have. He wanted to find her, and

he had me exactly where he wanted me – out for the count.

'I didn't know what to do. You were so tired.'

'Of course I'm fucking tired. You'd be tired if you hadn't slept properly for months. Just go, will you? Get out!'

He puts his hands up, backs into the opposite wall.

'Okay, okay. I'll go. I'm sorry. What's wrong with her?'

'Nothing. Babies cry. She's probably just hungry.'

He stands there, dumbly.

'I've asked you to go. Get out, Adam,' I say, pointedly. He hesitates. 'Get the fuck out of here!'

That gets him moving. He stumbles for the door, muttering, 'Okay. But I can come back, can't I?'

'No. No. It's better if you don't.'

'Sarah, please.' Those puppy-dog eyes won't fool me again.

'Don't you get it?' I shout at him. 'I don't want to see you again, bastard. I don't want you coming here. If you show your face again, it'll get fucking battered.'

He goes then, clattering down the stairs. I hear the kitchen door bang and the gate to the yard as well. I sit back on the bed and lift up my tee-shirt.

'Come on, Mia,' I say. 'Shush now. Are you hungry?' She is, of course. She searches furiously for a few seconds and then latches on. 'He's gone, Mia,' I say, 'the nasty man's gone. I won't let him hurt you.'

But sitting there, I'm thinking about what he said. All that stuff, about the numbers, I believed it when he was telling me. It made sense. At school, when I saw him with his notebook, he was writing the numbers down, I'm sure he was, like a trainspotter. If he does see them, he's living in a nightmare like me, poor sod. And his face . . . what he's been through.

I shake my head. I can't think about him. I've got this far.

Got away from home and had Mia, and made a sort of life for myself. I can't take on anything, anyone else. It's got to be about Mia and me. And maybe Adam's right. We should move away from here, right away. I'll take Mia right out of London, away from harm, away from him. Somewhere he'll never find us.

Adam

I'm such an idiot. The picture, the painting, I never ever wondered who the baby was. I was focused on me, only me. What a wanker! It's the baby, the baby she's terrified about.

Her baby.

I had no idea – she must have been pregnant at school, but I never noticed. I was hypnotised by her face, her eyes, her number.

It's still raining as I run through the streets. My feet slap against the wet pavement, and the words in my head fall into the same rhythm: *Sarah's child. Sarah's child.*

I thought it was bad enough being me, living with the weight of a thousand deaths around me. What the hell's it like for her – with the end of the year getting closer and closer, and a vision of her own child in flames playing over and over every night? Whatever I felt before, about the numbers and trying to change them, I feel it ten times more strongly now. I can't let Sarah's nightmare come true. I've got to fight it with everything I've got.

'You look like a drowned rat. Did you find it?' Nan's off her perch and hovering by the door when I come in.

'I found it and I found *her.*'

'Who?'

'The girl who did the painting on the wall. It's Sarah, the girl from school, the girl at the hospital.'

'So what's the deal with her?'

'She has nightmares and I'm in them.'

Anyone else would pull a face, frown maybe, ask what I'm talking about. Not Nan. She gets it straight away.

'The painting. It's her nightmare, her vision. She's a seer, Adam. She's got second sight.'

'She's got a baby as well.'

'A baby?'

'I saw it. Her. She's a twenty-seven, Nan. The baby's going to die with everyone else.'

I don't mean to tell. It's something about Nan, about the way she listens, that makes my mouth run away with me. And then it's out. It's said.

Nan's eyes spring wide.

'The baby dies? Oh no . . . and you're there with her. In the picture. Jesus, Adam. You know what this means, don't you?'

I shake my head. My legs are like jelly, I don't know how I'm still standing.

'It means that you must never see them again. I need to get you out of here, out of London, like you've been saying. You can't be here when it happens. You can't be anywhere near.'

'That's what she said.'

'The girl? Sarah?'

'Yeah, she told me to get out. Not to come back.'

'Did she do this to you an' all?'

Nan puts her hand up to my head. When she moves it away, there's blood on her nicotine-yellow fingertips.

'She did, but that was earlier. When she first saw me, before we talked. She threw a stone.'

'Nice, your friend is. Classy.'

'Shut up, Nan. You don't know her.'

She sniffs.

'Not sure I want to.'

'You won't never meet her now anyway. You're both right. I should stay away from her, from the baby. If I stay away, it can't come true, can it?'

Nan makes me sit down at the kitchen table while she fetches a bottle of disinfectant and dabs some on my head with cotton wool.

'Nan,' I say, 'has Nelson been back today?'

'No. Why?'

''Cause I think you're right, what you were saying before. We've got to warn people. We can't just let this shit happen.'

She stops dabbing and looks at me.

'Do you mean it?' she asks.

'Yeah. It's too big, too serious. I don't care if people think I'm a nutter. We've got to give them a chance to get out. And then we've got to get out too. You and me, Nan, out of London. Do you promise?'

'Yeah, I promise. We'll give it a try, and then we'll pack our bags and go. I used to like Norfolk before it disappeared under the North Sea. But we need somewhere hilly. Out in the middle of bloody nowhere. We'll sit on a hill, open a couple of cans and sit tight, yeah?'

Me and Nan on a hillside watching the end of the world.

'You can have a last fag if you like, I wouldn't deny you that.'

'I always thought I'd be the last smoker in England. Perhaps I will be.'

She puts the TCP away in the cupboard and starts rummaging through the freezer for something to eat.

'Adam,' she says.

'Yeah.'

'I'm glad you want to fight it, 'cause I've already done something.'

'Oh God, what is it?'

'I've booked an appointment.' She stands up from the freezer and sort of puffs her chest out.

'Who with?'

'Mister Vernon Taylor, the Emergency Planning Officer in the Civil Contingencies Unit at the Council.'

'Who the fuck's that?'

'Language. He's the person in charge of planning for disasters. I did some research. Aren't you proud of me?'

'Yeah, s'pose. I dunno. Shouldn't we be seeing that other guy, the one in a suit, MI5 or something like that? He gave me his card. Some geezer in the Council's not likely to believe us, is he? And even if he buys the stuff about the numbers, we don't know what's going to happen, do we? Only when.'

'It's his job to look after this kind of thing. Sort out this road, this estate. I don't like stiffs in suits any more than you do, but we can't let personal prejudice get in our way. We got to tell someone. We got to, Adam. We've got lives to save. It's our civic duty.' She's giving it the full upright citizen stuff now. I guess I must be pulling a face because she goes on, 'You're an ungrateful sod, you are. I thought you'd be pleased.'

'I am. I think. I just . . . I dunno. I am. Thanks, Nan.'

She sniffs a bit and then takes the cardboard off a packet and makes some holes in the top of the plastic with a knife.

'Dinner will be ready in ten minutes. Go and have a quick bath first, and put those filthy, wet clothes in the wash. You can wear a shirt tomorrow, look a bit smart for a change.'

'What for?'

'I just told you, you soft sod, we're going to see the Council. We've got to look the part. Don't want them thinking we're on day release or something.'

I haul myself upstairs and run a bath. It's only when I get in the hot water I realise how cold I've got. I let the warmth soak through to my bones and I close my eyes. It's still pissing down outside. I see Sarah's face and her number whispering a promise to me. *For richer, for poorer. In sickness and in health. Till death do us part.*

If I never see her again, if I keep away from her, how can that ever come true?

Sarah

I came here with just my school bag. Now I have no idea how I'm going to pack for the two of us. I suppose all I really need is clothes, nappies and wipes. We'll manage for everything else.

I don't know where we're going to go, just that we need to get away from here. I don't have enough cash for a train ticket, maybe a coach. Perhaps Vinny would give me some. But I couldn't ask – he's done so much for us. Been a real friend.

Mia's asleep as I gather up her things. I stop to look at her, with her mouth open, her arms flung up around her head. A flutter of panic starts to build in me. Will I cope on my own with her? What if I can't find anywhere to stay? It's stormy outside again, the glass is rattling in the window frames. I can't just set out in that lot with nowhere to go and no-one to go to. Not with a baby.

I sink down onto the bed, not defeated yet, but suddenly realising the truth of my situation. I need to think ahead, I need to plan.

The storm's so loud, I don't hear the knock at the door for a while. At some point, I realise that there's another sound on top of the rattling and creaking and groaning and I make my way downstairs. It's not coming from the back – someone's at the front door. No one ever comes to the front. I slide back the bolts, but there's no key for the lock. The door won't open.

I lean down and flip up the letter box.

'Who is it?'

I can see a shiny patent belt wrapped tightly around the middle of someone's coat. There's a pause and then the someone bends down and there's a chin level with the box.

'My name's Marie Southwell. I'm from Children's Services.'

Shit!

'What do you want?'

'I want to talk to Sally Harrison. Is that you?'

For a split second I feel a flood of relief. Sally Harrison? It's a mistake, wrong address. Then I remember that's me, the me that checked in at the hospital.

'You'll have to come round the back, down the alleyway and into the yard. I'll meet you.'

'Okay.'

I let the letter box spring shut and race into the kitchen, snatching up some of the dirty plates and mugs, shoving them into a cupboard and slamming the door shut. The woman who appears in the back alley is windswept, but still smart, with black patent boots to match her shiny belt. She shows me her ID and I lead her into the house, all at once painfully aware of how it must look to an outsider. Grease and dirt on the ceiling, mouse droppings on the floor, the baseball bat leaning up against the wall.

'Cup of tea?' I ask, hoping to distract her, but her eyes are everywhere, taking it all in.

She smiles. 'Yes please. Milk, no sugar.'

I'm all fingers and thumbs as I try to make the tea. The milk's out on the worktop. When I add it to the tea it forms white clots. I pour it down the sink.

'Shit. Milk's off. Sorry, I'll make some more. Can you drink it black?'

'Don't worry about the tea. Shall we sit down? It's just a routine follow-up. About you . . . and the baby. Is she here?'

'Yes, she's upstairs.'

'I'd like to see her. When we've had our chat.'

'Okay.' My palms are sweaty. I wipe them on my jeans and sit down. 'She's fine, the baby. There's nothing wrong with her.'

She looks up from the papers she's sorting on the kitchen table.

'No, no, of course there isn't. Just that you both seem to have slipped through the system before. It's just routine.'

'How did you . . . how did you find us?'

'She was chipped in the hospital, wasn't she? The baby, Louise.'

'Yes, but . . .'

'The hospital notified Children's Services and she was tracked here.'

Tracked. I'm speechless. Wherever we go now, we can be found.

'I never wanted her chipped. They just did it.'

'Well, yes, I know a lot of people don't like the idea, but it doesn't hurt them and it's a legal requirement now.'

'I know. Well, the law stinks.'

I can hear myself saying it, and I'm kicking myself,

thinking, *Stop it, act normal, act friendly, and she'll go away.*

The smile on her face goes a little tighter.

'Well, it's done now. And it means that we can give you the advice and support you need. Are you in contact with Louise's father?'

'No,' I say quickly. 'No. He never even knew.'

'I'll need his details, because there's child support to consider. He should be paying child support.'

'I don't want his money. I don't want anything to do with him.'

'But you could do with *some* money . . .' She looks around.

'I'm all right. I manage. I've got friends here, they help out.'

'You're entitled to money of your own.'

'I don't want it. I don't want anything off anybody. I just want to be left alone.'

'I'm afraid it doesn't work like that, not when you have a child. The local authority has a duty of care, to ensure the welfare of children in the borough.'

Care? *Care? Who cared about me when I was still at home? Who bothered to find out what was wrong when I started playing up at school? They didn't look further than the wrought-iron gates and the gravel driveway. Nothing wrong with that home, she's just a bad lot.*

'We can apply online now, if you like. I've brought my laptop.'

'I told you I don't want anything.'

'Maybe next time . . .'

'I'll fetch Louise down now, if you like. She's fine and I'm fine. We're fine.'

'I'd like to see her room, if I may? The baby's room?'

I sigh.

'Sure.'

And I lead her up the stairs, with the empty light sockets, the wallpaper hanging off the walls, the doors off the landing kicked in at the bottom. Mia's still asleep in her drawer. She's clean and safe and well. That's what they're looking for, isn't it?

'You're leaving,' Marie says, seeing the plastic bags full of clothes and nappies.

'No, just tidying up. It's not easy keeping tidy here . . .' *Shut up. It's fine here.*

'No,' she says, 'it's not easy. I can see that.'

My pictures are in heaps all over the place. She wanders over to one, picks a drawing up off the top of the pile.

'You're an artist. These are good.'

Then she notices the next one. It's Adam and Mia, in my nightmare. She bends to pick it up, frowns.

'What's this?'

'Nothing, it's nothing. Just a nightmare. I drew a nightmare.'

'It's . . . powerful stuff. Disturbing. Is this the father?'

I start to laugh but then blurt out, 'Yes, yes that's him. Scumbag. Dumped me before I even knew I was pregnant.' It's ridiculous. I'm obviously lying. There's Mia lying in her cot with her lily-white skin and blue eyes to prove it, but Marie doesn't seem to have noticed the evidence.

'We should be able to find him,' she says. 'His face is very . . . distinctive.'

'I don't want him found. I told you, I don't want anything to do with him.'

We both hear the back door slam. Vinny and the boys are back.

'Your housemates?'

I nod.

'I'll quickly examine Louise, and leave you to it, then.'

She kneels down by the drawer. The boys are on good form, I can hear them clattering about in the kitchen, and I start to wonder what state they're in.

'That looks fine,' Marie says. 'No need to wake her up.'

She stands up, dusting down her coat with her hands.

'I'll come back next week, we can talk through your benefits then. It's what you're entitled to. Okay?'

'Okay,' I say. I feel like I'm being bulldozed, back in the system, officially on the books, but it's fine. This time next week, I'll be long gone. We go downstairs, me leading the way. I'm cursing the lost front-door key – I could have let her out that way, and bypassed the boys altogether. It's no good, I'll have to take her through the back. But she's right behind me. There's no time for damage limitation.

They've got the foil and the spoons and the syringes all on the go. Vinny and Tom and Frank in the kitchen, cooking up a storm.

Adam

At twenty past two we're outside the Council One-Stop-Shop, and Nan's having a last fag for courage.

'Nan, what are we going to say? Have you thought about it?'

She tips her head back and blows a long stream of smoke up the sky, then drops the end of the cigarette on the floor and grinds it under her shoe.

'I've thought about it. I'm ready. Come on, Adam. Let's get in there.'

As well as a black polyester jacket and skirt, she's wearing shiny court shoes. They've only got a little heel, but that's five centimetres more than her usual slippers or crocs, and she's having a bit of trouble walking. She's tried so hard to dress up and look smart, but I can't help thinking the over-all effect is pretty close to a man in drag. She's made me put on some clean jeans and a school shirt. The collar's digging in, so I undo the top couple of buttons.

'Nan, we should've worn normal clothes. I feel stupid like . . .'

'Shh, we're here now.'

The automatic doors swish open in front of us and we go into a lobby area. There's a touch screen offering options. We pick 'appointment', '14.30' and 'Vernon Taylor' and then another set of doors opens and we're sent into a waiting room.

It's light and bright, with chairs grouped round coffee tables piled with magazines. The walls are mostly glass, so you can see through to the interview rooms the other side, but dotted about on them are screens, running films of people telling us how much the local council has helped them. In between clips, a slogan flashes up, 'Twenty-first century services for twenty-first century people'.

I look round the room at the other 'twenty-first century people'. There's a young woman sitting staring into space while her little boy runs round and round the chairs scream-ing at the top of his voice; there's a man in his forties or fifties, wearing a dressing gown over his clothes, talking to himself. The video loop is interrupted and a message comes up on screen.

'Mrs Dawson to Suite 3.'

I nudge Nan's arm.

'That's us. Look.'

'Suite 3. Where's that, Adam?'

Room 3 is in the corner to our right. Through the glass we can see someone already in there, waiting for us, a man in a crumpled suit with a crumpled face to match. He half gets up when we go in, wipes his hand on his jacket and holds it out towards Nan.

'Vernon Taylor,' he says.

'Valerie Dawson,' Nan says and shakes his hand. He don't offer it to me. The room is empty apart from a desk, three chairs and a laptop.

'Do sit down. Do sit down. Now then, Mrs . . . aah . . .'

'Dawson,' says Nan again.

'Quite. How can I help you?'

Nan takes a deep breath, and launches in. It sounds as lame as I thought it would. I mean, would you believe it if someone told you my story? I'm cringing as I sit there listening, embarrassed for all three of us. My eyes start roaming round, looking for a distraction. The little boy in the waiting room is looking in at us. He squashes his face against the glass, so it looks like the bottom of a slug. Nan and Mr Taylor take no notice, but I stick my tongue out at him. His face changes. He backs off from the window so quickly he trips over this own feet and starts to cry. He sits there, on the floor, while his mother carries on ignoring him.

I hate the way no-one's paying him any attention and I hate that my face made him cry. I turn back to Mr Taylor. Nan's got to the nitty-gritty now. Mr Taylor's making notes on the laptop as she speaks, but when she mentions the date, the first of January, he stops typing, and his eyes flick from the screen to Nan and then to me. I've already clocked his number, but it hits me again. He's one of them, a twenty-seven, but he's a drowner. I've seen quite a few more now, heard the rushing of water in my ears, felt it choking my lungs, filling my stomach, dragging me down.

He's still looking at me, and then he interrupts Nan, and talks to me directly for the first time.

'The first of January, New Year's Day. What do you think is going to happen?'

'I don't know. Something big. It's going to make buildings collapse and things catch fire. There's water too, lots of water.' I feel sick saying this to him, and there's a tell-tale tremble in my voice. 'And it's going to kill people. Lots of people.'

'Nothing more than that? No details? No *real* information?'

'It is real. All of this is real. I know it don't sound real, but it is.'

Nan leans forward in her chair.

'He's always seen them. The numbers. Always. I didn't think you'd believe me, so I brought these.' She fetches out the file of cuttings she showed me. 'His mum was the same, you see. She could see the numbers too. You might remember her. Jem, Jem Marsh – she was all over the papers. She predicted the London Eye bomb in 2009. Look, I've got the cuttings.'

'Nan?'

'Shh, Adam, it'll help. It will.'

She shoves the file across the desk. Mr Taylor fishes in his suit pocket for his glasses and starts to read.

'Yes,' he says in a low voice, like he's talking to himself, 'yes, I do remember. And this was your mother?' He looks up at me, like he's seeing me for the first time.

'Yeah,' I say.

'But she denied it later, didn't she? Said she'd made it all up?'

'She said that to get everyone off her back. That's all.'

He leans forward over the desk, and shuffles through the papers a bit more. Then he takes off his glasses and leans back in his chair. He closes his eyes and it's a long time before he speaks again. It's a long time before he even moves, and Nan and I are exchanging looks when he springs back into life.

'Let me tell you about my job,' he says. 'There are people

in councils all over the country doing what I do. We put the plans in place that make sure that we can cope with whatever life throws at us; flood, epidemics, accidents, terrorism, war even. It's all about risk assessment and forward planning. We have regular meetings with the emergency services and the government and the armed forces, and there are strategies and plans and procedures for every eventuality.' He's leaning forward again now, and his elbows slide on Nan's cuttings. 'I want you both to understand that if something happens at the New Year, we are well-placed to deal with it. I want you to go away from here feeling confident that the systems are set up to cope. I don't want you to worry any more.'

He starts gathering up the press clippings, bending right down to get a couple that have fallen onto the floor. It's obvious we're about to be dismissed. He's on auto-pilot now.

'We have early warning systems, you see. Long-range, medium-range and short-term forecasting, backed up by the most sophisticated computer systems. We . . .'

'It's not just me,' I cut in, 'there's other people too. There's a mural, a painting near Paddington. The girl that did it, she's seen it all in a dream. She's seen the same date as me. And it's all on the internet, people who know something's coming.'

He carries on stuffing the cuttings back into their folder.

'It's probably a film, or something on the television. Science fiction. Something that's stuck. Happens a lot. It can seem very real.'

'It's not a film, you patronising bastard, it's real! We need to get everyone out of London. Don't you understand?'

'Adam!'

'It's all right, Mrs . . . ah. It's all right. You feel that this is real, and worrying, but in fact, it's all under control. There's no need to panic, no need at all. You can leave it all to us now.'

'So you'll do something? Start moving people out?' Nan's trying to get him in her headlights, but he isn't fazed. His eyes are half-closed and he's trotting out the official line.

'There's no need to move anyone. We have the systems in place to cope with any eventuality.'

'You need to get people out!' I'm practically screaming now. 'It's not safe. It's . . .'

'The worst thing would be to panic. You know what the media are like. They could whip up a story like this in an instant, and then people will be running round like headless chickens. If everyone tries to leave at once, the transport system won't cope. It would be dangerous, so I must insist that you keep quiet about this, and leave it to the professionals.' He stands up and holds his hand out to Nan. 'Thank you for coming in today.'

She takes his hand and holds onto it, and she gives him one of her looks. She's got him now and I can feel how uncomfortable he is.

'So you'll definitely do something about it, will you?' Nan says. 'You'll take it further. You'll tell the police and the firemen and whoever else needs to know.'

'Yes. Yes, of course. I'll follow the procedures we have.'

'You will?' She's not letting go yet.

'I will. Thank you, Mrs Dawson. And if I were you,' he says in a lower voice, 'I'd think about booking a doctor's appointment. He's obviously agitated, *disturbed*.' His voice is down to a whisper. 'These things can run in families.'

I want to shout in his face, *I'm here, in the same room as you, you tosser,* but for once I keep quiet. I just want to get out of here, out of this bright, white shit-hole.

The boy and his mum are gone from the waiting room. I can see them in another interview room. He's quiet now, sitting on his mum's lap, sucking his thumb. She's got her arm round him. Does she care after all? Is he going to be all right? Suddenly I want to know his number. I want to know if this boy is going to survive. It matters. We didn't make eye contact before, he only looked as far as my scar.

Nan tugs on my sleeve.

'Come on, Adam, what are you gawping at? Let's get out of here.'

I let her lead me away and out into the wind and rain battering the High Street.

'Well,' she says on the way to the bus stop, 'at least we tried. Nobody could say we didn't try.'

'He just thought I'd got a screw loose.'

'Do you think so? Don't you think he was listening?'

'I dunno, Nan. He was full of it, though, wasn't he? Council-speak crap. Plans and systems.'

'Well, you need plans, don't you?' She don't sound convinced.

'Nan?'

'Yeah.'

'What happens if the guy in charge of dealing with an emergency dies along with everyone else?'

She stops walking then, and turns to face me.

'Is that right?' I nod. 'Shit.'

'What are we going to do, Nan?'

'I dunno, darlin', I dunno.' Standing there, she suddenly looks old again, and I think, *How the hell are we going to do this, save the world? An OAP and a sixteen-year-old kid. We're fucked, aren't we? The whole world is fucked.*

'I know what I'm going to do right now though. I'm going

to take these sodding shoes off.' She steps out of her shoes, picks them up and carries them till we get to a bin. Then she drops them in and sets off for the bus stop, striding along the wet pavement in her stockinged feet.

'Nan, you can't do that . . .'

'Can't I? Who says?'

We get to the stop just as a bus is pulling up, and it's not 'til we're sitting down that I remember Mum's cuttings, gathered up in their file, still lying on Taylor's desk.

Sarah

Marie doesn't say a word. Not one word. She doesn't need to: her face says it all. She picks her way across the kitchen and out of the back door. I follow her out. She's hunched up against the weather, clutching her files to her chest.

'Wait. Please wait!' I shout after her. She pauses in the gateway, and I catch up with her. The rain is battering into our faces.

'I'm clean,' I say to her. 'I've never done drugs. Never. Not interested. The boys do, but they don't involve me. I'm safe here. We're safe here.'

'How old are you, Sally?'

'Nineteen.'

I know she doesn't believe me.

'This is no place for a nineteen-year-old. And certainly no place for a baby. You know that, don't you?'

'It's our home. It's where we live. We're fine here.'

'We've got a duty of care, Sally. A duty of care. You'll be

187

hearing from us very soon.'

And with that, she's gone. The rain's so fierce and cold that it's hurting the skin on my face. The gate blows back on its hinges, flapping wildly in the wind. I take hold of it and slam it violently. I want to shut the world out. Why can't they just leave me alone? The gate bashes against the latch and flies open again.

'Shit! Shitting fucking shit!' My voice is swallowed up by the storm.

I go back inside. Vinny looks up from the table.

'Who's your friend?'

'My friend, you stupid, drug-soaked pillock, is from Children's Services. The Council.'

He stops what he's doing and puts the foil down on the table-top.

'Shit,' he says.

'Yeah, shit. Lots of it. Up to here.' I hold my hand up above my head.

'We'd better tidy up.' They all start gathering up their stuff.

'It's too late, Vin. It's too late for all of that. They'll come back. They'll take Mia, I know they will.'

'Mia?'

'They've got a duty of care, that's what she kept saying. They'll take her away from me.'

'No, we won't let them. We won't let them in.'

'What you going to do? Put up barricades? Wave your baseball bat at them? Yeah, that'll help.'

'What do you want me to do?' He stands there, flapping his long arms uselessly at his sides.

'I don't know. Nothing. I'm just going to go, get out of here. You should too. Let's face it, Vin. We're busted.'

I race upstairs and bundle up Mia in as many layers as I can, then I carry her down into the hall. I put her into her buggy and go back upstairs for the bags.

Vinny's in the bathroom, flushing his stock away. He calls out to me and I stop on the stairs.

'Where are you going to go?' Vinny asks.

'I don't know. I'll find somewhere.'

'I've got some cash,' he digs in his pocket, brings out a bunch of notes.

'No, Vinny, you've done enough.'

'Take it.' He stuffs it into one of the bags. 'I'll miss you, Sarah.'

'I'll miss you, too. We both will.' I put the bags down on the stairs and wrap my arms round his waist. He kisses the top of my head, like I was his child, his sister. 'I've got to go.'

I put the bags on the shelf under the buggy and wheel it out through the kitchen. There's no time to think, or be sentimental, I've just got to leave, but as I push the buggy down the back streets into the wind I wonder whether there's any point trying to run away. Because Mia's chip will tell them where we are. Wherever I go now, whatever I do, it's not a case of 'if' they find us, it's 'when'.

Adam

We realise there's been another power cut while we're still on the bus. It's starting to get dark, but the street lights are off and the shops are shutting up early. They know what to expect by now; the cuts can last for anything from a couple of hours up to about twelve. No point staying open in the dark, when your tills don't work and you can't take payment cards.

As we get nearer to our stop, Nan's face clouds over.

'I can't face it, Adam. Another night at home in the dark.'

'Where else can we go?'

She shrugs, gloomily.

'I dunno, stay on the bus until we find somewhere where the lights are on.'

'Do you want to? Really?'

'Nah,' she says. 'Can't be bothered. We'll sit up for a bit, shall we, see if they sort it out. Didn't bloody warn us this time did they, so perhaps something's up the creek somewhere. Perhaps they're working on it now.'

Back at the house, we make our way into the kitchen. We always keep candles out at the ready; we light a couple and sit at the table. The heating's off, so we keep our coats on. Nan finds her supply of 'emergency' chocolate, a couple of Snickers bars, so that's tea sorted.

'Nan, I think he knows something, that bloke, Taylor.'

'Knows what?'

'He weren't listening to you, not really, not 'til you said the date. That's when he woke up.'

'He didn't say, though, did he?'

'Well, he wouldn't. Not to people like us.'

'Do you think he will do something about it, Adam?'

'Shouldn't think so. He was pretty clear he wanted us to keep quiet, not to panic people. I reckon he'll do precisely nothing. He hasn't got a clue, Nan, how bad it's going to be. I did try to tell him . . .'

'I know you did. We both did.' The end of her cigarette is a red glow in the dark kitchen. 'Whatever happens, we done the right thing. We used the proper channels.'

'But it's not enough, Nan. It's not enough. We need to do more.'

'Well, you've got your little mate, whatisname, on the case.'

'Nelson. Yeah. I wonder how he's getting on.'

We drift off into silence. After a while Nan says, 'I'm sorry, love, I can't stand this any longer, I'm getting cold. I'm going to bed.' She takes one of the candles and goes upstairs. I press the button on my digital watch to light the display: 18:32. I can't go to bed at half past six! And I can't sit around doing nothing neither.

I keep going over our trip to the council. I should have said more, *made* him listen. How do you make people listen in a city like London? If I was still in Weston, I could've done something on the seafront, written a huge message in the sand, or hung a banner on the pier where everyone'd see. Why couldn't I do that here? Do something out in the open?

The wind's beating on the window – it sounds evil out there – but I can't sit still any longer. I can't do nothing. I pick up the candle and carry it through the lounge. In the hallway I blow out the flame and put the candle down on the floor. I wonder if I should tell Nan I'm going out, but she's already snoring up there. I'll be back before she even knows I've gone.

Outside, the car headlights make a stream of light in the dark. The buses are still running and as one crawls forward I sprint ahead to the next stop and flag it down. I swipe my card and find a seat. We trundle along for ten, twenty, thirty minutes – the whole of West London is dark.

I pull my hood forward and close my eyes. I don't know where I'm going and I don't really care. The sound of the engine, the rain spattering against the window, the coughs of the other passengers, all start to lull me into a sort of sleep. I'm shaken awake when the engine shudders to a halt and I open my eyes. Everyone else is filing off. I get to my feet and stumble forwards. We're at the end of the line, Marble Arch, where the bus terminates. The Arch itself is bathed in light, and the Christmas lights twinkle across Oxford Street for as far as I can see. The pavements are full, people jostling each other in that London way. It's like I've stepped onto another planet. Nan was right, we should have come here, sat in a cafe or something, been part of the normal world.

I wander through the crowds of late-night sales shoppers on Oxford Street. I keep my hood up and my head down. I don't want their numbers. I want to feel part of something, to be somewhere where it don't feel like everything's about to go wrong. Just for a few minutes I can pretend this is how it's going to be, with London carrying on the same, people working and shopping, eating out and having a drink, going to West End shows and sales.

A woman's bag hits my legs.

'Sorry,' she says.

Instinctively I look up. She's a twenty-seven. She's got four days to live. It all comes crowding back into my head, and suddenly this street is the worst place for me to be. I've got to get out, get away from all these people. It's choking me.

Breathe slowly. In through your nose and out through your mouth.

There are bodies all around me, pressing in from every direction. The air isn't reaching my lungs. It catches in my throat. My chest is heaving.

In through your nose.

I can't do it. Everything's starting to spin, the buildings, the faces.

Look down, look down.

Even the pavement's moving, shaking under my feet. I drop to my knees, and then I panic. I'll be trampled down here, squashed on the ground.

Except I'm not the only one down. All round me people are crouching, kneeling, holding on to each other. Everyone is on the ground. The woman with the shopping bag is screaming.

'Oh my God!'

And then it stops. Almost before it starts. No movement, no vibration, everything as it should be. People start getting back onto their feet.

'What happened there?'

'Whoah.'

There's no more screams, just nervous laughing. Everyone's okay. It was only a tremor. No harm done. Something to talk about when they all get home.

I stay down for a little while, breathing slowly, in and out, in and out, until I'm sure I'm okay. Then I ease myself up and look around. There's no sign it ever happened. The buildings are fine, no cracks in the windows, no signs fallen down. Everyone around me is fine, shaken but not stirred.

I stand still while Oxford Street gets back to normal around me. The blood's pumping through my body now, there are goosepimples all over my skin.

This is it. This is how it begins.

I should be thinking of Nan, whether she felt it in Kilburn, whether it woke her up. But it's not Nan in my head. There's a girl out there whose nightmares are starting to come true. If she felt what I just felt, she'll be as frightened as me.

Sarah.

Sarah

I don't know where to go. It's raining so bloody hard that I can't think straight. I need to get Mia out of it, that's all, so I come here, to the tunnel. At least it's sheltered and it feels as if it kind of belongs to me – I've spent enough time here. But when I get here, I do a double-take. The whole place is lighter, brighter and then I realise what's happened: someone's painted over my mural. The entire length of the tunnel is white. There's a smell of paint too, as though it's only just been done.

It doesn't feel mine any more. It's just a tunnel under a railway again, a bleak place. I don't want to be here, but where else should I go? At least I can take ten minutes to try and get my head together. But ten minutes turns into twenty, and then Mia needs a feed, so I end up camping out, sitting on a plastic bag on the floor, leaning against the wall. I can't believe it's over – my life at Vinny's. I didn't realise what I had there until now. A home. Mia's first home.

I'm not hidden at all here, and with Mia feeding I can't go

anywhere. I'm a sitting duck. I keep looking from one end of the tunnel to the other, checking for cars, checking for people. But what will I do if I see anyone? I've got nowhere to run to.

I look down at Mia. She's wrapped up in her padded all-in-one. Her head's inside my coat, but her bum and her legs are sticking out. She's gently twiddling her feet together. That's where they injected the chip: her left foot. It's in there now, invisible, silent, so tiny it can go through a needle. I feel sick at the thought, this thing inside my baby; active, alive, communicating with Them, the bastards that did that to her. They could be tracking us now; somewhere in an office in London or Delhi or Hong Kong – Mia could be a dot on someone's screen.

It's only a matter of time until they pick us up. And then what? Find us somewhere else to live? Send us home? Split us up?

If only I'd never taken her to hospital. If they'd never injected that thing into her, we could disappear. At least, we'd have a chance.

If she didn't have the chip.

It's only just under the surface, surely. I've got some scissors in my washbag . . . She stops feeding for a second, taking a breather. Her hand emerges from my coat, her tiny pink fingers searching for something to hold on to. Her skin's so thin, almost translucent. How could I even think of breaking it, digging below, to find that wretched chip? I've sunk to Their level. I'm disgusted at myself.

I tuck her hand back inside my coat, and I hold her tighter. *I'm sorry, I'm sorry. I won't ever hurt you and I won't let them take you, Mia. I won't.*

A gust of wind catches some rubbish and it blows into the

tunnel, scuffing against the gravel and the brick. I watch as a food wrapper dances its way towards me. Then I look beyond. There's someone there.

Adam

There's someone there. On the ground, in the tunnel.

The tunnel's been whitewashed: the painting, the nightmare, the date all covered over. It's still dim in there, but I can see that it's her. Sarah.

I went round to her house. I wasn't going to knock or nothing. I dunno what I was going to do, just wait there I think, I dunno. Anyway, I only got to the corner of the street, because there was a van and three police cars outside. Jesus! They were definitely at Sarah's because I saw that big, skinny friend of hers being led away, hands cuffed behind his back. I ducked out of the way before anyone saw me. Don't need that kind of trouble, but that left me not knowing: had Sarah been arrested too?

I wandered round on my own, and, of course, I ended up at the tunnel. I knew I would, and now here she is. Called me a bastard last time I saw her. Threw a stone at me last time we were here. I should turn round and walk away, but I can't. I can't keep away from her. I walk towards her, slowly, steadily, so she's got time to see me, time to move if she wants to. She don't. She's still sitting on the ground when I get to her.

It feels uncomfortable, me standing, her sitting, so I crouch down a bit away from her. She's cuddling the baby in to her, and then I twig – she's feeding her. There's nothing to see, just the baby tucked into her coat, but I still flush with embarrassment, the surface of my skin hot inside my clothes.

She's looking down at the ground, her hood pulled up around her face. I want her to look at me. I want to see her number again. I want that feeling.

'Sarah,' I say.

She keeps her eyes fixed down. She's pretending I'm not there. I can read her body language, I'm not stupid. She wants me to go away. But I won't. I can't.

'Sarah, it's me.'

No reaction.

'I saw your house, the police.'

Nothing. I don't know what to say next. I say what I'm thinking before I even know what I'm doing.

'Did you feel it? Did you feel the earthquake?'

She looks up then, and her number gives me that warm rush. She looks puzzled.

'What earthquake?'

'A tremor, about an hour ago. I was in Oxford Street. Everyone ducked down, then they were all laughing, like it wasn't anything, but it was.'

'I didn't feel anything. I was here an hour ago. I didn't feel a thing.'

'I'm not making it up.'

'I'm not saying you are.'

She's hostile. I expected that but she's unhappy as well. I

want to reach out to her. I want to get through her barriers.

'What happened?' I ask. 'What happened to you?'

She's looking at the ground again, but at least she's talking.

'I had a visit from the Social. They caught up with me.'

'Bummer.'

'It's more than that, Adam. They'll take her off me. She's all I've got.'

'They can't just do that.'

'They can. They will. I was living in a squat with drug addicts, a dealer. Doesn't look good. And now I've got nowhere to go. So I suppose I'm living on the streets.'

'You could go home.'

The baby must have stopped feeding now, because Sarah brings her up to her shoulder and then struggles to her feet. I offer a hand to help her but she takes no notice. She puts the baby into the pram.

'Goodbye, Adam,' she says, and starts walking away, like she means it.

I won't be shaken off like that. I'm trying to help her, for God's sake.

'I only meant . . . you've got somewhere to go, somewhere the Social would approve of.' But before the words are even out of my mouth, I remember her dad pinning me up against the wall. 'Sarah, I'm sorry.'

I run to catch up with her.

'Listen, I'm sorry,' I say. 'I can see why you wouldn't want to go back. Your dad . . .'

She stops and spins round.

'What about my dad?'

'He's . . . he's a bit of a case, isn't he?'

'You've met him?' She glares at me.

'Yeah. I . . . I went round there. When you stopped

coming to school.'

'Jesus, what are you? Some sort of stalker? Okay, you're officially freaking me out now, as if I wasn't freaked out enough already.'

She starts walking again, fast, really fast.

I jog along beside her.

'Sarah, I was worried about you. I only went round there to see if you were okay.'

'You shouldn't go round to people's houses. Not if they haven't invited you.'

'What was I meant to do? You drew me, Sarah, you drew me.'

'It was just a drawing. Everyone there was drawing.'

'It wasn't just a drawing and you know it. No one's ever looked at me like that, seen me.'

She hunches up her shoulders and leans forward, pushing the pushchair even faster. The wind and rain are still battering us. I'm almost shouting to make myself heard.

'Sarah, you leant across the desk and touched me. Touched my face. I couldn't just forget you.'

Still walking, she turns.

'Well, you should have,' she shouts back. 'I can't be anywhere near you. I've got to protect my daughter. It doesn't matter how I feel about you. You can't be near her. I can't let you.'

How I feel. How I feel . . .

'Stop a minute. Please, just stop!'

I put my hand on her shoulder to try to make her stand still. She jerks away.

'Get off me! Get off! You said we could fight the future, well, this is me doing it. I think you're going to hurt my baby, so I don't want to see you again. I'm trying to change things, Adam. I'm trying to do it my way.'

'I'd never hurt her. I'd never do that, Sarah.'

'How do you know? You can't know that. You see people's futures, but you only see part of them. Get away from me, Adam. Keep away. Leave us alone.'

I slow down and then stop.

'Where are you going?' I call after her.

'I don't know. Somewhere safe.'

She's speeding away from me. I'll never see her again. And suddenly that feels worse than the whole of London falling about my ears. It feels like the worst thing that could happen to me. I've got to make her stop.

'Sarah!' I call out. 'I know about your dad.'

I don't. I'm winging it, but I've got a gut feeling.

She stops again, and turns round. I catch up with her.

'He raped you, that's why you can't go home.'

She looks away from me, swallowing hard.

'That's it, isn't it?' I say. 'He hurt you.'

It's raining so hard, the water's dripping off the end of her nose.

'Yes, yes he did,' she says, almost to herself. She shoots a quick glance at me, testing my reaction. It's weird – she looks guilty, like she's done something wrong and I've caught her out.

I want to say the right thing, but I don't know what the right thing is. She's so jumpy, anything could be right or wrong with her, you can't tell.

'I'm so sorry.'

'Not your fault. Nothing to do with you,' she says, but there's still that look in her eyes, like she's expecting me to judge her for something. I step forward and put both arms round her shoulders. It's probably the wrong thing to do, but it's all I've got. Her whole body stiffens up, and I think, *Shit, I've messed up. She hates me.*

'I will never, never hurt you, Sarah,' I say into the top of her head. 'I promise you on my life.'

She's still standing there like she's made of stone.

'You can't promise things like that, no-one can,' she says.

'Yes, yes, they can,' I say.

Our faces are so close together. The rain on her eyelashes is making them stick together in clumps. I want to kiss them so bad, it's hurting me.

'Come home with me, Sarah.'

'No, no, I can't.'

'You got nowhere to go. I got somewhere. At least you can dry off, have something to eat.'

A gust of wind blasts a barrage of rain into our faces. I step back so I can see her properly.

'It's the twenty-eighth today,' I say. 'Your nightmare is on the first. So we're safe. You're safe from me, both of you. Come home with me tonight. Get out of this fucking weather. Get dry. Warm up.'

She's wavering.

'Come home. Get some sleep, and then you can go tomorrow. We can think of somewhere safe for you. Away from me, away from London.'

She doesn't say another word. Her expression's still grim and her eyes are firmly on Mia. She turns the buggy round, and we set off together.

Sarah

He helps us on and off the bus and then we walk along together, side by side, not touching. This is mad. I'm mad to be going anywhere with him. But where else am I to go? Who else, in this city of eight million people, would take me in?

'This is us,' he says. 'Electricity's back on anyway.'

'Here?'

He's stopped in front of a modern terrace. Three windows are lit up, cheerful yellow squares, one downstairs, two upstairs. It's tiny. There's a small wall at the front and a metal gate, with the paint peeling off it. The yard is packed with garden ornaments, little stone gnomes and windmills and shit. He sees me looking.

'My nan,' he says, 'she's mad.'

'Oh, right.'

He opens the gate and I wheel the buggy up the path. He pushes the front door, but it's not open so he gets out his keys. There's one moment when he's inside the front door and he leans out to grab the front of the buggy to lift it over the step, and I think again, *What the hell am I doing? This is the last place we should be – he's the last person we should be with.* He looks down at me, reaching for the buggy; the rain's dripping off him, and he smiles. And I think, *It's okay to be here, and it's okay to be with him. Just for tonight.*

Adam

We get the buggy into the front room. Mia's asleep, one hand flung up on either side of her head.

'Can I use your bathroom?'

'Sure, it's upstairs, straight ahead. I think my Nan's asleep up there.'

'Oh, right.'

While she's gone, I make a pot of tea and take a frantic look through the cupboards for something to offer her. The best I can find is an old packet of Pop-Tarts and a tin of tomato soup.

She comes downstairs looking better than when she went up.

'My hair's all fucked up. Mangy hedgehog, not a good look,' she says. 'I should just cut it off.'

'You could have a bath if you like, the water's hot enough. Wash it out and start again.'

'Could I? Could I use your bath? We never had much hot water at the squat.'

She looks back at the buggy in the front room.

'She'll be all right,' I say. 'I'll be here if she wakes up.' I have no idea about babies, not a clue. 'Do you want some clean clothes? I could find you some if you want. Nan's, not mine.' The thought of her in my clothes makes me melt inside.

'No, no, I'm fine. Just a bath.'

'I'll sort it out,' I say, and sprint upstairs. I run some bubble-bath under the hot tap. Instantly, the room fills with a sweet, chemical smell. I rummage in the airing cupboard and find the best towel I can. It's large, anyway, and clean.

'Thanks.' Sarah's in the doorway. She's followed me up.

'That's okay. Are you hungry? I've got some soup.'

'Yes. Starving actually.'

'I'll heat it up. You can have it after your bath.'

We go to squeeze past each other, but I can't help stopping beside her. She smells of the city, of traffic and grime, and unwashed skin. It's exciting. She's so close to me, I'd hardly have to move to kiss that place where her neck meets her shoulder.

'Thanks,' she says again, and I realise she's feeling crowded, she wants me out of the way.

I leave her to it, trying not to think of her peeling off her clothes, stepping into the foaming water, lying back and closing her eyes . . . I make myself do something normal, open the tin of soup and pour the contents into a saucepan. Then I put the tin opener down and lean against the kitchen bench so my crotch is pressing against the hard plastic of the cupboard door. I'm aching. *Don't think about it. Don't go there.* But I grow hard, hard, harder still as I think about pressing somewhere else, somewhere soft and unresisting. Saliva floods into my mouth, and I close my eyes and listen to the noises upstairs; her skin squeaking against the plastic as she shifts position, the shower being turned on and off, and then the gurgle of the water going out of the plughole and down the pipes.

The water going down the pipes. Shit! She's finished. She'll be down in a minute.

I stand up quickly, too quickly. I feel slightly dizzy. *Must look normal. Quick, get the soup ready.*

I light the gas ring under the saucepan, and just have time to grab a dishcloth to hold in front of my trousers when Sarah appears. She's got one towel wrapped round her body, and another round her hair like a turban. She looks so young; no make-up, just clean, pink skin. Pink legs, pink feet, pink arms, pink hands. I'm not expecting that. She's like a vision, an angel. I can't take my eyes off her.

She don't seem to notice the effect she's having on me.

'You were right,' she says, rubbing at her hair through the towel, 'my clothes were skanky. Do you think I could borrow some? Yours would be okay.'

'Yeah, 'course. I'll just do this.' The soup's boiling up the sides of the pan. I turn away from her to dish up. My dick's still fighting to get out of my jeans, so I hold onto the dishcloth while I put her bowl of soup on the table for her.

'I don't think we've got any bread. There might be some crackers,' I say.

'Don't worry. This is great. You having some?'

'No, I'm not hungry. I'll go and look for some clothes.'

In my room, I find a tee-shirt and some tracksuit bottoms that'll do, but when it comes to underwear, I can't take her my pants, that's plain wrong. I can't go through Nan's things either. For a start, she's asleep in her room and even if she wasn't I'd rather cut off my own hands.

I take the bundle of clothes downstairs. Mia's woken up

and Sarah's holding her, showing her some of Nan's ornaments on the mantelpiece. Mia's eyes are popping out of her head. Her hands brush against the polished wooden box that's got pride of place. Sarah moves her away.

'Don't touch, Mia,' she says. 'Don't touch the pretty things.' Then she frowns. 'What *is* that?'

'My great-grandad's ashes. Nan won't go anywhere without them.'

She takes another step away, pulling a face.

'Ew.'

'Here,' I say, holding out the clothes I fetched, 'these might do. While we wash yours.'

Mia turned her head when she heard my voice. Now she makes a kind of squawk. We're all taken by surprise. Without even thinking, I put my arms out for her.

'Is this all right?' I ask Sarah. She's as caught out as I am.

'Yeah, I suppose so.'

I take the baby's weight and hold her awkwardly.

'Put your hand on her back so she doesn't tip backwards.' Sarah moves my hand into place.

The baby's face is near my shoulder. I crane round, so I can see her.

'Hello,' I say.

She stares at me intently. My stomach flips over as her number hits me again. Why should someone so young, so beautiful, die?

Her hand brushes against my face, on the bad side and her fingers curl so they dig in.

'Mia, don't do that, you'll hurt him! Here, I'll have her back.' Sarah steps forward, ready to take her.

'No, it's okay. She's not hurting me.' It's a lie. One of her fingers has found a sore spot, but I don't want her taken off of me. I've never held a baby before. It's magic. Or maybe it's just this baby. She don't shrink away from me, or get upset at my face: she just looks.

When I glance over to Sarah, she's smiling, first time today. First time I've ever seen her smile properly. It transforms her face.

'You're good with her,' she says. 'She likes you. She normally screams her head off if I give her to someone else.'

'I'm a natural,' I say. It's a joke, but inside I feel like a hero.

And then we both hear footsteps on the stairs and Nan comes in. She looks from the pram to Sarah, standing there in her towels.

'Christ,' she says, 'it's full house here. What's all this?'

Sarah's shoulders hunch up again, on the defensive.

'Hello,' she says, 'I'm Sarah. I just . . .'

'You're the girl at the hospital. The girl who did the painting.'

'This is my Nan,' I say, 'Val.'

But Nan don't smile. She looks at me, and her face turns grey.

'Put the baby down, Adam. What do you think you're doing?'

'It's all right, Nan, she likes me.'

'Put her down!'

'Nan, stop it.'

She comes towards me and makes to take Mia out of my arms. Mia's scared. She burrows her face into my shoulder.

'What's wrong with you, Nan? She likes me.'

'What's wrong with me? What's wrong with you? You've seen her painting – you know what happens.'

We both look at Sarah then.

'I know, I know,' she says, 'but it's all right now. It's all right today.'

Nan wheels round.

'Do you want her to know him, to trust him, to turn to him on the first of January? Do you?'

Sarah's face twists up.

'No, course not. I don't know. I don't know.'

'Why are you here?' The hardness in Nan's voice is covering something else. There's fear in there too, but I don't s'pose Sarah knows that. Nan can be pretty intimidating, and she's turning it on now.

'Why am I here? The friends I was staying with, they've been arrested. There's no one else. I've got nowhere else to go. But I'll leave if you don't want me. It's fine. We'll find somewhere.'

She puts her hands up to Mia's tummy to lift her away from me, and one of them brushes my arm. It's so warm against my skin, smooth. I can feel her bones through her skin. The feeling's like an electric shock. It wakes me up.

'Nan, Sarah needs a place to stay tonight. I said she could stay here. She can have my room and I'll have the sofa. It's one night, Nan, and I've said it's okay.'

Nan looks at me. For a split second I can't tell if we're in for an almighty row. Then she gives a little shrug and looks away to Mia.

'Okay,' she says. 'I'm not going to turn you out on the street, but it's a mistake. I can feel it.' She takes a step towards me. 'Who's this, then?'

'Mia,' says Sarah.

Nan comes close. The baby shrinks away but she can't resist peeping at her.

'Don't be scared,' says Nan, gently stroking her cheek. 'I'm not a big, bad witch. I'm a good one.'

Sarah

Good witch, bad witch. What's the difference? It's not the bony, stained fingers or the spiky purple hair – it's the eyes. Once she fixes you with those eyes, you've had it. It's as if she's hypnotised you. You can't look away until she decides to release you.

Having shouted her head off, and frightened Mia half to death, she tries to make friends with her, but Mia isn't having it. She clings to me like a little monkey, and won't even look at her. So Val turns her attention to me. It's like a bolt of lightning going through me. She frowns.

'Lavender,' she says, 'of course, but also dark blue. And all bathed in pink.'

'Nan,' Adam says, 'don't start.'

'What? What is it?'

'It's your aura,' he says with a sigh.

'My what?'

'Your cosmic energies,' says Val. 'Bright pink, sensitive

and artistic. Lavender, a visionary, a dreamer of dreams. Dark blue, full of fear.'

I feel suddenly naked. Here's this woman, this strange, shrivelled-up woman, with hair three shades too bright for her, and she knows me.

'I'm right.'

It's a statement, not a question.

'Yeah,' I breathe, 'you're right.'

'Sarah,' she says, and I hold my breath, wondering what's coming next.

'Yes?'

'You're welcome here. You're welcome in this house.' And now I feel surrounded, wrapped up, a comfort blanket over my shoulders. I can't explain – it's not just relief, although I am relieved – there's something physical in the room, a warmth that feels like light and heat together. If you could bottle it, you'd make a fortune, and the label on the outside could read comfort or love or home. Yeah, I'd call it home. Not the one I came from, but the one everyone should have, in a perfect world. The place where you can be yourself, where you feel safe. I feel like crying, as if it would be okay to cry here, but I bite my lip. I've done enough crying in the last few days, and seen enough come to that. It's time to stop the tears.

'Thank you,' I say. Then, 'I'll go and put these clothes on.'

I give Mia back to Adam. She digs in a bit when she realises I'm handing her over, then she sees that it's him and relaxes, going to him willingly. The way she's taken to him is weird. She's never been like that with other people. She's shy, cautious. Perhaps my dream was only a means to an end. We were meant to meet Adam, and this is how it came about.

He found the painting and then I found him. Is that it? Is that all it is? Is there a happy-ever-after waiting for us, instead of a nightmare?

Upstairs, I put on the tee-shirt and joggers. As I pass the shirt over my head, I pause and sniff the material. It's his shirt. Adam's. I want it to smell of him, that slight sharpness, and it does, very faintly. I pull it down over my body. The thought of his smell on my skin makes me tingle in the places the shirt touches.

Later we drink tea and watch a bit of telly, and fuss over Mia. No-one talks about death dates or nightmares or auras. Instead, Adam teases his nan gently and she tells him to 'sod off', but it's all said with a smile and a twinkle in the eye. These two love each other. They might not know it, but there's love in this tiny, messy, run-down house.

The news comes on and we all fall silent for a while. It's the usual stuff: floods, famine, war. Japan's in trouble – there are three volcanoes threatening to erupt at once. A mass evacuation is under way. In London there's a big protest in Grosvenor Square against American threats of war against Iran. We all know Iran's nuclear. How fucking stupid would the president have to be to pick on them? Didn't she learn anything from Iraq, Afghanistan, North Korea? Right at the end they report on the earth tremor Adam felt in Oxford Street. It's a light-hearted item, you know 'And finally . . .' with a bit of footage from someone's mobile phone and some interviews with people who were there.

A crappy sitcom comes on after the news. We all sit looking at the screen, but none of us are watching.

'I think it's going to be an earthquake, Nan,' Adam says. 'Or it could be a bomb, a series of bombs.'

'The Japanese get it, don't they?' she says. 'They're not messing about.'

'Well, they have got volcanoes, they'd be mad not to evacuate, wouldn't they?'

'Yeah, but we've got you. We've got you telling us about it. People should listen. They should start getting out now.'

'It's not the same, is it? I was thinking about how to tell people, how to get publicity. Maybe a banner, climb up the Gherkin or Tower Bridge or something.'

'Like my painting,' I say. 'No one'll pay any attention. They'll just think you're a nutter. You need to get on the street screens. How many are there? A thousand? More? They're official, aren't they? People will take notice of them. You need to hack in.'

'Oh my God, you're right. If the council or the government won't do it, I'll have to. I'll have to hijack their screens.'

'Do you know how?'

'No, but I know a man who can.'

He's excited now, feet tapping on the floor, eyes shining.

'I'll try ringing him.'

I leave him to it. Mia's ready for bed and so am I. Adam's given me his room, says he'll kip on the sofa. I'm embarrassed, but he insists. I give Mia her bedtime feed and then put her down in a drawer on the floor, just like in the squat. I switch off the light and try closing my eyes. I wonder where Vinny is now. Adam said he saw him being led away. The thought of him lying in a cell somewhere makes me want to scream. He doesn't deserve that, not Vinny.

I think of the rain and the wind, of taking refuge in the tunnel. And I think of Adam, how we keep being drawn back together. And now I'm here, in his room. I told myself I'd keep away from him, but I've done the complete opposite. But it's not the New Year, not yet, so tonight I'm going to enjoy being warm and safe, and I'm going to sleep as long as Mia will let me.

Adam

I hear her screaming through my sleep. It cuts into my dreams and drags me up to the surface. It's a dreadful sound, tears at my heart. I know it's Sarah before I'm fully awake. I shove the blankets back and sprint up the stairs to my room and knock quietly on the door. She don't hear me – she's making too much noise herself.

I open the door and go in. Sarah's in my bed, sitting bolt upright with both arms out in front of her. Her eyes are open, and she's shouting Mia's name over and over again. Mia's in a drawer on the floor and, amazingly, she's still asleep.

'It's all right, Sarah,' I say, from the doorway. 'Mia's here. She's okay.'

She don't turn to look at me, but she's heard me.

'No!' she insists. 'She's in there. She's there on her own. Help me. Help me!' She starts sobbing. Her eyes might be open but she's not awake – she's deep inside her nightmare.

I walk over to the bed and sit down on the edge of the

mattress. I touch Sarah's arm gently.

'Sarah,' I say. 'It's a dream, only a dream. You need to wake up.'

She's still sobbing.

'Sarah,' I say, more loudly this time, 'wake up. Wake up now. It's just a dream.' I grip her arm more firmly and give it a little shake.

She turns her face then, and gasps.

'No,' she says. 'No, not you!'

'Sarah, you're at my house, everything's okay.'

'Adam?' she whispers, and she screws up her eyes, like she's struggling to tell if she's awake or still in her dream.

'It's me, Sarah. You're here with me. You had a bad dream, but you're safe now. Everything's all right.'

Her hands flop down onto the bed.

'Was I shouting?'

Only loud enough to wake the dead.

'Yeah, a little bit.'

'I used to wake Vin up too,' she sighs. 'In the end he got used to it.'

'You were shouting that she was 'in there,' the baby. Where are you in your dream?'

'I dunno. Some sort of building, a house, but it's collapsing and there are flames and . . .' She starts breathing heavily.

'Shh . . . it's all right. Don't think about it now. It's all right.'

'I'm so tired, Adam. So tired, but if I close my eyes, it'll all come back again.'

I shuffle up the bed a bit, but I don't touch her. I'm just there, if she wants me.

'No it won't,' I say. 'You'll be okay.'

'Will you stay here with me? Wake me up if I start again?'

I'll stay with you for ever. I'd swim the Channel for you. I'd walk on broken glass.

'Yeah, course. Here,' I say, 'shift over a bit.'

I'm next to her now, and she leans her head on me in that place between my shoulder and my chest.

I see her eyelashes dip and she closes her eyes. It's not long before she's asleep, but I stay awake for ages, watching over her. I'm drinking her in: the weight of her, her sweet smell, the way her body moves gently against mine as she breathes in and out. I want to remember how this feels, how I feel, every detail. I don't want to forget a thing.

I must have drifted off, though, because before I know it I'm waking up. Sarah's still there. She's tilted her head and she's looking up at me. She smiles.

'Hello,' she whispers.

'Hello, Sarah.'

I've got another hard-on, and the warmth of her, her closeness, it's almost too much to bear.

'Had a nice sleep?' I ask.

'Yeah.' She's relaxed, happier than I've ever seen her before. 'Thank you,' she says, 'for being here.'

We haven't stopped eye contact since I woke up. It's a peaceful thing, intense and intimate, beautiful. Her eyes flick down to my mouth and back to my eyes. She's thinking about it, I know she is, and suddenly so am I and I think, *It's now or never. Now.* And I bend forward just a little and I kiss her.

Her mouth is so soft. Half of mine is stiff with scar tissue, but hers is soft all over. Her lips are closed to start with. She lets me kiss her – she don't kiss me back – but then she makes this tiny noise, halfway between a grunt and a sigh, and she closes her eyes and opens her mouth, and her lips are pressing back against mine, and I know she wants me as much as I want her.

Her breath is stale from sleep, but I don't mind. I taste her on my tongue, and I can't get enough.

She puts her hand round the back of my neck, caressing me. Still kissing we move so that she's more underneath me. I run my hand down her arm, and then across. Her nipples are hard through the soft material of the tee-shirt, and wet. I realise with a shock that she must be leaking milk. Her tits aren't soft, like I expect. They're hard, too, and warm, almost hot.

'Careful,' she says. 'They're sore.' I move my hand away quickly, but she puts her hand on mine and places it back on her breast. 'It's okay, but gently.'

We kiss again. She moves her hands under my tee-shirt and runs them over my ribs and my back, exploring me with her fingertips.

I match her moves, feeling under her clothes, up around her back and down around the curve of her bum. She's stopped moving now, her muscles are tense, but I want more, I need to find out about every bit of her. I slide my hand round her thigh . . . and she twitches violently, trying to throw my hand off.

'No!' she says, and it's loud and there's an edge of panic in her voice.

'Sarah, I thought you wanted . . .'

She shoves me away from her.

'No, not that. I'm sorry. I thought I could, but I can't.'

I don't understand what's changed. She wanted me. She put my hands on her body.

'Sarah . . . ?'

'No! Leave it! I can't. I don't want to. Not with you. Not with . . .'

I stand up and back away.

'I get it,' I say. 'I'm disgusting. I'm the Elephant Man. Of course you wouldn't want to do it with me.'

Mia's woken up now and starts to cry. I stumble to the door. Behind me, I can hear Sarah, 'No, Adam, it's not that. Adam . . .' But I don't want to hear her excuses. I was stupid to think that anything could happen between us. Stupid to think it could ever happen with anyone.

I blunder out of the room and head for the stairs. Nan's standing in the doorway of her room, her hair all tousled and her eyes not quite open properly. She raises her eyebrows at me.

'Adam?' she says. 'What the . . .'

'Just don't ask. Not now, Nan. Not ever, all right?'

Sarah

I can't do it. I thought I could. I thought I wanted to, but I can't. I don't know if I ever will. I know Adam's different. He likes me, he really does and I like him, but that feeling of his weight on top of me, his hands running over my skin, freaks me out. It's not logical, it doesn't come from my mind, which is wanting him, excited to be with him. It's programmed into my body, as if that reacts all on its own, separate from anything else.

It's been a long time since my body felt like mine. At home, for years, it belonged to Him. He could have me, take me, whenever He wanted to. Now, it belongs to Mia. Magically, my body has done what it's needed to do to grow her, and give birth to her and feed her. I didn't know I could do this, but it happened. My body knew.

Sometime, one day, my body will be mine again. But who knows when that'll be, or who I'll be or how I'll feel. And in the meantime Adam storms off. He calls himself the Elephant Man. He thinks he's repulsive, but it's not that. It's not that at all. *It's not you, it's me.* Oh God, it's such a cliché, but it's true. I never meant to hurt him. Now what will he think about me – bitch, cow, cock-teaser?

'Looks as if we're out of here,' I say to Mia. 'Messed that up, didn't I?'

I pack our things up before going downstairs. Adam's on the couch, curled up, eyes tight shut. The telly's on, but he's not watching. Val's in the kitchen, perched on a stool and the room's thick with smoke. I stop in the doorway. Too smoky for Mia in there, too full of Adam in the lounge. There's nowhere for us to go – we'd better just leave.

'I'll just put her in the buggy,' I say, 'and fetch the rest of our things.'

'Why? Where are you going?' Val stubs out her cigarette.

'It was very kind of you to let us stay, but we should go and find somewhere else now.'

'You got somewhere, have you?' She looks at me, intently.

'Yes, I've got a couple of places I can try,' I lie. I don't want anyone feeling sorry for me or obliged or anything. I just want to go – I shouldn't have come here in the first place. We'll head out of London, and if we get picked up, well, I'll just have to deal with it.

I walk over to the buggy and try to lie Mia down, but she's not tired. She lets out a scream of temper.

'Please, Mia. Just lie down. I don't need this.'

She carries on screaming, but I strap her in and head upstairs for our bags. When I come down again, Val's standing by Mia, cooing at her. It's not helping.

'It's all right,' I say, 'we're going now.' I stuff the bags under the buggy and pull on my jacket.

'You don't need to,' says Val.

Behind her on the sofa, Adam's still got his eyes closed, but he can't possibly be asleep, not with this racket going on.

'She's going, Adam,' Val says to him. 'Aren't you even going to say goodbye?' He opens his eyes then, and looks straight at me. His face is blank. I feel like I've killed part of him.

I take a step forward. It can't end like this. Misunderstandings heaped up between us.

'Adam,' I say, 'it's not you. It's not you, it's . . .'

He slams his fist into the sofa.

'Stop it!' he yells. 'Don't say that, don't ever say it!'

'Okay, okay, I'm going.' It's no good talking to him. I've upset him so much, it's better to leave him to it. I go to the front door and wedge it open, so I can get the buggy out. I manage to bump it down the step. Mia's still crying, but I can't pick her up until we're well away from here. I turn to shut the door behind me, and suddenly Adam's there, in the doorway. I've no idea what he's going to do – shout at me, hit me, kiss me. He's fizzing with energy, right on the edge. His hands are balled up into fists. He thrusts one towards me.

'Here,' he says. He turns his hand over and opens his fingers. There's a couple of notes and some coins in it.

'No, don't be stupid,' I say.

'Have it. Get out of London. There's three days to go. Get Mia away from here. Away from me.'

He's looking down as he speaks. But when he says 'me' his eyes flick up to meet mine, and now they're not dead or lifeless. The spark's back and it's a spark I recognise – a pinprick of fear dancing in his eyes.

'Take it,' he says again, and he puts his hand on top of mine. His touch is so warm. My body reacts to it instantly; a blush spreads over my skin, there's a sweet ache between my legs. I don't want to go any more. I want to stay here and fight whatever it is that's trying to tear us apart. I want to touch his burnt face, kiss it, so he knows I don't mind.

'What are you going to do?'

'I'm going to start making a noise. I've got to get people out of London.'

'On your own?'

'Yeah, I dunno, whatever.'

We're both standing there now, like there's unfinished business between us. I've taken the money, but he hasn't taken his hand away. I don't want him to take his hand away.

'I could help you,' I say.

We're looking at each other now, and for a second or two I wonder if he's thinking what I'm thinking – that we're meant to be together, that we can do this.

He moves his hand away from mine, and gently touches my face, the way I once touched him.

'No,' he says, and his voice is low and gruff. 'You need to get away. That's the best thing you can do. Take Mia somewhere safe.'

He's right. I've known it all along. The only way to escape the future, my nightmare, is to be nowhere near Adam on the first.

'Okay,' I say, 'I'll go. But I'll keep in touch, shall I? Maybe when this is all over, we can . . .'

I can't imagine what's the other side of the New Year. I don't know what the world will be like. I don't know if any of us will still be alive. Adam knows. He's seen my number.

'Adam . . .?'

'Yeah.'

I suddenly realise that I don't want to know if I've got a week, or a month, or a year. He said he'd never tell me, and he's right, it's best that way. I don't want to know my own death sentence.

'Take care.'

I dart forward and kiss his cheek, the one with the scarring. He closes his eyes, and I turn and walk quickly down the path. *Don't look back. Don't look back.* I can't help it – I look over my shoulder and he's still standing in the doorway. His eyes are open now, and he's standing there, watching. He raises his arm and drags his sleeve across his eyes, and his face distorts – a smile that's not a smile. I can't watch him cry. I turn away and I walk on.

Adam

She's walking away, and perhaps it's the best thing for both of us, for all of us. I want to scream, 'Come back!' I want to run after her and spin her round and hold her. But part of me, the good part of me, is happy she's going – because now she'll be safe and Mia will be safe. And if they're not, it won't be me that's hurt them.

We're doing it, I think. *It doesn't have to end the way we've seen. We're changing it.*

I go back into the house and get dressed properly.

'Where are you going?' Nan asks.

'Churchill House,' I say. 'I'm going to see a man about a screen.'

She reaches for her coat.

'No, Nan. Stay here. I'm going to do this on my own.' I'm buzzing with it all now: the possibility of changing things; the chance to save lives, hundreds, thousands of lives.

She's still got her coat in her hands.

'Nan, I won't be long. I'll see Nelson and then I'll come

home.'

'It feels like it's getting close, Adam. I don't want to let you out of my sight. I made that mistake before. I let your dad go . . .'

She's twisting the coat in her hands, wringing the life out of it. Before I know it, I've stepped towards her to give her a quick hug. Her arms go round me and she hugs me back, keeping me there a bit too long for comfort.

'I'll be back soon,' I say, and she lets go.

'Okay,' she says, 'okay. I'll see you later.' She turns away but she doesn't head for her stool in the kitchen, she sits down on the sofa, in front of the news. And I'm out of there, jogging along the road. I suppose I'm half-hoping to catch up with Sarah, but there's no sign of her on the main road.

Churchill House is only five minutes' jog away. When I get there, I realise I don't know Nelson's number. I go into the lobby. The place is huge; fifteen floors and thirty flats on each level. I get my mobile out and try his number again. This time he answers.

'Nelson, it's me, Adam.'

'Adam.'

'Hi. I'm at your place, downstairs. What number are you?'

'You're here?'

'Yeah, I need to talk to you.'

'I don't know, Adam. I don't think it's a good idea.'

'What?'

'I don't think you should be here.'

'Nelson, what's up with you, man?'

'Things have been . . . difficult . . . weird. We shouldn't even talk on the phone, Adam.'

'That's why I'm here. To see you, talk face to face.'

'I'm not sure . . .'

I've had enough of this.

'Nelson, stop fucking about. I'm coming to see you if I have to knock on every fucking door. What number's your flat?'

There's a pause and I think for a moment that he's hung up on me.

Then, 'Nine two seven. Ninth floor.'

'Right. Cheers. I'm coming up.'

The lift's not working, so I head up the stairs. I pass three lots of people on the way – a couple of young guys, a woman with a toddler and a baby in a sling, and an old granny with a shopping trolley. They're all the first of January. Every single one. This place, this building, is going to bury them all.

The first four or five floors are okay, but I'm flagging by the time I reach the ninth. Number 927 is towards the end of a walkway, open at the side. The door's on the latch. Nelson's hovering inside the hallway, out of sight.

'Come in,' he hisses at me. 'Quickly.'

'Hi, Nelson. Nice to see you too,' I say.

He hardly seems to hear me, just closes the door behind us.

'Did anyone see you?' His voice is still low.

'What?'

'Did anyone see you come in here?'

'I dunno. There was a few people on the stairs, but no one on your landing. What's with the whispering? Why are you so jumpy?'

'I'm being watched. They're on to me.'

'Who are?'

'Dunno. MI5 probably.'

There's no light on in the hall, and all the curtains are

closed, so it's pretty dingy in there, but even so I can see the twitch on his face is going mad and his eyes are flicking around all over the shop, looking anywhere except me.

'What are you talking about?'

'I put it on the para-web, Adam. Like I said I would. I put it on and it spread like wildfire. There's tons of stuff out there about the New Year. Tons. People want to read it. They want to find out. There's so much evidence now – you're right, Adam, something big is going to happen.'

'What is it, Nelson? Do you know?'

He shakes his head.

'Could be natural. There's a lot of seismic activity going on. A lot. The radon levels are up apparently.'

'What's that?'

'A gas held in the rocks in the earth's crust. If the levels go up, it means there's activity. This guy, this professor, is posting them up on the para-web, but even that's being shut down. Only they can't stop us knowing about the volcanoes. Have you seen them, Adam? They *did* make the news.'

'Yeah, but they're in Japan. We ain't got any volcanoes here.'

Nelson sighs.

'What year are you in? Eleven, twelve? You've done plate tectonics, haven't you?'

My mind spins like a fruit machine. Plate tectonics, geography, school. It all seems like a million years ago. Nothing stuck then and nothing comes to mind now. But I don't want to look stupid.

'Yeah, course.'

'So Japan is on the other end of the Eurasian plate,' he says.

'Right. I knew that.'

'So if something happens at one end of the plate, some- thing's likely to happen at the other end. In Europe – Greece, Turkey, Italy. Here. Like an earthquake. And we've got the gas and we've had a tremor already.'

'What about fire?'

Nelson's twitch is taking over his whole face. He swallows hard.

'You get fire after earthquakes. Broken gas pipes, electrical fires. In San Francisco in 1906, the fires burned for three days after the quake. More people were burned to death than crushed.'

We're still standing in the hall, but my legs are starting to feel wobbly. Fatal combination – nine floors of stairs and the end of the world.

'Nelson, can we go and sit down?' I make to go past him, find his lounge or his kitchen. He steps across the hallway, blocking me. 'What're you doing?'

'You can't come in. My mum's in the kitchen and my brothers are here.'

'Can't you have friends back?'

'No. Not you. I don't want them to see you. I'm in enough trouble as it is.'

'What sort of trouble?'

'They traced my online posts here. They know it was me. We've had people round. Counter-terrorism, Children's Services, Immigration.'

'What?'

'They all came, the whole lot of them all at once. Went through the flat like a swarm of locusts. Interviewed my mum and dad. My mum was terrified.'

'Are they illegal? Your mum and dad?'

'Course not, but they came here twenty years ago, before

ID cards, before anything, so all their paperwork is out of date. They've done nothing wrong.'

'So they're okay? Nothing happened? You just got searched.'

'They're *not* okay. *I'm* not okay. They've taken my computer. They've cautioned me.'

'But you haven't done anything illegal.'

'Haven't I? Conspiring to promote fear.'

'What?'

'It's in the Terrorism Act 2018. Conspiring to promote fear. They could lock me up, Adam. Up to ten years.'

He's on the edge, anyone can tell that. Right on the edge. And I've done it to him.

'Nelson,' I say, 'I'm so sorry. I didn't know.'

'Neither did I. I didn't know what I was getting into.'

'I shouldn't have asked you. I'll go. I'll leave you alone. Only . . .'

He finally looks at me, and his number hits me again. 112027. That shitty number. He don't deserve it.

'What?'

'Only, promise me you'll get out of this place.'

'I can't leave without my family.'

'Get them out too, then.'

'It's not easy . . .'

'Do it, Nelson. Just do it.'

'I will. I'll get them out.'

I turn to go.

'Adam,' he says. 'What did you come here for?'

'I wanted to ask you something.'

'What was it?'

I can't ask him about the screens. He's done enough already.

'Nothing. It's not important.'

'It must have been something.'

'Yeah, but it doesn't matter now.'

'Tell me, Adam. I'm in trouble already. If there's something I can do, some way of getting back at those bastards.'

'Nelson!'

'They're bullies, Adam. They've frightened my mum. That's low. That's immoral.'

'I just thought . . . I just thought we could do something with the public information screens. Hack into them or something.'

He smiles.

'Of course. Of course we could.'

'Only not without a computer.'

'There are computers everywhere, Adam. There are even computers outside London, or so it's rumoured . . .'

'You don't have to . . . you've done enough already. Look after yourself now. Yourself and your family.'

'I don't have to, but I want to. They're going to let thousands of people die, Adam. It's not right . . .'

'Take care, mate.'

I make a fist and hold it out to him. He looks at it for a few seconds then he clears his throat and does the same, and we touch knuckles. I wonder if he's ever done that before. I wonder if he'll ever do it again.

'Bye, Nelson,' I say.

I hear the door closing behind me. I'm not the praying sort, but as I jog along the walkway I send a little prayer out into the courtyard and up into the grey sky. *Let him get out. Let him be all right.* And maybe he will, because he may be quiet and he may be geeky, but I reckon Nelson's got more balls than a snooker hall.

Sarah

I'm only a few minutes' walk from Adam's house when they pick me up.

The speed of it is shocking; one moment I'm pushing the buggy along the pavement, the next a car has drawn up by me and I'm bundled into the back seat while someone unclips Mia and straps her into a baby seat beside me. Then people get in either side of us, doors are slammed shut and locked, and we're off.

The buggy and our bags are left behind.

'What the hell are you doing? Who are you?'

The man next to me flips a wallet open and flashes his ID at me.

'Children's Services. Viv here is from the police. Family support.'

'Why the hell did you grab me off the street? What sort of country is this?'

The woman the other side of Mia cuts in, 'We had to come to you because you've been running away from us. You

234

weren't at Giles Street. No one there knew where you'd gone.'

'You can track Mia's chip. You've done it before. There's no need for all this drama.'

'There's every need. We've charged your housemates with possession of class A drugs with intent to supply. Last night you were staying in a house with the widow of one of west London's most notorious armed robbers and her great-grandson who is currently suspended from school for a savage and violent attack, and has been interviewed as part of a murder investigation. And who knows where you were going next.'

It doesn't sound so great when she puts it like that.

'Where are we going now?'

'We're going to Paddington Green police station, where we will interview you about activities at Giles Street. Louise will be taken to foster carers. We've got someone standing by right now.'

'Take her? Take her? No! No way. I'll go to the police station. I'll answer your questions – I've got nothing to hide. But I won't let you take my baby away.'

'It's not your choice, Sally. We've got a court order. Your baby needs to be in a safe, stable environment.'

'I'm still feeding her,' I say. There's silence, and I think, *I've done it. They can't take her away now.* Then the woman says, 'We'll make sure she's fed and comfortable. They're very experienced carers.'

And I suddenly realise, as if I didn't already know, what a cold, cruel world it is and what cold, cruel people I'm dealing with.

You think you can run away, and you can't.

You think you can have some control over your life, and you can't.

They'll get you in the end.

The car's travelling at a steady speed. I'm hemmed in, not even next to a door. I can't think of any way out of this. All I can do is sit there, and let myself be taken to a place where they'll take my baby away from me.

We pull off the main road, and down a ramp into an underground car park. I hold Mia's hand in mine. Part of me still doesn't believe they'll actually do this. But they do.

We're unloaded from the car. I ask to hold Mia one last time, and they let me. She's fussing after being lifted out of the car seat. I try to talk to her, 'This isn't the end, Mia. I'll see you again, soon. I promise.' But she's got her eyes closed and she's thrashing her head from side to side. And the words don't come out right anyway: they're squeaky, blurry, teary words. It's all wrong. Someone reaches in and puts their hands between my arms and her body, and then they lift her away from me.

All I can see is two people hurrying away; one carrying the car seat, one carrying Mia. The policeman next to me says, 'This way, please,' and puts his hand on my shoulder to turn me round. I'm thinking, *'Get your filthy hands off me,'* but it doesn't come out in words. It's a scream, a roar, and I don't punch him, I raise my hand up and drag my nails down his face, and then he's screaming too, high-pitched, horrified. He puts his hands up to the five red steaks and I start running.

Across the car park, an engine starts up. It's the car they're taking Mia away in. I run towards it. They've seen me – the tyres squeal as they accelerate up the ramp. There's a metal gate at the top, and they have to wait for it to open. I can catch them. The gate slides to one side. I'm almost there. I reach forward and my fingers brush the boot and then the brake lights flash off, the car moves away and it's gone, joining the stream of traffic on the Edgware Road. I start following, but I soon lose sight of it. I slow down and stop, leaning forward with my hands on my thighs as I try to catch my breath.

I glance behind me and there are half a dozen cops streaming out of the police station. I watch, almost detached, and then it sinks in that they're after me.

I've got more than a hundred metres' head start on them, but they're closing in fast, and suddenly the thought of their hands on me, grabbing me, shoving me, is too much. Anger surges through me again, together with a kick of adrenalin. I don't know where I'm going to go, but I'm not going to just stand here and let them get me. I start running. My coat is making me too hot, so I shrug it off and drop it. Then I'm away, arms and legs free to stretch, feet pounding into the pavement, splashing through puddles. I run down alleys and passages, cut through a car lot and round the back of a pub. I don't look back, not once. I just keep going, one foot in front of the other. My chest starts to ache, it's like my lungs are going to burst, but I'm not stopping. I run through a market, through the smell of wet cabbage leaves and frying burgers, and finally, I find a path down to the canal, a dreary strip of grey water. I keep looking round, but there's no-one behind. There's a pile of railway sleepers at the side of the path. I stop running and sink down onto them.

All I've got is the clothes I'm wearing. I have nothing else left. When they took Mia away, they were taking my life. *Bastards! Bastards! Bastards!* The only thing in my head is her, the absence of her, how my arms are missing her weight, how my breasts are hot and full with milk she'll never drink. Being there, sitting there without her, is unbearable. I want to run again, do something, move – but I can't. Even sitting down my legs are shaking. They're not taking me anywhere for a while. And so I have to stay here, alone with my despair.

Unbearably, utterly, alone.

Adam

I don't go straight home when I leave Nelson. I should do. I should go home, pack my bags and get on the first coach out of London, with or without Nan. But at the back of my mind, I don't want to leave it all to Nelson. I want to try and do something, like the Gherkin thing or the Tower Bridge thing, so I set off into town for a last attempt to wake the city up.

I end up in Oxford Street again, and I can hear this chanting some way off. So I follow the noise. There's a voice booming through a megaphone, the crowd backing it up. I don't get what they're saying to start with, then when I make out the words I realise where I am. This must be Grosvenor Square. It's the demo we saw on the telly last night.

'No war, no war, no war.'

The sound echoes off the buildings even in the streets all round. In the square it's overwhelming. There are uniformed police posted every few metres. I squeeze past and into the crowd. The guy with the megaphone is at the front somewhere – I can't see him, but I can hear him all right, and suddenly I know what I've got to do. I've got to get to him and I've got to grab the megaphone. It don't occur to me to wonder if I can. I just go for it.

It's a big crowd, but the atmosphere is great. There's lots of young people, some families, even really young kids and some oldies, even older than Nan. Everyone's there for the same reason. These are people who think that if enough of you shout loud enough, people will listen.

I make my way through them, getting closer to the centre of the noise, and then I spot him, the man with the megaphone. He's middle aged, one of those guys who's in denial about their hair, so it's thin on top but down to his shoulders. I worm my way between backs and shoulders and arms until I'm right next to him. I could grab hold of the megaphone from here, but that's Plan B. I'll try Plan A first.

I tap the guy on the shoulder. He looks round at me, does a double-take when he sees my burn, then releases a button on the megaphone to turn it off.

'All right, mate?' he says.

'Yeah, cool,' I say. 'Can anyone have a go?'

He's not sure. He don't like war. He don't like the Americans. He don't like the government, but he likes to have control of the megaphone.

'I wanna be like you, man,' I say. 'I wanna change the world.'

A grin spreads across his face.

''Course you do. 'Course you do. Okay, young fella,' he says. He holds the megaphone out towards me. 'Press the red button and keep it down when you speak into the end. Don't be shy. Give it some welly. I'll introduce you.'

He turns away, holds the mouthpiece up to his face and presses the red button.

'We've got a young warrior for peace here. I want you to give a warm welcome to . . .' he pauses and leans his head back towards me.

'Adam,' I whisper.

'. . . Adam. Let's hear it for Adam.'

The crowd all cheer like crazy. They haven't got a clue who I am, but they'll cheer anything – it's that sort of morning and that sort of crowd. I take hold of the megaphone. It's heavier than I'm expecting, but I take a deep breath, hold it up to my mouth and press the button.

'No war!' I shout. 'No war!' I stop, and the crowd chants back at me. I do a couple more rounds of that, until they're really on my side. Baldy slaps me on the back and then holds his hand out for the megaphone, but I'm not done yet. I've only just started.

'No-one wants this war,' I shout. The sound booms out across the square and it's great. 'No-one wants this war, but in three days' time London's going to be flattened. The whole city's going to be destroyed.' The crowd's gone quieter now, there's even a few jeers. 'Yesterday's tremor was just the start. There's much worse coming. Much, much worse. We need to get out of London. We need to get out by New Year's Day.'

There are more jeers now, and booing.

'Keep yourselves safe. Keep your families safe. Get out of London. Go today. Go now.'

All around me people are trying to shout me down.

'No!'

'Get lost!'

'No war!'

Baldy tries to grab the megaphone, but I'm holding on tight.

'People are going to die here. Save yourselves. Save your families. Get out of London.'

There's other people jostling me now. Someone prises the megaphone out of my fingers and I throw a punch. They're crowding in on me so I don't know who I'm hitting, but they're giving as good as they're getting, feet and hands flying at me. I hold my arms up around my face but that leaves my body open and someone catches me in the stomach. The air's punched out of my lungs and I slump forward.

The violence is rippling through the crowd now. People are pushing forward to get to me then being pushed back and there's panic in the air. I try to keep on my feet. I've got to get out. I put my head down and charge through. It's difficult 'cause we're packed in so tight, and people are grabbing at me, but in a few minutes I make it to the edge.

In front of me there's a row of polished boots. I unbend a bit and look up, into a wall of riot shields.

'Let me out!' I shout. 'I've got to get out before they kill me!' The wall doesn't move. 'Let me out! Let me out!'

I step forward and hammer a fist onto one of the shields. The shield next to it moves towards me. Great, a gap, I'm going to get out of here. A baton crunches down on my shoulder. One hit and I'm on the ground. They don't follow up – they don't need to. The guy steps back and the wall's solid again. My face scrapes into the concrete, and for a few seconds I don't know what's happening, where I am, whether I'm alive or dead. I should move, I should get on my feet, but it's beyond me. I don't even know which way is up.

The people behind me, the ones that were punching and kicking me, they've changed their tune now. They're shouting their heads off, roaring and raging at the police.

'Civil liberties!'

'Police brutality!'

'Fascists! Take their pictures! Get their numbers!'

There's hands all over me again, not pulling and pinching like before, but holding me, reassuring me.

'You all right, mate? Can you hear me?'

I open my eyes slowly. At least half a dozen lenses are pointed at me, with a mass of faces behind them, a jumble of numbers.

'We got it all on film, mate. They won't get away with it. What's your name? How old are you? We'll get it on the lunchtime news.'

I don't want all the fuss. I want to get out of here, get home to Nan, but slowly their words filter through. *All on film. Lunchtime news.* And I remember why I'm here.

'The first of January,' I say, looking straight into the nearest camera. 'Get out of London. It's all going up on New Year's Day.'

People start trying to shush me. It's not what they want to hear, but I keep going.

'London's in danger. Yesterday was just the start. It will be worse than that. Ten times worse. A hundred times worse. People are going to die here. Get out. Get out of London.'

The cameras are trained on me as I'm helped to my feet. People are firing questions at me. Who hit me? How many times? I don't answer them, I stick to my own script. Blood trickles from my face into my mouth, but I don't stop. This is my chance. This is my moment. I'm broadcasting to the nation. Pray to God the nation listens.

They keep us in the square for six hours. They don't let nobody in or out. You have to pee where you stand. Women crouch down, while their friends make a barrier round them. We ask for water: they don't bring it. We ask to be allowed to leave, quietly, without any fuss: they tell us we're being kept here for our own safety.

From time to time, someone loses it. They start arguing, or try and barge their way out through the wall of shields. They get the same treatment as me – sticks and boots coming at them till they're down – and then the wall's back in place.

Once the cameras move away from me, I try talking to people, just one or two at a time. The thing is I like them. Before I'd have taken no notice or scoffed at them – long-haired hippies, thinking they can change the world. But listening to them, I realise they think about things, the big things – the future of the planet, people in other countries going hungry, being oppressed. They care. Makes me feel like I've gone through my whole life with my eyes shut.

A lot of them are the first of January. I tell them they need to get out. I walk through the crowd, having the same conversation, over and over again.

'Get out? We can't even get out of Grosvenor Square.'

'Yeah, but after today. Go home and pack some things and just go.'

'Why are you saying this?'

'I can see it. I can see the future, man.'

They don't know how to take me. Some of them are kind – they think I'm crazy, and if they're nice to me, I'll go away. Others just shake their heads and wait for me to move on.

'Promise me,' I say, 'promise me you'll get out of London.' A few people do. I've spooked them, I suppose, or they're humouring me. But as I work my way from person to person, I can predict who will say they'll go – and none of them are twenty-sevens. I start to get a bit obsessed. I've got to get one twenty-seven to say they'll leave. But however hard I try, I can't do it. It's getting frustrating and I suppose I'm getting agitated. I can tell I'm starting to get people's backs up, but I can't stop. In the end, someone stops me.

I'm talking to a woman. She's pretty, in her twenties and she's got just over a week to live.

'Come on,' I'm saying. 'You've got to promise me you'll go. There's only days left now. You've got to get yourself safe. A lot of people are going to die here, you know?'

She doesn't want to make eye contact, keeps looking away from me into the crowd, and then someone steps in, a big bloke, several inches taller than me, not a hair on his head.

'She don't want to talk to you, okay? Leave her alone. You're frightening her. It's bad enough here as it is without you bothering everyone. Why don't you keep your mouth shut for a bit and give everyone a break?'

Another day, somewhere else, I might have taken him on. But I've been battered enough today.

'It's life and death, that's all,' I say, holding both hands up in surrender. 'I'm trying to save lives.' Then I turn away from them both, and look through the crowd towards the shields keeping us in.

It's a long wait until they let us go. People start to sit down, even though they know that the dampness on the ground is piss, not water. The talking slowly tails off, 'til hundreds of us, maybe a couple of thousand even, are sitting there in silence and waiting.

In the end there's no great drama. A few minutes after it's got properly dark, the police just walk away. No announcement, no instructions. One minute they're there, the next they're filing down the side-streets and getting into their vans.

I look around me. People are getting wearily to their feet. They're angry about the way they've been treated, but they're too tired and uncomfortable to go on about it apart from muttering under their breath. My legs are beyond stiff. When I stand up they feel like they'll give way. I shift my weight from one to the other, trying to get the blood flowing again, while pins and needles shoot up from the soles of my feet.

I shamble out of the square and head for the bus stop. It's only when the queue starts filing on to the bus and I'm two from the front I reach into my pocket and realise it's completely empty – no wallet, no Oystercard. Sometime over the last six hours, one of that nice, moral, save-the-world lot has cleaned me out. I've still got my phone and about twenty-five cents. But who would I ring? Nan? She can't get me home from here – I'm going to have to walk.

I work through my other pockets, but there's nothing useful and I'm holding up the queue. People are starting to tut and tsk behind me. Then someone just barges past and I'm pushed out of the way. I can't be bothered to lash out this time. It'd be pointless and I haven't got the energy. Everyone's tired. It's been a long day and they want to get home. So do I. I move away from the bus stop, and start walking. It's miles home, but I don't even think about it. I just put one foot in front of the other, head down, through streets and garden squares and shopping parades. All I see is paving slabs and concrete, feet and legs. Which is how I nearly miss it. A miracle, the only thing that could put a smile on my face at the end of this long, long day.

I come to a place where the feet aren't moving. A crowd's gathering on the pavement. I have to look up to find my way through, and then I see what's stopped them. There's a message flashing on the public information screen above a row of shops: "URGENT: EVACUATE LONDON NOW." Then another: "LEAVE LONDON NOW. MAJOR INCIDENT WARNING: EVACUATE LONDON."

'Oh my God, he's done it!' I want to punch the air, but instead I look around the faces in the crowd. They're puzzled. They're scared.

Then the phone in my pocket starts vibrating. A text. I take it out, and it's the same thing. The messages on the screen are being texted to my phone. It's happening to everyone else here too. All the way down the street, people are looking at their phones and then looking at the screens.

I dial Nelson's number, but all I get is his voicemail. The excitement's fizzing through my voice as I leave my message.

'Nelson, you beauty. You done it. I don't know how, but you done it. Thanks, man. Keep safe.'

People are starting to leave now. Some of them are breaking into a run, pushing other people out of the way. I was knackered when I left Grosvenor Square, but now I'm firing on all cylinders again. I break into a run myself. I'm going to get home and I'm going to pack my things and me and Nan are out of here tonight.

Sarah

I was stupid to dump my coat. So stupid. I'll freeze to death out here. Part of me doesn't even care. I've got nothing left to live for. They've got her now – they won't give her back. She'll be tucked up somewhere in a nice, clean cot in a nice, clean house, with a foster mum and a foster dad, drinking formula from a bottle.

It's the last bit that gets me. Of course I want Mia to be warm and safe and looked after. She should be with me, but if she isn't then I want her to have the best. But the thought of her drinking milk from a bottle kills me. I've fed her from the start. It's our thing, it's what we do. Now that link, that connection's gone.

How could they do that? How could they take her away when we physically need each other? It's the cruellest thing.

I slide off the sleepers and onto the ground, curling up in a ball, hugging my knees into me. I'm shivering violently, but I hardly notice. The pain in my body doesn't count. It's the pain in my head that will kill me – her loss, her absence, her *not being here*, is worse than anything I've ever felt before.

I get so cold, I stop shivering. My body's still and stiff. I should move, go somewhere else, anywhere that might be more sheltered and offer a little warmth. Or I should walk through the night, get my arms and legs moving, keep my blood circulating. But I've gone past it now, that moment when I might have used some common sense, made myself get up – the cold has sapped it out of me – and now I'm stuck here.

My arms are folded up into my chest. One of my hands is resting against my neck. I can feel a pulse there but it's faint and slow. I should move: I can't. I should sit up: the ground won't let me. I should call out for help: my throat is dry and full of dust. The pulse beneath my fingers is getting slower, and slower. If I can count it, it's still there, but I can't remember the names of the numbers any more. I can't remember . . .

Adam

It's quicker going along the canal. More direct and there are no people, not at this time of night. I've jogged all the way, the adrenalin's still pumping. You can see some parts of the path in the lights from the buildings alongside, but most of it's dark, so I can only see a few metres ahead.

I'm on a darker stretch now, getting near the alley that goes through to the main road and home. There's something on the ground, up ahead, a heap of clothes maybe. Then I make out a foot and a few centimetres of pale leg between a shoe and the bottom of some trousers. My stomach turns over. What is it? A dummy, most likely, something out of a shop window, dumped by the side of the canal. God, that's creepy.

I realise I've stopped running. I've stopped altogether. I don't want to go near this thing. It's freaking me out.

Don't be so stupid, I tell myself. *It's plastic, a doll, that's all.*

I make myself walk on. But it's so lifelike. As I get nearer I can see the arms and the head. One hand's resting on the jaw, hiding part of the face. It's only got a tee-shirt on, so you can see nearly all the arms. The plastic's pale and smooth, almost white.

My stomach flips again. A dummy can't hunch up like that. It can't make that shape. My guts twist into a knot. It's a body. I've found a dead body. Shit! I take another step so that I'm level with it. Half the head is shaved and there's a bristly line running over the top.

'Sarah!' I gag on the word as it comes out of my throat.

This thing, it's Sarah. She's on her own, in this dark, cold place. There's no sign of Mia.

She can't be dead. Her number is 2572075. Numbers don't change. Or do they? Is she the proof they can?

I crouch down next to her and touch her hand. It's icy cold. I take it away from her face, cradle it in both of mine, then bring it up to my mouth. I kiss her fingers.

'Sarah. Sarah.' I say her name, over and over again. My breath's like smoke in the dark air, threading through her fingers. I stare at her face – with her eyes closed she looks so young. I stare and stare until my eyes start to lose it. I'm brimming up with tears and her mouth goes blurry. I blink and the tears spill down my face so I can see clearly, but her mouth is still hazy, like there's a mist round it.

There *is* a mist! Shit! I put her hand down gently and lean forward. I hold my fingers close to her lips and I can feel the warm breath coming from them. I rip off my jacket and drape it over her. I fumble for the phone in my pocket and dial 999. Nothing happens, then I see that the low battery sign's flashing and it cuts off altogether, the screen blank and useless. I can't leave her here while I go to get help – she's only just alive now. I put my arm under her back and lift her so I can get my jacket on her properly, pushing her arms into the sleeves like I'm dressing a child. Then I hold her as close to me as I can, rubbing her arms, rubbing her back, trying to pass the warmth from my body into hers.

'Sarah! Sarah! Come back. Come back to me.'

Her eyes are still closed, and I'm getting cold now. I've only been here a few minutes and I'm shivering. How long has she been here?

I stick one arm behind her back and the other one under her legs and heave her onto my lap. Then I put one leg forward and stagger onto my feet. We sway wildly for a few seconds before I get my balance. I'm desperately aware the water's only a step or two away. She's a dead weight in my arms, with her head flopping down. I hitch her up so her neck's resting on my arm and her head's tucked into my shoulder, then I set off as fast as I can.

I find the alleyway and soon I'm up to the High Road and half walking, half running along the pavement. People look, but no-one offers to help. No-one tries to stop me. They just turn away and carry on with their business. When I get back to Carlton Villas, the gate's open and the door's on the latch. I edge through the door and into the front room. Nan's there.

'Good God, Adam, what's this?'

'Just get out the way. Let me put her down.'

She shifts so that I can lay Sarah down on the sofa.

'Oh my God, look at 'er.'

'I know. Get some blankets.'

Nan rushes upstairs and fetches the duvet from my bed. She tucks it round Sarah, making sure her arms are underneath.

'You'd better get something on too,' she says. 'Wait here.'

She brings me a thick hoodie.

'I'll get the kettle on,' she says. 'Sit over there, near the fire.'

I do as I'm told. The telly's playing in the background, but it takes me a while to realise that the pictures they're showing are from Grosvenor Square. Even then it don't really sink in 'til a face comes onto the screen – a mad-eyed boy with blood on his face is shouting something at the camera.

'People are going to die here. Get out. Get out of London!'

'You've been on the box all day.' Nan puts a mug of tea in my hands. 'Careful, it's hot. I been sitting here, watching you, wondering when the hell I'm going to see you again. Those bastards had you penned in there all day. Pigs!'

It's all on screen; the rally, me getting whacked with a baton and falling to the ground. I know it's me and I know it happened, but it's the weirdest thing watching it on Nan's TV. For a start, I'm a sight, a proper sight. Face messed up, staring eyes. And the stuff I'm saying – I sound like a nutter. I put my mug down on the floor next to me and lean forward with my head in my hands, groaning.

'What's up, Adam? You poorly?'

'No, it's just . . . just . . .' I can't put it into words. How huge it all is, how hopeless it is trying to do something about it, how frustrating it is to be me, trapped in this body, with this face.

'Drink your tea up, you've only had half.'

I reach for my mug. As I sit up, I look towards Sarah on the sofa. She's awake, at least her eyes are half-open, and her number, her precious number is there. I put my tea back down and scrabble over to kneel beside her.

I stroke her forehead.

'Sarah,' I say. 'You're home with us. I found you, and I

brought you home.'

I don't know if she's heard me. She don't say nothing. There's a deadness in her eyes and she looks straight past me.

'Sarah,' I say, 'it's all right now. You're going to be all right.'

I want her to look at me, but she won't. Instead, she closes her eyes again, but her lips are moving. I lean closer to hear what she says.

'She's gone,' she whispers. 'They took Mia. She's gone.'

Sarah

It takes a while to explain. I'm numb from the cold, and numb from what's happened to me. So it's not until I've had a Cup-a-soup, and the warmth from the fire has really soaked in that I can tell them what's gone on. Adam and his nan listen in silence.

After I've finished, Adam says, 'We'll get her back, Sarah. We will. We'll get her back.'

'They won't give her back to me.'

'You're her mum. You're a good mum, I seen you with her. Why wouldn't they?'

'I'm sixteen. I've been in trouble in every school I've ever been to. I ran away from home. I lived with drug dealers and I just hurt a copper, scratched his face from his eye to his chin.'

'You must have had your reasons for all that.' Val coolly lights another fag, and I think how lucky Adam is to have her. She's not judging me or telling me what to do.

'Tell Nan the rest,' Adam says. 'About your dad.'

I can't. She may be a diamond, but I don't know her well enough. Not for that. I shake my head.

'Do you mind if I do?' I shrug, and he tells her. The cigarette burns down towards her fingers, unsmoked, as she listens.

'And Mia's . . .?'

'Mia's His,' I say. 'Well, He's the father. But she's not His, she never will be. She's mine.'

'Sweetheart,' Nan says, 'go to the council. Tell the truth and don't stop telling it 'til they listen. She's your baby. She should be with you. We'll go with you. We'll help, won't we, Adam?'

'Course. Course we will.'

'We'll do it,' she says, bathing us both in her nicotine fumes. 'We'll fucking do it. We can't let the bastards win.'

But it's not that easy. Because the next day when I do go to the One-Stop-Centre and finally get to see a social worker, they call the police. And I'm taken down to the station and charged with assault.

The worst thing is they charge me under my own name. The smokescreen I thought I'd created around me and Mia has been blown away. They picked up my coat when I ran off from Paddington Green, and, of course, my ID card was in the pocket. I can't believe I was so stupid. I should have binned it, or shredded it. Why did I hold onto it? What did I think I was holding on to? Did some part of me think I was going to go back to my old life one day?

So they've been piecing together my story, the police and the Children's Services. They've put together the bits of the jigsaw: home, school, Giles Street, Mia, except no-one knows she's called Mia. Vinny and the boys obviously haven't told them anything. So they keep calling her Louise, and I think *I've still got that. Her real name. Who she really is.*

And through all the questioning and the hanging around and waiting, I keep her in my head – her face, the feel of her in my arms, the way she smells, her smile. It kills me to think about her, but it's the only thing that will keep me going through all this.

Now they've got me, they don't want to let me go. They're running through the options: foster care, a place for young offenders . . . or home.

'We've told your parents that we've found you. They're on their way here.'

I feel like I'm dropping into a black hole.

'No. No. I don't want to see them.' The woman frowns. She's fifty-something and looks as if she was born fifty-something.

'They're your parents. You're sixteen.'

'I ran away. Don't you get it? I ran away from them.'

'You ran away because you were pregnant.'

'No, it wasn't that. Okay, yes, it was, but it's not what you think.'

'What was it? Tell me.'

And I can't do it. In this bare interview room. With this stranger. I can't tell her about my dad, what He did to me. I know it was a crime, and this is the place where you report crime, these are the people you tell, but I can't. It's personal.

'Tell her, Sarah.' Val is sitting in with us. She leans forward in her chair.

It's no good. I clam up. The social worker carries on asking questions, but I stay silent, and all the time I'm thinking that Mum and Dad are in a black Mercedes somewhere, getting nearer and nearer. This is what piles up the pressure in my head. This is what finally makes me speak.

'I know I've done things wrong,' I say. 'I know I shouldn't have hurt that policeman. I hold my hands up. I did it and I'm sorry. I'll apologise to him face to face, if you like. I'll write him a letter. Anything. They'd just taken my baby away from me. I was upset.'

They're listening.

'I need to see my baby. I need to be with her. If she's with a foster mum, perhaps I can go there too. You can watch me twenty-four hours a day, I don't care. See how I am with her. Let me prove I'm a good mum. I have been up to now. You don't believe me, but I have been.'

I can hear the pleading tone in my voice. I hate myself for it, to be crawling to them like that, but I'd do anything to get Mia back. Anything.

'Louise is safe now, and her safety is our number one priority.' The social worker says. 'You've been leading a very . . . unstable . . . life. She needs stability, routine. Obviously, while we're . . . helping you, if we can place her with family, then that's the best solution.'

'With family . . .?'

'Your mother and father. Louise's grandparents. It's an option, one we'll discuss with them when they get here.'

'My parents. Are you mad?'

'It's often the best solution. When clients, parents like you, are finding their feet, grandparents often step in to help.'

'You've got to be fucking kidding!'

'You may have had a difficult relationship with them, but they . . .'

I jump to my feet and the chair clatters backwards onto the floor behind me.

'Do I get a say in this? Do I get any say?'

'Sit down, Sarah. Please.' I stay standing. 'We'll obviously listen to your views, but ultimately the decision will be made by the Children's Panel in consultation with the Children's Magistrate. Above all, we have to think of Louise.'

'I can't stay here. I can't see them. If you're going to lock me up, just do it. I'd rather be in a cell than here.'

'We don't want to lock you up. You're being bailed for the assault on PC McDonnell, so we're looking for somewhere suitable for you to stay, assuming that you won't go home.'

'I won't go home. I'd kill myself first.' She looks at me then, and, too late, I realise that that is just the sort of thing you don't say in front of a social worker. 'I didn't mean it,' I blurt out quickly. 'I'm not going to kill myself.'

'I'll have her at mine. I'll look after her.'

'Mrs Dawson, I'm not sure . . .'

'She won't go anywhere, run off, not without the baby. She needs somewhere clean and warm, some good home cooking. I'm used to teenagers. Brought up enough of them.'

'It's not that. It's the father . . .'

'The father?'

'Your great-grandson, Adam Dawson. Louise's dad.'

Val's ready to bust out laughing now. Her face twists up and she starts to say, 'Adam? No, he never . . .' but then she looks at me. I've got my eyes wide open and I'm nodding at her.

She raises her eyebrows and says, 'Right . . . yeah, Adam . . . and Sarah.'

'He's been in trouble.' The woman looks back at her screen and starts scrolling down. 'Quite a bit of trouble.'

'Yeah, he's been in trouble. What sixteen-year-old hasn't? He's a good lad, though. Good with the baby. You don't need to worry about him.'

I guess it's not easy to find places for delinquent teenagers like me, because two hours later they end up agreeing that I can stay at Val's. I have to sign a load of forms, and so does she.

On the way out of the police station, we walk past another interview room. The door's slightly open and I glimpse the two people sitting on the other side of the table. My mum looks smaller and older than I remember her, even though it's only three months since I left. But my dad's just the same. The sight of him makes me want to vomit. I have to swallow to keep down the bile rising up inside me. He glances up and our eyes meet, just for a second. There's nothing there, no spark of recognition, no warmth, no hate. Nothing. What does he see when he looks at me? I don't know and I don't care. But the thought of him seeing Mia, holding her, turns me inside-out.

'Get me out of here,' I say to Val, and I clutch her arm.

'Was that them?' she asks.

'Yeah.'

'I'd like to skin him alive, what he did to you. You need to tell people. They need to know.'

'I can't, Val. I can't. Let's go. Please. Please.'

Outside, I have to stop to be sick.

'It's not right,' Val keeps saying. 'This isn't right. It's not fair.'

I can't say anything, even when I've cleaned myself up a bit. I hold onto her arm as we walk to the bus stop. I like the fact that she's so fired up – it feels good to have someone on my side. It feels good that that person is Val.

Sitting next to her on the bus, she has the tact not to say anything about Adam, but I'm not so controlled. There's something about her. She understands so much.

'Val,' I say, 'Thanks.'

'What for?'

'For letting me stay. For sticking up for me. For keeping quiet about Adam – I had to say something. They found a picture of him at the squat. It was the first thing that came into my head.'

She snorts.

'That's okay. He'd make a nice dad, Adam would. He'll make someone a nice husband one day. Can't go wrong with a Dawson. Bit wild, sometimes, like my Cyril and Terry, of course, but they're solid underneath.' She's looking straight ahead, hands fiddling with the clasp on her handbag. She'd be happier with a cigarette in them.

'Val?'

'Yeah.'

'He knows, doesn't he? Adam knows your number and mine and Mia's.'

She sighs.

'Yeah,' she says, 'he does, poor lad.'

'Would it be better to know?'

She looks up then.

'No, Sarah. What good would it do? Better to live your life how you want to, take each day as it comes.'

She's right, of course, but as the bus trundles along I can't help thinking. 112027. Adam. Val. Me. Mia. Will any of us see the second?

Adam

'You did it, Nelson, you're a star! You did it!'

'You did too; you've been all over the media. Forty million hits on YouTube.'

Forty million? That's colossal.

'We're doing it, man. We're doing it!'

'I gotta go, Adam. I just wanted to check in with you. Say goodbye . . .'

'Where are you, man? Are you safe?'

'I can't say. I can't talk for long – I think they're listening to my phone.'

'Are you out of London, though?'

'Not yet.'

'Nelson. Go. Go now.'

'Yeah, I will. You need to get out too, though, don't you?'

'We'll go. Just a few things to sort. But we're going. Nelson?'

'Yeah?'

'Thanks, mate.'

'That's okay. We did a good thing. We—'

The phone goes dead. I redial straight away, but there's nothing, no voicemail or anything.

'That your mate?' Nan asks.

'Yeah, but we was cut off.'

'Happens, doesn't it?'

'Yeah. S'pose. He said he was being listened to. On his phone. Do you think they picked him up?'

'No, it's just the bloody phone system. Don't make something out of it, Adam.'

'I wouldn't want anything to happen to him. He put himself out for me.'

'You can't worry about him now. We got things closer to home to think about.'

Nan tips her head towards Sarah. She's sitting like a zombie on the sofa, eyes on the telly though she's not really watching. She's been like that since she and Nan got back from the police station. Nan's been trying to cheer her up and so have I, but she's so down, she don't hardly speak.

'We'll get her back, Sarah. We will. If they won't let you have her, they'll at least let you visit, and then we could . . . grab her.'

Nan's flapping her hands, trying to shush me. Sarah looks at me.

'They won't even let me see her,' she says, with scorn in her voice. 'Not for ages. Maybe not ever. And I don't know where she is. Not for certain.'

'We can think of something . . .'

She shoots me a look then that says 'Shut up' as clearly as if she'd shouted it in my face. So I do. I perch on a chair and pretend to watch the TV. We're on a news channel, showing different scenes from various bus, coach and rail stations around London. There's an unconfirmed report of someone crushed on the tube. Panic's starting to spread across the city.

'I didn't want this. People getting hurt trying to get out. That's not part of the deal.'

The screen cuts to the pavement by King's Cross tube. There's a body carried out on a stretcher, and their face is covered.

'Oh my God! This isn't right. This isn't right.'

'It's not your fault, Adam,' Nan says. 'You can't blame yourself.'

I'm up on my feet now.

'Of course it's my fault! I got it out there! I got half of London trying to leave.'

'People have to take care, look after theirselves.'

Two steps and I'm over to where Nan's standing.

'Shut up, Nan! Just shut up! What if everyone else is right and it's just screwed-up stuff in my brain? What if I'm mental, disturbed? Nothing's going to happen on the first. Only now people are dying trying to get away from something that isn't going to happen.'

'Calm down, love, calm down.'

Everything she says makes it worse. I thought she understood, but she can't. If she understood she wouldn't tell me to calm down.

'Don't tell me that! It's in my head, Nan. It's inside me. All this stuff. I thought I could do a good thing, but it's turning into a bad thing. I don't want it! I don't want people to die! Why are people dying? Why are they dying, Nan?'

She's backing away from me, but I can't stop shouting. There's so much rage inside me. It's like the cork is out of the bottle now.

'I'm killing people, Nan. I'm killing them. I never meant to. I . . .'

'Adam, look. Look.' It's Sarah. Her voice stops me in my tracks. 'Look who's on now.'

The screen has cut from King's Cross to the Prime Minister.

'Oh God, not 'im,' Nan growls.

'Shh . . .'

'He was bloody useless the first time. God knows why they voted him back in, pompous prat.'

'Nan, shut up. I wanna hear.'

I sit on the arm of Sarah's sofa.

'People of Britain, it's become my custom to talk to you at New Year, to reflect on the past twelve months and look ahead to the year to come. I'm talking to you now, a little earlier than usual, to appeal for calm.' His face is flushed, his bald head's shining in the TV lights. 'I know you will have heard the rumour that London is facing a crisis. I want to assure you that it is not.'

'Look at 'is hands. He can't keep them still. He's lying.'

'Shut up, Nan.'

'This is a pernicious rumour promoted by people who wish to spread terror throughout our nation. They will not succeed, and I can assure you that we will find those responsible and they will feel the force of British justice. We have the most advanced monitoring systems in the world, the most sophisticated intelligence service. For your reassurance, I have raised the country's security level to red which means that all government personnel are now fully engaged in maintaining your safety. I urge all of you to go about your everyday business calmly. London is safe. You do not need to leave the capital. I will be here today, working in Downing

Street as normal, and I will be here tomorrow. The best thing you can do for yourself, for your family and for our country is to keep calm and carry on. Thank you.'

The channel switches back to the news studio. Nan reaches for the remote and turns the sound down.

'It's all right for him, I 'spect he's got a bloody great bunker under Number Ten, don't you?' she says.

'Do you think anyone will listen to him?'

'I dunno. Someone must have voted for him. Perhaps they'll listen.'

I feel so churned up. There's a million thoughts flooding through me.

'I don't know if I want people to go or to stay now,' I say.

'We want people to go, don't we? You've seen it. You and Sarah. You've seen what's going to happen. You're not mad. You've been given something. You've been given a chance to make a difference. Anyway,' she sniffs, 'it's not up to you now, love. You've set the ball rolling but it's on its way now. I reckon it's out of your hands.'

Sarah sits up a little.

'They're going to find the people responsible,' she quotes the Prime Minister's words. 'That's us, isn't it?'

'Us and Nelson.'

'What'll they do? What'll they do to us?' Her questions hang in the air and then someone batters on the door. Sarah gasps. Nan swears and I close my eyes. What next? What now? I want it all to go away.

'Open up! Police!'

'Shit, better get it. Adam?' Nan says. 'Get the door before they break it down.'

I drag myself to my feet, put the chain on and open the door enough to see out. There are half a dozen uniformed coppers in the front yard.

'Adam Marsh?' the one at the front asks.

'Yeah,' I say.

'Open up, please.'

'What is it?'

'Open up, sir.'

I push the door to, unhook the chain. I'm about to open the door properly when it's pushed into my face and a hand grabs my wrist and puts a handcuff round it.

'What the fuck . . .?'

'Adam Marsh, I have a warrant for your arrest for the murder of Junior Driscoll on the sixth of December 2026.'

Sarah

They take him away, just like that. Val goes with him and I'm left on my own. It was bad enough being without Mia when everyone else was here, but it's ten times worse on my own. I sit, numb, for a while, then I wander into the kitchen and look for something to tidy up, but it's all neat and clean. I empty Val's ashtray into the bin, wash it and dry it with some kitchen paper.

Back in the lounge, the TV is full of the same story. Panic and paranoia in London, people on the move, people criticising the government, police leave cancelled, army on standby. Adam is a side-story now – it's got bigger than him, although they do show footage of him being arrested, and marched down Val's front path watched by an army of silent gnomes.

I leave the telly on and go upstairs, wandering into Adam's room. I feel so useless. I don't know where Mia is. I don't know what's happening to her or to Adam. I pace from one side of the room to the other, bouncing off the walls, then hitting them with my fists, screaming.

I don't know how long I carry on like that. I've lost it, completely lost it. It's frightening letting go, and now I've started I can't seem to stop. At some point I pick up the chair by the door and fling it. The back breaks off as it hits the wall. I keep moving, hitting, screaming until the adrenalin's gone and I finally see how pathetic it is, how pathetic I am.

I flop down onto the floor near the bed and lean against Adam's bedside table. It digs into my back but I'm too exhausted to move. My throat is sore from all the noise I've been making. What good did it all do? What difference did I make? None of it got me one centimetre nearer to Mia. She's out there somewhere, without me. Is she missing me at all? Has she noticed I'm not there for her?

I look around me for something, anything to distract from the misery of being me right now. It's a room full of boy's things – posters, heaps of old clothes, trainers lying around. There's something on the floor under the bed, a book maybe. I'm thinking it's going to be porn – that's what boys keep under the bed, isn't it? I slide it across the carpet towards me, and I feel a little shiver run down my spine. It's not a printed book, or a magazine – it's a notebook. It's the notebook I saw Adam with, that very first day at school.

I pick it up and rest it on one palm, brushing dust and fluff off the cover with my other hand.

I know it's his.

I know it's private.

I shouldn't look.

I open the cover.

His writing is messy. It's joined up and slopes strongly to the right. The horizontal lines on the book are printed, but he's ruled vertical ones on every page to make columns, and he's recorded names and dates and descriptions and more dates. There are pages and pages of them.

I scan down just one.

'Junior, 4/09/2026, at school, violent, a knife, the smell of blood, a sick feeling, 6/12/2026.'

Junior. He's the one Adam's been arrested for. Adam wrote his death down in this book on the fourth of September, three months before he died.

This is dynamite. I honestly don't know if Adam killed the boy or not, but this could convict him.

I turn over the page and I gasp as I read the name in the left-hand column.

'Sarah.'

Adam

I can't do this. There's two days to go and I'm in a cell. At the back of my mind I knew they'd do me for Junior. How could they not? I wrote down his death date – on my palm-net, my dad's computer, in my book. It's there. I can't deny it, and how can I make anyone understand that although I knew it, I didn't plan it? Who's going to believe me?

I knew they'd do me, but I didn't think it would be now. I thought I'd be with Nan, with Sarah, helping them, finding Mia, keeping them safe. I feel like I've let them down. I'm not there for them.

The cops say I'll be sent to court tomorrow and, like as not, the magistrates'll put me on remand 'til the trial. Only God knows how long I'll have to wait for that.

And the men in suits are back. Just before they lock me up in here, the two of them come into the interview room, the fat guy and the one with ginger hair.

'Turning up at Grosvenor Square,' says Big-gut, 'not a smart move. You've seen the panic you've created. You and your "friends". We know who they are: Sarah Halligan, Val Dawson, Nelson Pickard. We know where Sarah and your grandmother are,' – my stomach lurches and I feel the panic rising – 'but Nelson, where is he, Adam? Where's Nelson?'

I shake my head.

'You don't know or you're not telling? You're in a lot of trouble. We could maybe . . . help you.'

A glimmer of hope. Maybe this is my way home.

'Get me out?'

He shakes his head. 'You're being charged with murder, Adam. Even we can't get you out of that. No, we could make things easier though, get you moved to a hospital. Hearing voices, seeing numbers, and a family history of it. Your mum and everything. We could make sure they offered you treatment.'

I look away.

'We just need to know where Nelson is, that's all.'

I hate what they're saying and I'm scared for Nelson, what I've got him into. I look the guy straight in the eye.

'I'm not telling you,' I say. 'Nelson's a hero. He's worth ten of you. He reached people. He got them moving. You did nothing. You knew about it, and you did nothing. I'm not talking, not even if you pull my fingernails out.'

He laughs then.

'We don't do that, not in this country.' He pauses. 'Pity.'

The two of them exchange a smile. S'pose that's their idea of a joke. I want to wipe the smile off their faces. I want them to go away.

'I don't know why you're wasting your time here,' I say and I look them both in the eye, one after the other. 'You should be on that motorway yourselves. You haven't got long left.'

The older one frowns at me.

'That sounds like a threat.'

'Not a threat, man, I just say what I see.'

He scrapes his chair back and makes for the door.

'Get him out of here,' he says to the copper outside. 'Get him out.'

Sarah

Val comes home just past midnight. She looks exhausted, the skin round her eyes sagging, her mouth set in a grim line.

'They've charged him. They say he'll be taken to some young offenders' place bloody miles from here. God knows how I'll get there to see him.'

I help her off with her coat and put the kettle on. The book is on the kitchen table. She doesn't seem to see it. She's concentrating on lighting her cigarette. Her lighter's nearly out of gas and she flicks and flicks at it with increasing ferocity.

'Come on,' she growls, with the cigarette dangling out of one corner of her mouth. 'Light, damn you. Why won't you light?'

'There's another one somewhere. Here . . .' I snatch up a new one from the top of the microwave, spark it up and hold it to the end of her fag. She's clutching the old lighter so hard it looks as though she might crush it. I take it gently from her and put it on the table next to Adam's book. And that's when she sees it.

'Where d'you get that from?'

'I found it. Under his bed. I wasn't looking or anything. It caught my eye.'

'Do you know what it is?' Those hazel eyes are searching mine now, warily.

'Yeah.'

'Have you read it?'

I can't lie to her. She can look right inside me.

'Some.' *Enough. Too much. My number. Mia's.* 'Have you?'

She shakes her head.

'No. Don't want to. Well, I do, but I don't.'

I know exactly what she means.

'Sarah,' she says, 'get rid of it.'

'What?'

'We need to get rid. He's in enough trouble as it is. Won't help if they find this. Here . . .' She picks up the new lighter and holds it out towards me. She wants me to burn it.

'It's Adam's. It's personal.'

'Is there anything in there about that lad, Junior?'

Violent, a knife, the smell of blood, a sick feeling, 6/12/2026.

'Yes. Yes, there is.'

'So do it. Burn it, Sarah. I know he never done it. He's told me that and I believe him. I think they got some stuff off of his computer, but this'll send him to prison. This could send him to the gallows. The death penalty kicks in at sixteen. They could 'ave 'im, Sarah. My boy. My beautiful boy.'

I take the lighter from her, and look around. The bin is plastic, so that's no good. I can't go outside because of the press gathered there. I don't want a bloody audience; and I don't want to be caught on camera destroying evidence. It'll have to be the sink.

I hold the notebook up in one hand and the lighter underneath it, concentrating the flame on one corner. It doesn't take long to catch. I keep hold of it as long as I can, but when the flames start licking my fingertips, I let the burning book drop into the sink. Val and I stand watching the pages curl, tormented in the heat, until all that's left is a pile of black and grey flakes. Then I scoop them up in my bare hands and dump them in the bin.

'Gone,' she says. 'Thanks, Sarah.'

I run my hands under the tap, rubbing at them to get rid of the fragments of ash clinging onto my skin. If only I could wash away the contents of the book so easily. But they're in my head, now, like they've been in Adam's for so long – death sentences, numbers, my own number and Mia's.

1/1/2027.

Oh.

My.

God.

Adam

Up the front of the courtroom three stiffs in suits are sitting behind a sort of desk, on a raised-up platform – two men and a woman. The woman's in the middle and it looks like she's the one in charge. She's got a sharp red jacket on and evil-looking, black-framed glasses.

There's some desks in front of the judges and then at the back of the room a little partition with a couple of rows of chairs behind. There's a guy with a notebook sitting there and there's Nan and Sarah.

I wasn't expecting to see them. It never crossed my mind they'd be here.

I don't want them to see me like this.

I can't look at them.

Nan raises her hand, starts waving, but I turn my head the other way and walk past.

I'm shown to a chair next to my solicitor. She smiles at me as I sit down, gives my arm a little squeeze.

'All right?' she says.

I can't answer. I'm numb. I don't believe this is happening to me.

Red-jacket says, 'Right, let's start,' and a bloke in a shabby suit stands up and starts firing questions at me. Name? Address?

I mumble my replies and then they read the charge out.

Murder.

There's more talking, but I don't know what it's about. 'Committal . . . remand . . . preliminary hearing . . .'

Then everyone's standing up, the guards are back and it's time for me to go again. What now? What's happening?

My brief leans over. 'I'll see you in Sydenham. Tomorrow or the next day. We can talk then.'

'Sydenham? Where is it? What's going on?'

'Young offenders' institution,' she says. 'You'll be there until your trial. Keep your head down. Don't do anything silly. I'll see you tomorrow . . .'

Nan reaches over the barrier as I'm led past. The guard blocks her and pushes me forward so I almost trip.

'Adam . . .' she calls out, but there's no time. I'm out of there and down the steps and back in the cell. They uncuff me and then the door's slammed shut, and I can hear the guards' footsteps echoing down the corridor.

'What's happening? What's happening to me?'

I bang on the grill. They said I was gonna be taken somewhere, and now I'm back here again.

The footsteps stop.

'Quiet in there. We'll move you when there's a van ready. It's fucking chaos in London today. Just sit tight and shut up.'

How can I sit tight? We're running out of time. I can feel the seconds ticking away in my head, a non-stop countdown.

The clock in the court said half-past eleven. Just over twelve hours 'til New Year's Day. What are Nan and Sarah doing now? What the hell am I going to do, banged up in a fucking cell?

Sarah

New Year's Eve. Val and I spend the morning at the Magistrate's Court and the afternoon on the phone. I'm ringing Children's Services trying to find out where Mia is. Val's ringing the police, Adam's solicitor, anyone else she can think of. For both of us, it's like talking to a brick wall. Everyone is telling us that there are procedures to follow, that procedures like this take time.

I'm told that I will be interviewed 'within the next week or so'. It's a Bank Holiday tomorrow, so there'll only be on-call staff there, dealing with emergencies.

'But this is an emergency.'

'Your daughter is safe. She's being cared for. After the Bank Holiday we will call you in for an interview. This will probably be one of a series. We need to get the full picture of you, your circumstances, your experience as a parent. Realistically, we're looking at a case conference in early February, then a long-term custody decision sometime after that.'

'Sometime? I need to see my daughter now. I need to see her tomorrow. I can't wait.'

'That's the system, I'm afraid.'

'Can't I see her? Just see her. I don't mind who else is there.'

'We'll be able to look at interim visitation rights after your first interview.'

'At least tell me where she is.'

'She's safe.'

'Please.'

'Your daughter is safe. We'll be in touch after the New Year.'

And the phone is cut dead. That's it. Dismissed. Sit tight. Do nothing for a couple of days. Do nothing while the world crashes down around us. Do nothing while London is torn into bits. I stare out of the kitchen window. It's got dark outside. People are putting their lights on in the tower blocks around us. Each light means there's somebody home, but there aren't nearly as many as you'd expect. I reckon a lot of people have already left.

Val doesn't have any more luck trying to get to Adam or get him out of the Young Offenders' place they've sent him to. I lean in the kitchen doorway while she talks. I can tell it's not going well, but when she puts the phone down, she lets rip with a string of insults that even I'd be proud of.

'They won't even let me see 'im, Sarah, not for a couple of weeks. He's a young lad. He's going to be going mad in there. I know 'im. He'll be worried about you, and Mia, and me. He's got a temper on 'im an' all. He could do anything.'

'What can we do?'

'I dunno, love. I dunno.'

We heat up some food, though neither of us eats much of

it. We sit and stare at the TV as it moves from news updates to reviews of the year to so-called 'entertainment' shows filmed weeks ago in studios with big clocks in the background.

'Of course, it's New Year's Eve, love. I was on me own this time last year . . .'

'I was at home. At my mum and dad's.'

There are some big cans of worms here, and neither of us wants to open them.

'Do you want a drink of something? I'm going to.'

'I don't really drink.'

'I'll just give you a drop then.'

She scuttles into the kitchen and comes back with two thin glasses with rich, dark liquid in, and a bottle tucked under her arm.

'Drop of sherry,' she says, handing me one.

'Right. Thanks.' I sniff it. Just the vapour catches in the back of my throat. I cradle it in my hands, with no intention of drinking the vile stuff. Val's got no hesitation in getting stuck in.

'Shouldn't we be getting ready?' I say. 'For tomorrow?'

'What do we think it is? Earthquake? Bomb? S'pose we should head for the Underground, that's what they did in the Second World War.'

'Shall we do that, then? Go and camp out there?'

'Don't fancy it much. They make me feel hemmed in at the best of times. What if we couldn't get out again? I reckon I'll take my chances here. Hide under the kitchen table or something. What do you want to do?'

Reckon I'll take my chances. I saw her number in Adam's book. I saw mine too. We're going to be okay, me and Val. It doesn't matter where we are when it hits – *we're going to survive.*

But Mia's different. Mia's only got hours left. My daughter. My baby.

'I've got to find Mia.'

She pours another glass of sherry for herself, looks at mine, untouched, and puts the bottle down.

'I've been thinking about that,' she says. 'I reckon you know where she is.'

'What?'

'It's in your nightmare, your vision. You've seen it over and over. There must be clues to where you are. Tell me about it.'

'It's just flames and fire, a building collapsing around us. We're trapped. Adam's there. He takes her from me. He takes her into the fire.'

'That's what happens, but where are you? Think, Sarah, think. It's in there.'

She's staring at me now, willing me to remember. I look into her eyes, and they take me deeper into myself.

'Think, Sarah, think. Close your eyes now. What do you see?'

Adam

There's no way out of here. You can't bust out through the window. You can't bust out through the door. My only chance is going to be when they transfer me.

When they brought me here my hands were handcuffed in front of me and I was in a van with several others. It's gonna be difficult to beat up a guard and break away with my hands together. Would the others join in? The best time would be before I'm shut in the van, when they're leading me out of here. I pace around the cell and I think about elbows and knees and feet – the damage I could do with them. I've got to do it. If I end up in Sydenham, I'm stuffed. I'll spend New Year's Day banged up. I can't let it happen, a sitting duck, stuck in a cell. Not seeing, not hearing, not knowing what's going on. Buried by the walls, maybe. My last resting place, a fucking prison. It's not going to happen. I'm not going to let it.

They took my watch and my belt off me when they arrested me, so I don't know how long it is before they come for me. Must be ten or twelve hours, though, because they've brought me two meals, if you can call them that, and the little square of window in my cell got dark a long time ago.

It's not what I'm expecting, though. This time I'm cuffed to a guard. He's a fat bastard, about ten years older than me, with a smear of a moustache on his top lip. With two more guards in front and behind, we're into the yard and locked in the van before I know it. The engine starts up and we're away.

Damn, damn, damn. I missed my chance. What the hell am I going to do now?

'What's the time, mate?' I ask him.

'Quarter to midnight.'

'Shit!'

'What's the problem? Missing a party? You and me both. Bloody New Year's Eve and they cancelled all leave.'

'What they done that for?'

'Where've you been? In a cave? The whole city's gone mad. People clogging up the roads, trying to get out, and the rest of them, the ones that are staying are treating it like it was 1999. They've set up a field hospital in Trafalgar Square to deal with all the drunks. Jesus, people in this town are mental.'

'I could do with joining them. Honest, mate, I need to get out of here.'

He looks at me, warily, and I catch his number. First of January. I'm handcuffed to a guy who's going to be dead within twenty-four hours. I don't get any clues from his number, though, it's just blackness, blankness, that's all. A strange one.

'Don't start with that,' he says.

'It's important. I need to get to my family.'

He shakes his head.

'Not tonight, mate. You're going to Sydenham, end of. We're over the river now, take us fifteen minutes max. There's no way out of these vans.'

'They don't stop for nothing?'

'Nothing. No fag breaks. No comfort breaks.'

'What if I hit you?'

He snorts.

'One, I'd hit you back so hard you wouldn't know what was happening to you. Trained, you see. Two, there's a camera up there. The guys up front can see everything that goes on in here. You start getting out of line and they put the sirens on, put the pedal to the metal and we go to the nearest cop shop, and then you get the beating of your lifetime.' *But they'd have to open the doors to do that, wouldn't they?* 'It's not worth it, honest, mate. It only makes things worse and . . .'

I ball my hand up into the tightest fist that I can, duck away from him and thump him hard on the side of the head.

He lurches sideways, then reaches into his belt and brings out a baton.

'Fucking moron!' he shouts. He makes to swing the stick at me, but I scramble to my feet and jam the heel of my foot into his crotch. He crumples forward, and I snatch the baton out of his hand and bring it down on the back of his head. There's a sickening crack as it hits. 112027. Is it past midnight yet? Is it me that kills him?

I drop the baton and put my hand to his neck, pressing into his skin to try to find a pulse. He's still alive.

The alarm starts up then, a deafening sound, filling up the inside of the van, and we're both flung towards the back as it accelerates sharply. I've got to get out of the handcuffs. The guard is slumped over with his head between his knees. I push him off the bench, get on my hands and knees and start going through his pockets. I can't find a key anywhere.

The baton's rolled to the other side of the floor. I reach across, dragging the guard's arm with me, scrabbling with my fingers 'til I can close them round the handle. Then I kneel up and heave his arm to the edge of the bench. I pull my hand as far away from his as I can so the chain of the cuffs is tight. I smash the baton at the chain. It dents the links but doesn't break it.

'Shit! Shit!'

The van's lurching wildly now. I topple backwards, hitting my head on the floor. We rock back the other way. This thing's unstable

'Stop the van!' I'm shouting now, though I know they wouldn't take any notice of me even if they could hear me over the siren. 'Slow down, for Christ's sake!'

I claw my way up to the front, dragging Fatboy with me and bang on the cab wall with the baton.

'Your mate needs help! Get us to a hospital!'

I'm slammed against the bench as the van tips again, but this time it doesn't right itself. With the siren still wailing we tip up and suddenly the wall's the floor and the floor's the wall and we're over again. My travel buddy's on top of me, crushing the air out of me and then everything flips and he's underneath. The van's bumping and banging and there's an almighty noise and the floor – or it could be the wall or the ceiling – hits my chin and I black out.

Sarah

I close my eyes. The telly's blaring out the countdown. 'Six, five, four . . .' I can't see anything. I can't get there. 'Three, two, one . . .' Big Ben's chimes ring through the lounge. 'Happy New Year!' Outside fireworks are going off like Kilburn's a battlefield.

'Think, Sarah.'

The flames are behind me and in front. I can't find Mia. I can't find her. The building's creaking, something's breaking away. Oh God, the roof's falling. It's hot. Unbearable. The paint's blistering on the stairpost. The stairpost. *The stairpost.* With the smooth curves carved into it, worn smoother by the hands that have swung round it as the children clatter downstairs and jump the last three steps. The children. My brothers and me.

I open my eyes.

'It's my house. She's with my parents. They gave her to them.'

Val's still looking at me, and her eyes are oceans of sympathy and strength.

'That's where we'll go then. We'll fetch her back. Come on, Sarah, no time like the present.'

'Now?'

'Now. I'll just fetch me bag from the kitchen.'

And then, with a 'pop' the TV switches off, and the house is plunged into darkness.

'Bloody hell, not again!'

The fireworks carry on for a bit, brighter than ever now, and then peter out. It's dark, but there's something eerie about the darkness. I look past Val towards the kitchen window.

'Oh my God!'

'You all right?'

'I'm fine. It's the sky. Look at the sky.'

With the electricity out, there are no reflections to stop us seeing out. The tower blocks are black fingers, outlined by a sky that's going crazy. Ribbons of green and yellow light are pulsing in the air. They shift in front of our eyes, glowing and fading, dissolving and reappearing.

'What the hell . . .?'

'It's awesome, Val. What is it?'

'Dunno, love. I've never seen nothing like it. Have you noticed something else?'

'What?'

'That bloody dog's stopped yapping.'

She's right. All day we've heard its constant yip, yip, yip through the walls, but now there's quiet. Everything's quiet.

'Thank goodness for small mercies,' she says. We lapse into silence again, and then a whining howl starts up.

'Spoke to soon, love. God, that thing's a pain. Don't know what Norma was thinking, getting that bloody pug.'

And then there's the biggest bang I've ever heard in my life, and the floor rears up underneath me, hurling me into the air, and I don't know what's up and what's down, and my ears are full of banging and crashing and splintering, and my head and shoulder hit something hard, and there's a red flash in my head and then nothing.

Adam

One side of me is cold and wet. I shiver and sit up. Above me the sky's exploding; there's rockets bursting like mortar shells, stars showering over me. I can see the colours reflected in front of me – it feels like I'm surrounded. It sounds like a battleground. *Bonfire Night's always like this,* I think. But then I look up again. *It's not the fifth of November. It's midnight on New Year's Eve. It's past midnight. It's the first of January.*

I put my hands on the ground to support me. A metal bracelet slides down my wrist. A bracelet? I don't wear jewellery, never have. My hands touch slime and I realise it's mud under my fingers. I'm by a river, with the water a metre or two away from me.

I look around me. Another rocket lights up the sky and in its flash I see a van lying on its side by the wall. The cab's smashed in, the back door's open.

I stagger to my feet, wincing at the pain all through me. I take a few steps towards the van. Its siren is quiet now.

There's a heap of something on the ground nearby. I crouch down. It's a person. A body. My guard. The matching half of the handcuffs is still on his wrist, the chain broken on impact.

'Sorry, mate,' I say. I can't find any other words.

I stumble to the cab. The ground's soggy. It drags at me, putting me off balance. Two more bodies inside the van. Their airbags inflated okay, but they didn't save them.

I turn away.

Where the hell am I?

I blunder forward and my hands hit something cold, rough, slimy – the river wall. I follow it along, treading on rubbish and God-knows-what washed-up at the side. I reach some steps and collapse onto them, breathing hard, trying to get my head round everything.

The fireworks are easing off now, just a few rockets in the distance, but the water's shimmering, green and yellow. It's the weirdest thing. I look up and there's ribbons of colour glowing and fading in the sky.

'What the hell . . .?' I murmur, and then I hear the loudest bang I've ever heard in my life and the ground's lifting under me and I'm thrown into the air. I land in water, ankle-deep. The sky's still full of shimmering colours, and now it's the only light there is.

Everything else has gone.

The whole city's in darkness.

And it's quiet. No traffic, no sirens, only a few shouts and screams echoing across the river.

The water around me drains away, taking some of the mud from under me. I feel like I'm being drawn into the ground, like I'll disappear, swallowed up by the bed of the Thames. It's like the seaside, like Weston, when you stand at the edge of the beach and the waves come and go, sucking the sand from under your toes, making you wobble.

The water's gone now, all of it. There's wet mud there now, not river. I start walking back to where I think the wall is. If we crossed the river, I'll need to be back the other side to get to Nan's. But, wait a minute, there's no water. I could walk across. I don't need to find a bridge. I turn round and head off the other way, but I've only gone a few steps when a little voice in my head takes me back to Weston again.

The waves come and go.

The water hasn't just disappeared. There's no plughole in the Thames. It's a river, a tidal river. It's gone now, but it'll come back.

And suddenly my head is full of the twenty-sevens I've seen with watery deaths, lungs filling up, helpless, drowning.

I turn round again and try to run, but the mud's so sticky it's like I'm running in slow motion. Off to my left, I can hear a sound, a rumble or a roar. *Come on, come on.* I'm pushing myself on, lifting one foot up then the other. I've got to find the steps and get out of here and then climb up somewhere, get higher, out of the way.

But it's too late. I look over my shoulder. I can't see it, but I can hear it. There's tons of water barrelling up the river, a monster raging towards me. I stop in my tracks, take in a lungful of air, but it's here before I'm ready. It hits me as I'm breathing in and blasts me off my feet. All I can do is shut my mouth and close my eyes as my body's being tossed around like a rag doll. The water holds me 'til my chest is bursting. I can't hold on any longer. I've got to breathe. I've got to open my mouth.

I can't.

I have to.

Sarah

I hurt everywhere, not just inside my head. I don't know where I am. I think I'm lying on my front. I can move my arms but not my legs. There's stuff in my mouth, hair or fluff or something, catching on my tongue, making me gag. I retch a bit, and try to spit my mouth clean.

Someone's shouting in the darkness.

'Adam? Adam?'

It's Val. She's alive, and not far away, but I can't see her.

I try to shout back, but my voice comes out as a whisper.

My legs are caught under something. I twist round and stretch towards them, groping to find out what's there. I can't see a thing, but it feels like one of the armchairs, not that heavy, but awkward to shift from this position. I get both hands on it and push. There's a slight movement and I manage to manoeuvre my legs round so I'm sitting up properly. Another push and there's a scraping noise and a crash, and my legs are free. Pain shoots up them, as though someone's sticking foot-long needles into me.

'Jesus!' I can't help crying out, and now my voice is back.

'Who's that?' Val's voice is gravelly and wary.

'It's me. Sarah.'

There's silence. Then, 'Who are you? What are you doing in my house?'

'It's me, Val. Adam's friend. Sarah. It's me.'

'Whoever you are, can you get me up? I feel like a bloody beetle. I'm flat on me back here.'

She sounds like she's only a couple of metres away. I don't trust my legs, so I start to crawl towards her. Underneath me, things crunch and move and dig in as I shuffle forward. All Val's ornaments, thrown about and broken; all her souvenirs and mementos, all the little things that had caught her eye. I try not to think about it as another one shatters under my knee.

Reaching in front of me, my hand touches something soft.

'That you, Adam?'

'It's me, Sarah.'

'Sarah.'

She says it deliberately, like she's feeding it into her brain, trying to remember.

'Sarah with the baby,' I say. 'Sarah who paints.'

'Sa-rah.' It sounds like the light's dawning now. 'Sarah with the baby.'

'Yeah, that's right.'

'Oh my God, I remember . . . Where's Adam?'

'I don't know, Val. They locked him up, remember?'

'Oh shit. My boy. My beautiful boy.'

'Can you move? Are you hurt? We need to get out of here.'

The building is groaning and sighing around us.

'Val,' I say, 'are you hurt?'

'No. I dunno. Help me up.'

Our hands meet in the dark, hers bony and desperate. They cling onto mine like they'll never let go. We manage to get to our feet.

'Let's get out of here,' I say.

'Okay, love, where's the door?'

'We don't need a door, Val, we just walk.'

'What do you mean?'

'The front of the house has gone, Val.'

'Don't be silly. We had a bit of a bump, that's all. We're still here. The house is still here.'

'We are, but half your house isn't. Keep walking.'

Arms linked, we pick our way over the debris. There's a half-moon above us, giving enough light to show shapes in the gloom, but you can't see any detail. Someone out on the street is shining a torch around and they flash it our way for a few seconds. And now we can see it: a mound of rubble where the front wall of the house used to be, spilling out into the yard. We have to scramble up and over it to get out, but there's no other way.

The beam of light moves away from us and we're walking blind again.

We wobble our way over the last of the stuff that used to be a house. A stretch of garden wall is still standing, so we perch on there, looking back where we have just come from.

The air is full of dust, thick with it, but as the moonlight filters through we can see what's happened. The front walls of all the houses in our row have gone. It's like a crazy doll's house where you can see inside the rooms.

'We were lucky to get out of there,' I say.

'Lucky,' Val repeats. 'Lucky.'

Something moves on the ground next to me. I catch the

movement out of the corner of my eye and yelp.

'What is it?'

I'm expecting to see a hand or an arm or something, but it's not human. It's a small, black thing wriggling and squirming. Then it makes a noise, halfway between a grunt and a whine. I get off the wall and crouch down next to it. I put out my hand and touch dust, but there's soft fur underneath, and warmth. The thing responds, lifting its head, and in the moonlight I can see an empty socket where its eye used to be.

'It's a dog, Val.'

'A dog?' says Val. 'Norma's dog?'

I run my hand down his back. He's panting hard. There's something wrong. His back end is flat against the ground, his legs splayed out.

'Come on,' I say, 'Come here.' I move a little bit away from him and click my fingers. He shuffles towards me using his front legs, like a commando wriggling on his belly. His back legs trail uselessly behind. 'His legs are no good. They're not working.'

Val kneels down next to me.

'Let's have a look.' She runs her hands over the dog.

'His back's broken,' she says. 'Better tell Norma. Where's Norma?'

We look towards next door. It's just a shell. Unlike Val's house, the ceiling's fallen in. The whole thing's gone.

'Oh, shit,' she says. I can't see her face, not the expression on it anyway, but it's there in her voice. 'Poor Norma. Adam told us. He told us this was coming. I always believed him, but I never thought it would be like this . . .'

'We'll have to finish him off. We can't leave him like this. Sarah?'

She wants me to kill him. The hair on the back of my neck stands up.

'I can't, Val. I just can't.' She leans forward and I hear her scrabbling in the rubble. She's got something in her hand now.

'Okay. Okay. Good boy, good boy.'

She moves in the dim light, bringing her hand high above his head. Then she smashes it down. There's a dull thud, that's all, a thud. She doesn't say anything, but scoops up the body and stumbles back towards the houses.

'What are you doing?'

'I'm going to bury him where he should be, with Norma.'

I scramble after her and together we pile stones and bricks on top of him. Then we make our way back to the wall and sit down.

'Thank you,' Val says. She finds my hand and takes it in hers. We sit in silence for a while. I'm numb. I can't take in what's happened. It was quiet to start with, but now the night is filling up with noise; sirens, shouts. There are people in this street shouting, people desperate for help, and I suddenly wonder if the person who's got Mia is shouting too. Are they trapped somewhere, or are they safe? Is she crying, or could she possibly have slept through it all? Or is she dead already? Her number is imprinted in my mind, the number I read in Adam's book. 112027. It's today. It's here. I might be too late.

'Val,' I say, 'I've got to find Mia. It's the only thing that matters now.'

'Mia,' she says. 'The baby.'

'Yeah, I've got to get to her.'

'Of course,' she says. 'We should go now. It's just . . . it's just . . .'

'What?'

'I don't want to leave without Cyril's box.'

Cyril? Cyril's box? I want to scream. She's worried about the ashes of someone who died years ago while somewhere in London my baby needs me now.

'Val, please, leave it. We'll never find it in that lot. Please, I need to get to Mia.'

'It's all I've got left of him.'

I think my head's going to explode. *It doesn't matter. He's gone.* But it does matter.

'Val, I don't think it's safe to go back in. You'll never find it anyway, not in the dark.'

'It'll be light soon. We could stay 'til it gets light.'

I try to stay calm, but my frustration's building up as each second ticks away.

'Val, I've really got to go.'

'We won't get far in the dark, safer to travel in the day-time . . .'

I look down the road. With the moonlight, it's not completely pitch black. I take a few steps along the pavement and I step into thin air. The pavement isn't there. My foot goes down, down, down and I'm clutching wildly for something to get hold of, trying to fling myself backwards. Finally, when I'm up to my thigh in the ground, my foot hits something.

'Shit!' I call out.

And suddenly Val's there.

'Sarah? Sarah? What's happened?'

She finds my shoulder, her bony hand gripping, holding me.

'I've fallen down something.'

She helps me to clamber out.

'Don't go, Sarah,' she says. 'Don't go 'til it's light.'

From the other side of the road, someone's shouting.

'My wife. She's in there. Help me. Help me!'

My heart's pounding in my chest. I know what I'm going to have to do, and it's killing me.

'Stay there, Val,' I sigh. 'I'll try to help these people, and the moment it gets lighter, we'll get Cyril out and we'll go.'

'I can help too,' she says. And so we do stay. We crawl across the road to Val's neighbours, and help them to move stones and bricks and timber. And between us we manage to pull the woman out of the wreckage of her house. She's not hurt too badly, but she's in shock. Her husband sits next to her on the pavement, in his pyjamas and dressing gown, holding her hand.

Our eyes get accustomed to the dim light, so we hardly notice dawn breaking, the sky turning from black to grey. I've been leaning forward, my head in my hands but my back's hurting so I straighten up and look around me.

'Oh my God, Val. Oh my God.'

'What is it? Have you found something?'

'No. Look.'

She, too, straightens up. She puts her hands on her hips and stretches her back. Then she looks down the street, and a noise comes out of her mouth, somewhere between a sigh and a whistle.

'Sweet Jesus.'

The houses around us are wrecked, but it's not that that's shocking. It's the road, or rather the hole where the road used to be, the one I found earlier. It's ten metres wide and a hundred, two hundred, three hundred metres long, like someone took the biggest knife in the world and ripped it through the surface of the earth.

And I feel like that knife is ripping through me too, and I know that I can't stay here for another minute. My daughter's out there, in this damaged, ripped-up city.

'Val, please, please, let's get out of here.'

'Yes, Sarah, we will. I'll just nip home. It won't take a minute.'

'No, Val, look at it. It's not safe.'

She starts making her way over there anyway. I catch up with her.

'Sit down a minute. I'll go.'

'You know what you're looking for, don't you? A wooden box. It was on the mantelpiece.'

'Yes, okay, I'll get it.'

I set off across the rubble. It's difficult to find my footing. I keep stumbling, my ankles turning this way and that as the debris shifts. The back wall of the lounge is still standing and the side walls. The ceiling is still in, just. The mantelpiece is still attached to the wall at one end. The other end has come free and is sagging down towards the floor. The carpet has disappeared under a layer of broken furniture and ornaments. Everything is covered in dust. I bend over and start picking through stuff.

The ceiling creaks and a stream of dust falls down beside me.

'Have you found it?' Val's voice drifts across the rubble.

I don't reply. My fingers are already scratched and sore from helping the rescue effort through the night. I'm taking the tips off them again, as I scrabble through. This is hopeless. I don't want to admit defeat, but each new groan from the building around me sends waves of panic up and down my spine. I don't want to be buried here.

'Come out!' she shouts. 'Leave it. It don't matter.'

I can't find it. I stand up and start to turn around, when something catches my eye, something white and shiny wedged under a picture frame. I crouch down and examine it – a little china swan, intact, still perfect. I put it in my pocket and pick my way out of the room for the last time.

Val comes to meet me. She puts her hand on my arm.

'I thought it was going to go. I thought you'd be buried. I'd never have forgiven myself. Don't know what I was thinking of, selfish old cow.'

Behind me the building is creaking again.

'We should move further away,' I say.

We get out onto the road.

'Sorry about Cyril,' I say, 'but I did find this. It's not broken.'

I dip into my pocket and produce the swan. I put it in Val's open hand. She looks at it and runs her fingers all over it.

'We got this on our honeymoon,' she says, quietly, talking to herself as much as me. 'A week in Swanage, on the south coast. He was as hot as axle-grease that week. God, I thought I'd never walk again!' She must sense me cringing because a throaty laugh starts up, which rapidly turns into a coughing fit. 'Too much information?'

I nod, too embarrassed to say anything.

'Thanks,' she says. 'For this. It's something, innit? Shame about the box though.'

'It's only ash, Val. It's not really him.' I'm trying to say the right thing, if there is a right thing to say at a time like this.

'I know that, love,' she says, 'but I put eight thousand quid in there with him.'

My jaw drops open.

'Eight thousand? What did you do, rob a bank?'

302

'Not me, love, it was Cyril's. Rainy day money, he called it.'

'Do you want me to go back?'

We both look over to the house, and somewhere inside there's a loud crack and the chimney on top of the roof tilts.

'Oh shit, it's going.'

The chimney falls sideways punching a hole in the roof, and then the whole lot goes, crashing through the bedroom floor, down into the lounge. Debris is flying out of the place. Instinctively I turn away and put my arms round Val. It's like a blast from a bomb. We're showered with dust. I keep my head down and my eyes closed for a long time. When I look up again and turn around, the whole house is just a heap of rubble.

Val's as pale as a ghost.

'You could have been in there . . .'

'I wasn't. I got out.' I give her a reassuring squeeze, but I'm shaking, arms and legs trembling uncontrollably. She squeezes me back, wrapping her arms round me, rocking me gently from side to side. Then she pulls away a little and wipes the dust from my face.

'Come on, Sarah,' she says. 'We've got a baby to find, haven't we? Come on, love. Let's go. Let's find her.'

Adam

My head breaks the surface just as I breathe in. I get a mixture of air and water; it catches in my throat and makes me cough and retch.

I dip down again, underwater, but I know now what I'm aiming for, and I push my hands through the water forcing my body up. I cough and spit and take a deeper breath in. It helps me float, and I lean back, face clear of the surface and carry on getting air in my lungs. Above me the green and yellow lights have almost gone, but there's a half moon in the sky, and its light means I can make out dark shapes either side of me. I don't have a clue where I am. I've no idea how long I was under, but I can feel I'm still being moved along.

The water is raging and powerful. I've got no choice. I've got to go with it. I start getting a feel for it, I'm almost comfortable with it, when a side-wave hits me and I'm under again, caught in a current, swept along. And then my arm's scraping on something, something hard ripping through my sweatshirt. My foot hits something else, gets hooked and my leg's pulled backwards and I'm jerked to a standstill while the water carries on blasting past me.

I try and reach down, but my body's fighting the current. My face breaks the surface and I gulp down some air and duck under again to find out what's going on with my foot. It's caught on a railing – my shoe's wedged in there. The water's so strong, it's sapping my energy. I know I'm getting weaker. I go up for more air and duck down again and this time I manage to get my fingers into the back of my trainer. My foot doesn't want to come, but I wriggle it about and pull the shoe looser 'til suddenly I'm free, and the water snatches me and takes me further on.

If there was a railing, the river's flooded over the streets, but the water here will be shallower. I've got more of a chance of getting out. I start kicking with my legs and whirling my arms over my head and into the water. At first, it feels hopeless, but then I can tell that I'm moving and the water is flatter. I cut my way through – *keep going, keep going* – till at last my fingertips graze against the bottom. I stop swimming and put my feet down. The water's only knee deep here. It's still moving but the current is gentle, so I can sit and not get swept away.

My chest is heaving painfully. I can't believe I done it. I've escaped. I'm alive. If I was going to die today, surely that was Death's chance to grab me. I never even got my twenty-five metres badge at school. They used to laugh at me: 'Black kids can't swim.' I had no idea I could do that.

I try standing so I can wade out of the water, but my legs don't have the strength, so I shuffle along on my bum for a bit, and then crawl a bit more. I bump into something. It floats away from me, a dark shape in the water, with two pale hands picked out by the moonlight. After a bit the water is down to a few centimetres and I drag myself up to my feet and start walking.

It doesn't take long to work out where I am. After ten minutes I can see the big circle of the London Eye standing out black against the sky. It makes me think of Mum.

Don't go to London. Don't let Nan take you there.

Where is she now, Mum? Is she looking down at me? Was she there with me, giving me that little extra bit of energy to drag myself out of the river? We forgot what she said, Nan and me. Nan 'cause she's a contrary old cow. Me 'cause I met Sarah, and I had to try to help her. We forgot what she said and now we're suffering for it, though God knows what's happening to Sarah and Nan. In my heart, I think they're okay, 'cause after all, I seen their numbers. I know they're both survivors. But even so I get the jitters when I think about them and I start running. I'm going to get through these dark streets and I'm going to get home.

It takes me hours. I have to get across the river, and half the bridges in London have gone. There are police at Vauxhall Bridge keeping people off it because it's not safe, but I barge past them and belt across as fast as I can 'til I'm over and through the police cordon at the other side.

It's just getting light when I find the High Road, but as I get to Nan's street, I can't believe my eyes. Half the road's disappeared. There's a massive hole, hundreds of metres long. The houses have collapsed. It takes me a while to work out which one is Nan's, which one *was* Nan's. It's been ripped open at the front, and the roof's fallen in, so all that's left is a couple of walls and a heap of rubble. A few of her gnomes are lying spread-eagled at the front of the heap, like little corpses.

'Oh my God,' I say out loud. No one could have survived that if they were inside the house. And where else would they be? I don't get it. I thought they were both survivors. I thought Sarah was my future.

My legs can't hold me any more. I sink down to the ground and close my eyes. This isn't right. It can't be right.

'They got out, you know.'

'What?'

I look up and there's an old man, in his pyjamas and dressing gown. He clocks the handcuff on my wrist, but he don't say nothing about it.

'Your nan and a girl. They got out before the roof came in.'

'Are you sure?'

'Sure I'm sure. They stayed to help me and my wife. They were heroes.'

The news washes through me like another tidal wave. It knocks the air out of me all over again.

'Was there a baby? Did they have a baby with them?'

He shakes his head.

'No, just the two of them.'

'Where are they now?'

He shakes his head again.

'Sorry, I don't know. They left here a little while ago. Twenty, thirty minutes. Didn't say where they were going.'

Twenty minutes. That's nothing. I can catch them up. I can find them. If I knew where they were going. *Think, Adam. Think, think.* I close my eyes again. I try to focus on Sarah, what'll be going on in her head. If they didn't have Mia with them, she'll be desperate to find her. So where is she? Where's Mia?

Her mum and dad were there at the police station, the day they charged her with assault. She saw them. They could have taken Mia back with them that same day if the Children's Workers let them. And why wouldn't they? Two decent citizens. Nice house in Hampstead. Nice car. Nice life.

'You all right, son?' Pyjama-man is still watching me.

I'm knackered. I feel like I could lie down in the road and sleep right now.

'Yeah,' I say. 'Yeah, I'm fine. I've got a couple of ladies to find.'

'Ah, cherchez les femmes,' he says. 'Good luck, son,' and he winks and turns away.

My whole body hurts; my arm's bashed about, my wrist's sore, my ankle's bruised and twisted, my lungs are aching. But it's my foot that's letting me down now. I bend my leg and twist my foot to have a look. I brush the crap off it with my hands – bits of brick and stone, dust, pieces of glass, splinters of wood. I wince and gasp. There's some deep cuts there now.

I'll never get to Hampstead like this. I need a shoe. I spot a curtain, still attached to a rail lying on top of the rubble. I crawl over the debris and tear at the material, ripping it into long bandages. Then I start wrapping one round my foot. My hands are shaking, but I can't stop now. I try to keep them under control so I can circle the material over and under from the toe right up to the ankle, 'til I've made a sort of cloth boot, then I tie it in a knot at the front. It's genius. I take a deep breath, get up and test my weight out. It's still painful, but nothing like it was before. Yeah, this'll do it.

I start to walk, and it feels okay so I step it up and start jogging, away from the house where my dad grew up, my home too, for a while. There's nothing left, but I don't feel anything about that, 'cause it's people that make a home, and the three people that'd make it home for me aren't there any more.

But I'm going to find them. I'm going to find them if it's the last thing I do.

Sarah

We head across town, but the place we walk through isn't London at all, at least not the London I grew up in. Nothing is as it should be. It's completely, utterly changed. It's not exactly quiet because there are car alarms and burglar alarms going off, and miles away there are sirens, but the background hum of traffic is gone. The noise that you go to sleep to at night and wake up to in the morning – it's missing.

My head plays tricks on me. As we walk along, my mind is seeing the place how it used to be and I start to feel kind of spaced out when there's sky where a building should be, where walls are missing, or where the pavement has disappeared under a heap of rubble. We find two more holes in the road. One cuts across the street, making a chasm too wide to jump over, so we have to go back on ourselves and find a different way round.

Everywhere we go, people are shouting for help. Gaggles of people gather where there's any reason to hope; families, neighbours, strangers pitching in to try and rescue the ones still alive. They form lines straggling across the rubble, passing bricks and blocks and timber from one to the other. There's no sign of the police or the fire service or even the army. Not round here, not in Kilburn. We've been left. We're on our own. If we don't do it ourselves, it won't get done.

It's tempting to help, but it's nearly eight in the morning now and Mia is all that matters, Val and I agree on that.

The first fire is a few streets away. Some flats above a row of shops are blazing away, flames streaking out of one of the windows up towards the sky. Two figures are in the very top window, trapped by the fire below. People have piled up cardboard boxes, anything they can find, in the street below, and they're yelling, 'Jump!'

As we watch, the figures climb out of the window and, hand in hand, they launch themselves into the air. They land on the makeshift mattress, but it's not enough. They land and they stay down, hands entwined, necks broken. We stay for longer than we should do, as people cover over the two bodies with the clothes that were meant to cushion their fall. Then we turn and walk away, silent, numb with horror.

The streets are full. Everyone who could get out under their own steam has done so, and no-one's going back inside. There aren't that many 'insides' to go back to, and the buildings left standing aren't to be trusted. Some people are wandering aimlessly, others sitting by the side of the road, head in hands. Most are joining the rescue effort, going where they're needed, responding to the cries and shouts all around.

Of course, not everyone's trying to help: some are helping themselves. We pass plenty of shops with their windows smashed. Nature may have broken some of them, but crowbars and baseball bats have done the rest. People are going in and out like it's the January sales. Only no-one's buying. They're just taking it all away.

I keep looking at my watch. We've only gone about a couple of kilometres and it's already quarter past nine. I stop again.

'Val, this is no good. We won't get there in time. What are we going to do?'

'Do you want to go on ahead without me? You'll be quicker.'

That's exactly what I want, but it seems ungrateful.

'Not really,' I say. 'I want to get there, but I don't want to be on my own.' Then I hit on something. 'Val, can you ride a bike?'

'Course I bloody can. I was young once, you know.'

There are Freebikes all over London, a row of them just along the street, some of them a bit mangled, most of them okay still.

'Come on,' I say, and we scurry up to them. I've got some change in my pocket and I put my hand out to put a Euro into the slot, when behind me Val makes a noise like a startled bird. I spin round. There are other people screaming too, and a noise like thunder. It's not coming from above us, though, it's underneath us, all around, and then I see what everyone else is seeing – a wave spreading along the road. I don't mean water on top of it, the road itself is the wave, the whole thing rippling like it's a ribbon or a sheet or something.

We don't have time to run anywhere, so I grab Val and I pull her down to the ground. As soon as we're down there we're pitched back up into the air. I cry out as something hits me in the back. Anything not fixed down is being tossed about like a ship at sea: cars, bikes, people.

All around us windows are popping, glass is showering down, and then buildings themselves, the ones that survived the first quake, start to collapse.

'Stay down!' I shout. 'It's not over!' But it is. As quickly as it came, the movement stops. Was it really only a couple of seconds? The noise carries on for a while though, and I wait until it's faded, before I open my eyes and lift my head up. Beside me, Val's doing the same, slowly unwinding.

'Oh shit.' Val's voice is still working anyway.

'Are you okay?' I say. 'Are you okay?'

'Yeah,' she says, 'think so. You?'

'I don't know.'

I'm so battered by it all, not physically, but in my head. I don't know if I can do this. I don't even know if I *should* be doing it.

'Come on, Sarah, we've got a little girl to find. We need to find Mia.'

Tears brim in my eyes when she says Mia's name.

'Look at me. Look at me. We can do it,' she says. 'We can do it, Sarah. We can change things. But not here. We need to find her.'

'What if we should be keeping away from her? If Adam's not there and I'm not there, maybe her future will be different, her number will be different. I read it, Val. I read Mia's number in Adam's book.'

'It's today, isn't it?'

She knows. How does she know?

'You said you didn't read it.'

'I didn't. He told me.'

'He *told* you. I don't believe it. He said he never tells people's numbers.'

'It was after he saw her for the first time. He was so shook up when he got home. It just came out.'

'Doesn't matter anyway. I've seen it every night since I fell pregnant with her. The end. How it happens.'

'Except that it won't be like your nightmare, because Adam's not here. So it's different already. Whatever happens, Sarah, you should be there. She's your daughter. I wasn't there for Terry, and I regret it more than anything . . .'

The two of us are on the edge of tears now.

'Come on, Sarah. Let's do this.'

She grunts as she gets back onto her feet and I wonder whether it's just her normal aches and pains or if she's been injured. She sets her mouth in a thin line and reaches for a bike.

'You lead the way,' she says to me. 'I'll follow. I'll be right behind you.'

It takes us about half an hour to get to Hampstead. As we get nearer, my spirits start rising. I've been dreading this, but the houses round here aren't too bad. There are whole rows still intact. If you ignore the odd broken pane here and there, tree branches where they shouldn't be, you can almost imagine that the earthquake hasn't hit here. Almost.

Then I see it – a column of smoke rising up from the rooftops two or three roads away. I stop the bike and stand watching, as my guts turn to water inside me.

'Is it . . .?' Val's drawn up alongside.

I put my hand up to my mouth and nod.

'I can't do it,' I say, and my words are whispers. 'I don't think I can.'

Val reaches over and puts her hand on my shoulder.

'You have to. She's your daughter.'

'The house . . . my parents . . .'

'I'm going to be there with you. We're here now. We're here.'

I swallow hard.

'Okay,' I say. 'Let's go.'

Adam

I'm so close behind them. If I was a dog I could pick up their scent. I wish I *was* a dog – then I'd know I'm on the right track.

I'm full of doubt, worried I'm chasing across London to the wrong place, and all the action will be somewhere else, somewhere I don't know about. But I try not to think about that. I've decided what to do – I've got to do it now.

Getting to Nan's it was so dark I couldn't see the big picture. Now, in the light, what the quake's done is mind-boggling. Something so solid, so big, so complex – a whole city – is just a pile of rubble. With so many buildings down, there's more sky in London now. And today is sunny, the first bright day for weeks. Too bright for comfort. It's hard enough working out which way to go, without being dazzled as well.

I keep my eyes down, away from the sky and I try not to look at the people gathered here and there, the bodies laid out in the street. There's so many stories here. I've seen them coming, they've lived in my head for months, and it was true. It was all true. Maybe I should be pleased? What I tried to tell people has happened. I was right, wasn't I? But I don't feel like that, not even a bit. I feel the horror of it, right through me, in my bones. I feel empty and useless. I tried to help and people died just the same, hundreds and hundreds of people. They're still dying all around me.

Only I don't want to stop trying. I don't want to give up. I look up every now and again, searching ahead of me for Sarah or Nan. I'm getting close to Sarah's neighbourhood now. Some of the houses seem okay, and I start to let myself believe that it's going to work out. I'll get there and find them, Sarah and Nan and Mia, and maybe they'll be having a row with Sarah's parents, and maybe Nan will be giving them a piece of her mind . . . and then I see the smoke, a column of black billowing up into the blue sky.

And I remember . . .

Sarah's nightmare.

The flames.

The heat.

The terror.

I stop for a moment, and put my hand up to my face. The flames. The heat. I've been there before. I know what it feels like. Sweat's pouring off of me from my run, but I'm cold as ice inside.

The smoke rises and I think, *This is the one place I shouldn't be. I should turn and walk away and maybe Mia will be saved.* But it's the chicken in me talking. I'm scared of fire. I'm scared of dying. But I know I've got to do it. Sarah's seen it, a vision of how it's going to be. I'm there with her, in her nightmare. She's terrified. She hates me. I take Mia away from her.

But I'm not here to hurt anyone. I'm here to save Mia. I hate the numbers. I want to change them. I want to wipe them out, and if I can't, then I'll die trying.

Sarah

All I want, all I've wanted since they took her away from me, is to see Mia again. To hold her in my arms.

When I see the smoke rising up over the rooftops, I know it's my house, and I'm plunged back into my nightmare. It's been running on a loop inside my head for a year, while outside, in the real world, life has been teasing me: *Here's your daughter, here's Adam, it's coming, it's coming true.* Now, I know that this is the time when the two come together, fantasy and reality, the future and the present. But it's twisted, unexpected. I'm here with Val. There's no Adam. But with or without him, I'm going to have to do it. I'm going to have to walk into my nightmare.

I feel sick to my stomach.

I don't know if Mia's alive or dead. I *feel* that she's alive but maybe that's wishful thinking. I know her number now. I've seen her death sentence.

As Val and I cycle up to the house, it's as though I'm outside it all, watching a film . . . or a dream. The muscles in my legs tense as I press the pedals. My hands, sore and bleeding, grip the handlebars, but I don't feel the pain. The air is full of the acrid smell of smoke – burning buildings, burning furniture, burning people. The sounds are the sounds of people and fire, no traffic, no aeroplanes, just the crackle of flames, and the cries and shouts of people in distress.

I don't have time to think about coming home. I don't have time to notice that the street is pretty much the same, except for two trees and a lamp post lying across the road. The gates to the house are open.

The roof timbers are ablaze, belching black smoke into the sky, crackling and popping.

I drop my bike on the drive and run towards the house. There's a crowd of people gathered there. I push my way through. In the middle of it all are Marty and Luke. They're sitting on the ground, among a sea of legs. I dive down next to them on the gravel.

At first they don't seem to realise it's me. Of course, I've shaved most of my hair off since I left, and it's been a few months.

'Luke, Marty, it's me, Sarah.'

Two pairs of eyes search my face, and then Marty lurches forward and flings his arms round my neck, while Luke starts crying.

'Where's Mum and Dad?' I ask.

'In there.'

'Is there a baby?'

Marty nods.

'The baby was staying with us. She kept crying all the time.'

'Is she in there?'

'Yes.'

'Where? Upstairs? Downstairs?'

He shakes his head. I look over to the house. The front bedroom has collapsed onto the room below.

'Were they at the front? In the sitting room?'

He shrugs.

Someone taps me on the shoulder. I look up and see a woman, Mrs Dixon, who lives a couple of doors down the street.

'Sarah?' she says. 'Is that you?' She's looking at me like I've just landed from another planet.

'Yes, it's me. I'm back.'

'Where did you . . .? Your parents . . . your parents.' As she looks towards the house, there's a blast from inside and a window is blown out, glass, frame and everything.

'Get back. Get back everyone!'

'Mrs Dixon,' I say, 'will you take the boys out onto the road for me? It's too dangerous here.'

She frowns.

'Of course, but where are you going . . .?'

The front of the house is blazing, so I sprint towards the side, shielding my face from the heat as I squeeze down the path. The kitchen's at the back. Peering through the door, I can see a man lying face down on the floor. 'Oh God.'

It's my dad. I know it is.

'What is it?' Val's next to me.

'Nothing. There's someone in there. On the floor.'

'Jesus.'

'Val, go back. Go somewhere safe.'

'I'm not going anywhere. I'm here to help.'

I haven't got time to argue with her. I try the handle of the kitchen door but it's locked. I pick up a plant pot and smash through the glass. Then I reach through and turn the key, and I'm in.

Dad's sprawled on his front, motionless. I bend down and put my hand on His neck. It's cold. I press down, trying to find a pulse. There's nothing. He's gone. The kitchen's a mess, but there's nothing to show He's been hit by anything. It looks like He just fell where He was.

Even dead, I'm scared of Him. I'm expecting Him to suddenly open his eyes, grab my hand or shout out.

Stop it, Sarah. Stop it. Leave him. He's gone. Where's Mia?

Val's standing behind me.

'Is he . . .?'

'Yes,' I say.

I walk towards the hall, and shout out, 'Hello? Hello? Is there anyone here?' The hall is blocked with fallen masonry. There's no way through, no way Upstairs.

I cup my hands and try again. 'Hello?'

There's no answer, except the creaking of the timbers above our heads, the steady trickle of debris and ash down in front of us. There's heat too, coming from above.

Then I hear it. I stand perfectly still, and listen. It's a sound I know so well, it's part of me. Val's behind me in the hall. She's shouting too. I turn round and put a hand on her arm.

'Shh. Listen.'

'It's too dangerous, Sarah. We should get out of 'ere.'

'Can't you hear her?'

She stands and cocks her head to one side.

'No, Sarah. I'm sorry, I can't.'

There's an almighty crash above us, and the sickening sound of timber being torn apart. We grab each other and duck down together, arms protecting our heads.

I cry out as something big hits my shoulder. The noise

seems to go on for ever; splintering, groaning, stuff showering down all around us. When it finally goes quiet again, I
open my eyes a fraction and peek through the shield of my
arms. I can hardly see the hall any more. More of the ceiling
has come down, taking the banisters and half the stairway
with it. The front of the house is on fire, but so's the back
too now. There are flames all around us. I uncurl a little and
look up. I can see right up into the roof where there's a
hole, three or four metres across, open to the sky. The gap's
creating a draught because there are flames too, being sucked
in from all around it and roaring out and up.

'Oh shit,' Val says, 'we've got to get out of 'ere. Sarah,
we've got to get out.'

Her hair is covered with dust and ash, and there's more
raining down on her, settling on her face, her eyelashes.

'I heard her, Val,' I say. She looks up at the roof and then
down at me again. Her eyes are wide with fear.

'I don't think you did,' she says. 'I think you *wanted* to
hear her.'

'Don't you think I know my own daughter's voice?'

'Yeah, but . . .'

'She's alive somewhere. I know it.'

She puts her hands on my shoulders.

'Half this house has gone already. She could be anywhere.'

'She's near. I heard her. I can't leave her. She needs me.'

'It's not safe. We've got to go.'

'I can't leave.'

'Sarah, if she's under there,' and she nods towards the heap
where the sitting room would have been, 'then we can't get
her from 'ere. We'll need to go in from the top. We need to
go back outside while we still can.'

There's a loud bang above our heads.

321

'Please, Sarah.'

We both look behind us at the way we came in. There's a wall of flame filling the doorway to the kitchen, yellow and orange tongues licking up through the roof, reaching for the sky. But at the heart of it, there's a darkness, a dark shape, a shadow. The blurred edges become focused and we both gasp. It's a man, walking towards us through the flames.

My dad. My dad's here.

But it can't be. He's dead. I've seen Him. I felt the chill of death in his neck. It's not Him, it's . . .

'Adam,' breathes Val. 'Oh my God, it's Adam.'

She stumbles forward and falls into his arms as he emerges from the fire. He looks different, older maybe. I blink and my nightmare fills my head. *The stranger with the scarred face takes my baby from me and walks into the flames.*

My baby. My baby. Where is she?

'It's only four steps and you're through the flames,' Adam's shouting to be heard above the noise. 'Get out of here, Nan. I'm here now. I'll deal with it.'

She holds onto his arms, her deep hazel eyes searching his face.

'Nan, I'm not arguing. Go. Four steps and you're out. We'll be right behind you.'

She nods. 'Okay,' she says. 'Adam . . . ?'

'Not now. Just go. I'll see you in a minute.'

He puts his arm around her shoulders and gently points her in the right direction. She glances up at him again, and then half-walks, half-runs towards the kitchen. She's silhou-etted, like he was, for a moment, and then she's gone.

'Adam . . .' I say, but then I stop. I hear it again – a weak cry, almost like an animal – and Adam does too. I see it in his face.

It's muffled and to one side of us. We both reach for the door to the under-stairs cupboard at the same time. There's a small round handle and you press a button in the middle. My hand gets there first. The button burns the end of my thumb as I touch it. I pull the door open, and cry out, bringing my sleeve up to my nose. There's an overpowering stench: vinegar and booze and shit.

It's dark in the cupboard and it takes a while for my eyes to adjust, and then I see them. Mia: alive, pink, squirming in the arms of my mum. One side of Mia's face is spattered with blood, but it's not hers. There's a big wound on Mum's scalp, and cuts on her face. The blood has trickled out of her and onto Mia, and she hasn't wiped it off, because she doesn't know it's there. Her eyes are open and she's looking right at me, but she can't see a thing. She's dead.

I crawl in next to the two of them. There's glass all over the floor, broken bottles and their contents; whisky, gin, pickles. Shards like knives cut through my jeans, slicing the skin on my knees and shins. I lean forward and gently take Mia from Mum's arms.

'It's all right, all right,' I coo to her, 'I've got you now.'

I hold her close, bent over so I can kiss her face, feel her warmth, smell her baby skin. She's red-hot. Her clothes are wet in my hands, where her nappy's leaked, and she smells of sick and pee. But it's her sick, her pee, and I breathe it in gratefully.

My little girl.

My life.

Alive and back in my arms.

Adam

Sarah dives into the cupboard. I can't see what's happening. 'Is she there? Have you got her?' I shout out. Above my head the burning rafters are so hot I can feel it from down here. I'm trying to stay calm, to think not feel, to be in charge, to make the right decisions, but I've heard this noise before. My body remembers this burning heat, my skin's shouting at me: *You know this. Not again! Get out! Get out!* The sweat's pouring off of me. Every creak, every movement above me makes me flinch. *This is it. It's coming down.*

'Sarah!' I shout, but my voice comes out in a scream of terror. 'Sarah! Have you got her? Bring her out now!'

I can hear Mia's cry. I duck down to peer into the dark space. There are three people squeezed into there – Sarah, Mia and her mum.

'Jesus!' Sarah's mum is dead, half her head caved in.

Sarah's got hold of Mia. She's still crying, but at least she's alive.

'For God's sake, Sarah, come out of there now!'

I back up, to make room for her to get out, but there's a hissing, wrenching sound above me. I look up and a beam of wood is dropping out of the sky towards me.

'Shit!'

I launch myself into the cupboard, knocking into Sarah's mum. She slumps sideways, as Sarah screams, and the beam crashes to the floor half a metre from my foot.

'Oh my God! Oh my God!' I twist round and look behind me. The rafter's lying across the hallway, still burning, sending its heat and flames towards us. More debris falls on top, the pieces that aren't already on fire soon catching alight.

Sarah won't stop screaming. In this tiny space she's making as much noise as Mia. I look back to the flames. They've got us trapped in here. It's getting hotter and hotter, and soon the doorframe will catch and the flames will be inside with us. Orange and yellow and white. It's too bright, much too bright, but I can't look away. There's a face in the flames. *Junior staggers backwards, clutching his stomach and I fall, fall, fall. The flames are all round me. They're melting my skin, cooking me from the outside.*

The first flame comes licking round the doorframe. I slide away from it through broken glass, until I'm right against Sarah. Her mouth is close to my ear and she's screaming still.

'Sarah,' I shout. 'You've got to stop. You're frightening Mia.'

Her screams turn into words.

'The fire! It's here. We're trapped.'

'I know.'

'What are we going to do?'

Looking out of the cupboard door is like looking into a furnace. It's madness to go out there. I should turn my back on it, put my arms around Sarah and Mia, and hold them until the end. I should tell them I love them, and close my eyes, and keep them closed. They'll find four bodies here.

'Adam? Adam?'

She's looking at me for an answer. I don't have one. I haven't got a plan and I'm as terrified as she is. But then her number comes to me again and I remember what it means. We're going to be old, together. She's going to go peacefully. We aren't meant to die in here. Sarah's is one number I don't want to change. I've held on to it since the first moment I saw her. I'll hold on to it now.

'We'll have to go through the fire.' It's our only option.

'I can't. I can't.'

'I'll go out first, see what it's like out there. Then, when I say, you come out. We'll get through it together.'

She's not screaming any more, but she's crying, a high whimpering noise.

'We can do it, Sarah. We can do it.'

I know what this is going to feel like. I've been here before. *Don't think. Don't think. Just do it. Do it. Do it now!*

I shuffle away from Sarah and put my hand at the bottom of the doorframe. The paint's blistering in the heat. I lever myself forward and out, trying to keep low. The heat takes my breath away. It looks like we're surrounded by flames. I know the front of the hall is blocked, so our best bet is the way we came in, back through the kitchen, the way I sent Nan. The fire's so close I can't see what's happening the other side of it. Has the kitchen roof caved in or is it clear? There's no time to check. The hair sizzles on my head. I'm burning up where I stand.

'Sarah, we've got to go now!'

She stares at me out of the darkness like a hunted animal, but she don't move.

'I can't.'

'Nan got through. It's fine. You've got to go now though. Quickly!'

She moves forward on her knees, holding Mia close to her body. I take her elbows and help her up and out. Her eyes are red. She struggles to keep them open against the light and the heat.

'Oh my God, I can't. I can't.'

She crouches down.

'It's four steps and then you're through. Four steps.'

'We won't make it. Oh my God.'

'We haven't got time for this.'

I'm hunched over her, standing between her and the flames. I can feel the flesh on my back getting scorched in the heat.

'Give me the baby. Give me Mia.'

She looks at me then. I see the flames reflected in her eyes and in the middle of this chaos there's a moment of stillness between us. We both know we're smack in the middle of her nightmare.

This is it.

This is how it happens.

She hesitates for a second, two seconds. The back of my sweatshirt is on fire, I can feel it.

'Sarah! Give me the baby!'

She passes Mia to me. Mia wriggles in my arms, but I've got her.

'Now go!'

She steps away from me. For a split-second her body is a black shape against the flames, and then she's gone. Mia's crying. I'm crying now. I thought I'd known pain. I thought I'd known terror. I was wrong.

This is pain.

This is terror.

I gather Mia into my body, curling round her, shielding her with my arms.

She's as hot as I am, and as I hold her, her body goes rigid and her eyes roll back into her head. Her arms and legs start to twitch.

Mia. Mia. Not now. Not today. Hold on, Mia, hold on.

I gather her in closer and I walk into the fire.

Sarah

He says it's only four steps. One, two, three, four. The numbers are in my head as I walk away from him, as I walk away from Mia. My mind is screaming them as the heat hits my body. I close my eyes and I walk.

One, two, three, four.

I open my eyes, but I'm still inside the fire. It's raging all around me. He lied! He lied to me! I trusted him and he tricked me and now he's there, with her and I'll never see them again.

I turn around. I need to go back. I should never have left Mia. The heat forces my eyes closed again, and instead of Mia, I see Adam, his dark brown eyes, looking straight at me, straight into me. I feel his face, the first time I reached across the desk at school and touched him, his skin so smooth then. Adam. The boy who came looking for me, once, twice, three times. Who took me home. Who gave me his bed. Who stayed in London when he should have run away. Who kissed me.

And then someone takes my hand and pulls me round, bony fingers squeezing mine.

'It's this way. Only a few steps more.'

I keep my eyes closed and I start walking again. The floor's a mess and my feet keep bumping into things. I lift them up, trying to step over, step through, step round – all with my eyes tight shut.

And suddenly, the heat isn't there any more. The roaring has gone from my ears. I'm out the other side, in the kitchen.

There's a space where my father's body was, and a trail through the debris to the back door. People come rushing forward. Hands pat me where my clothes are alight, and lead me outside. Voices shoot questions at me. Fresh air hits my lungs, forcing its way through the smoke inside me.

I try to get clear of the hands, the voices. I want to go back. I want to be with Adam and Mia. I need to fetch them.

The voices join together in a chorus, a collective gasp.

'Look!'

I turn around and Adam is walking through the kitchen door. He's on fire, trailing flames from his clothes and his hair as he walks.

'Oh my God!'

Then he's surrounded by people. I can't see him through the wall of backs and legs and feet.

'Adam!' I scream. 'Adam!'

The wall breaks and I catch sight of him, down on the ground, wrapped up in something from head to toe. They're rolling him from side to side. And through all the noise, the cries and shouts, my ears pick out the voice I need to hear, the voice that's so dear to me that it's part of me. Mia. She's crying. She's alive.

I run across to the crowd, work my way into the gap.

They're unwrapping Adam now, peeling away the blanket. People fall silent as he is revealed; his head, his shoulders, his chest. He's on his side, with his back to me. All his hair is gone at the back of his head, and his clothes have burnt away. His skin is blistered, melted.

His eyes are closed, but the front of him, his face and his arms, aren't so bad. It was his back that caught the heat and Mia is still in his arms. Her arms and legs are stiff, odd-looking.

'Let me,' I say and I gently reach under her body and lift her away from him. As soon as I pick her up, I feel her body relax. The crying subsides, and with a few last shuddering sobs, she stops and opens her eyes.

'Mia,' I say. 'Mia.'

She stares at me with her blue, blue eyes.

'Mia. You're safe now. It's all right. You're safe now.'

'Is she all right?'

Adam's voice is whisper. His eyes are open too.

'Yes,' I say, 'she's fine. Look, she's fine. You saved her.'

I hold her down close to his face, so that he can see her, but he closes his eyes again.

'I can't,' he says. 'I can't look.'

'Yes. Yes, you can. She's fine.'

Mia coos and stretches her arms out towards him. The tiny hairs on her skin are singed, but her skin is pink and healthy and perfect. She touches his face, and he opens his eyes.

'Oh my God,' he breathes.

'What is it?'

'Mia,' he says.

He says her name and he starts to cry.

Adam

The fit didn't kill her. She's upset, but she's fine and she's back in Sarah's arms, where she should be.

There's just one thing that's different, and it blows my mind. I can't take it in. I don't understand.

My eyes fill up with tears. I try to blink them away. I don't want to stop looking at her face, her eyes.

'It's all right,' Sarah keeps saying. 'She's fine. You saved her.'

And it looks like I did. That's what it looks like. And yet. And yet . . .

She's close to me. Her hand is on my face, touching me. She doesn't smile. She looks at me, all solemn. She's calmer now and she stares at me and I stare at her.

I've heard people talk about old souls and I never knew what they were on about. Now I think maybe I know what it means. There's something timeless about the person looking at me. She can't be only a month old – she's seen things and been places. She knows. She understands.

Her face is the last thing I see before I pass out and it stays with me as I sink down and away. It floats in front of me and goes through my eyes and into my head. It changes inside me, fading from colour to black and white and then into negative, light where it was dark, dark where it was light. It turns inside out, its features break apart from each other and dance, then join back in the wrong order, teasing me about what a face should be. It's a game. I know it's only a game, but more than anything I want her face back how it should be. I want it to turn out right. The pieces have to fit back in a way that makes sense. If I can't get them to do that everything will be wrong. If I can't do it, I might as well die.

There was noise before – crackling flames, hissing and groaning from the building on fire, cries and shouts.

There's no noise now, only a silence that feels like a scream.

Sarah

It's like a movie, a disaster movie. I'm in it, but I'm also watching it, as things play out around me.

The house is completely ablaze now. There's no chance of saving it. In the back garden people are huddled in groups; around Adam, around Mia and me. All the things you see in a suburban back garden are still there; a couple of swings, a climbing frame, a trampoline. Dad's body lies a metre away from a space hopper. It used to be mine and then the boys had it. Its mad eyes and grin are facing me. Dad's face is covered up. Someone's put a coat over him, but his hands and legs are sticking out.

Looking at him, I wonder what I should feel. I don't feel anything, not yet. It's just a body under a coat. It's more upsetting thinking about Mum, slumped in the under-stairs cupboard. The flames will have got to her now. She's being cremated. It's too horrible to think about.

I owe her. Whatever went on when I was at home, she saved Mia. Even when she was dead, she protected her.

I look back towards the house.

'Thank you,' I say inside my head. 'I love you, Mum.' *Do I? The woman who turned a blind eye? Did I – do I – love her?* The flames are roaring now, like some sort of animal, sending glowing ash and smoke high up into the sky. I crane my neck back, trying to see where it all ends, but I can't.

'We're losing him,' someone says. The words drag me back onto the ground. It's Adam. They mean Adam.

He's still lying on his side, but his eyes are closed now. The skin on his back and shoulders has turned pale – burnt white by the fire.

'He's gone into shock.'

All these weeks and months in my nightmare, I felt so desperate about Mia. My panic, my terror was focused on her. That's what haunted me. I was sure she was going to die.

I never thought it would be Adam.

'Don't go, Adam. Don't go.'

He doesn't react. His eyes are open now but they're fixed firmly on one spot. His face starts to relax. He's almost gone.

I put Mia down on the ground gently, then I cup Adam's face with my hands and half-crouch, half-lie down, so that my face is in front of his.

'Adam. Look at me. Look at me, now.'

His eyes are open, but he's not seeing me. The connection isn't there.

'Adam. Please, please!'

I lean forward and kiss him gently. His mouth tastes of smoke. He doesn't kiss me back.

'It's over,' someone says.

'No! No, it can't be!' I stretch forward a little more and kiss his eyes. As I pull back my tears fall down, spilling onto his lashes, splashing like rain.

Adam

I used to hate seeing numbers. They scared me. I didn't know why I'd got this gift, this curse. But it's a number that saves me now. Sarah's.

I'm in a tunnel, a long tube of darkness, but there's light at the end; light and warmth and someone waiting for me. Mum. She's how she used to be – not how she was when she died. She holds her hand out, and I reach towards her, but our fingers don't touch. She's smiling, and it feels so good to see her again. I never thought I would. She's talking to me but her lips aren't moving. I can hear her thoughts.

'What you doing here, darlin'? It's not time yet.'

I can hear other voices too, shouting, crying, but they're miles away.

'It's over.'

'No! No, it can't be!'

And then someone's close to me, really close, and I open my eyes, but I can't see them. I can only see the light, and somehow the light is Mum and she's the light. It's all I want to see. I've missed her so much.

Something splashes in my eyes, and it stings. I blink it away and now there's another face. Sarah. And her number floods through me and it's like the first time I ever saw her. It shocks me, how someone can leave this world so easily, bathed in love and light. And I know I'm going to be there. I'll be with her, holding her in my arms. I'm part of it, part of her life. So I can't go now, I've got to stay.

The tunnel's gone, Mum's gone, but it's okay. Just seeing her was enough.

Sarah

He blinks. Once. Twice. And then he looks at me.

'Adam,' I say. 'Come back. Come back to me.'

And in that moment, that fraction of a second, he's with me again. I want to keep him so badly. The feeling's so fierce, it's like a pain, but I know that all I can do is look. All I've got is my eyes looking into his, his eyes looking into mine. And everything else goes away. It's the two of us again. We've got now, this minute, this second.

'Come back to me, Adam. I need you.'

His mouth is moving now. I strain to catch his words.

'I love you, Sarah.'

'I love you, too. I always have, only I was scared.'

'I'm scared now . . .' He's trying to say something else, struggling to find enough strength to get the words out.

'Shh,' I say. 'Don't worry. Tell me later.'

'The numbers . . .' he whispers.

'Don't worry. Don't worry about them. Not now.'

'But Sarah, you don't understand.'

'What? What is it?'

'Mia's number . . .'

I freeze. Her number was today. *Oh my God, oh my God.* I lean closer, so my ear is next to his mouth. He's talking under his breath. A list of numbers. I can't make them out.

'Two. Twenty. Two . . .'

'Adam? Adam, what are you saying?'

'Mia's number,' he says, his voice no more than a whisper, 'it's changed.'

'Oh my God. Do you mean she's all right? She's going to be okay?'

'I dunno. I don't get it.'

'Why? If it's not today, then she must be okay, mustn't she? Adam, tell me. Tell me Mia's number.'

'2022054,' he murmurs. 'It's the same as Nan's now. I've got to tell her. Where is she? Where's Nan?'

I sit up and look round the crowd of faces peering down at us. She'll be somewhere close at hand, but she's not. I bend and twist, trying to see through all the legs, through to the others behind them.

And then I realise – I haven't seen her since Adam put his arm round her shoulders and sent her off into the flames. She wasn't there in the garden when I got out, but I heard her in the fire. I felt her hand guiding mine. Didn't I?

'Sarah.' Adam's looking straight at me now. 'Sarah. Where's Nan?'

Sarah

He won't leave her in the wreckage. He's hurt, badly hurt. We need to get him to hospital so someone can treat the burns on his back, but he won't let us.

'She's in there,' he says, looking towards the house. 'Nan's in there. I'm not going anywhere.'

If he had the strength he'd go back inside, but the flames are too intense, and, besides, Adam's beat. He only just escaped with his own life. His own and Mia's.

There are no fire crews to put out the flames, only a gaggle of neighbours watching helplessly as the house is incinerated. One by one they drift away, back to their own shattered homes, or to see if they can find help. We stay in the garden – Adam, Marty, Luke, Mia and me – and we watch and we wait. We wait until the flames die down, and the column of smoke dwindles away to almost nothing. We spend the night camped out while metres away from us the embers glow.

In the morning, the hopelessness of our task is clear. The whole house has collapsed, reduced to a mixed-up pile of ash, charred wood and metal . . . and, somewhere, human bones. My mum's in there, as well as Val.

Adam stares and stares at the smouldering remains.

'Adam,' I say, 'we can't.'

I want to get out of here. Find some help for him. Overnight the skin on his back has puffed up and blistered. He says it doesn't hurt, but it hurts me to look at him. I don't know how someone so badly burnt can still be alive. But I'm glad he is. It's true what they say: you don't know what you've got till you lose it. And I came close to losing Adam. I think I did lose him. He went away and came back again.

'She's gone,' I say, as gently as I can. 'I'm so sorry.'

'We can't leave her there.'

Suddenly I'm back at Carlton Villas, and Val's staring into the rubble where her home used to be. She didn't want to leave, but I made her. And now I'll have to make Adam leave her.

'There's nothing else we can do for her,' I say. 'We need to find a doctor. You need a doctor.'

'Why?'

I think he's asking about his burns. He can't see them himself, not properly, so he doesn't know how bad they are, but then he says, 'Why did she die, Sarah? How did her number change?'

'I don't know. Val thought that you could change numbers. She told me that, and I think you did, Adam. I don't know how many people got out of London, but it must be hundreds, maybe thousands. You saved them. And you saved Mia.'

He looks at me then.

'I don't know about the hundreds and thousands. I don't know what their numbers were, but Mia . . . Mia's different.

341

You knew about Mia's number,' he says.

'Yes. I saw it in your book.'

'I was wrong. The numbers I saw were wrong.'

'No, you saw them, but they changed. You changed them.'

He looks away from me then and his eyes fill with tears.

'I wanted to save Mia, but I would never . . . I never . . .'

He doesn't have to say the rest. I know. He would never have hurt his nan.

'Did I do it, Sarah? Did I kill her?'

'No, of course not. You saved people, you . . .' I stop. He's looking at me again and his eyes are so tortured. I want to say the right thing, make it all better. But there are some things that no-one can make better. And there are some times when bullshit just won't cut it. 'Adam, I don't know. I don't understand about the numbers. I don't know what the rules are. Maybe it was you. Maybe it was Val. She wanted to help. She loved you so much, Adam. She was a powerful woman.'

'I hated her, Sarah. I hated her . . . but I loved her too. I never told her.'

'You didn't need to. She knew anyway.'

'Did she?'

'Course she did.'

He shakes his head and looks away.

'Adam,' I say, 'you saved thousands of lives. You're a hero.'

He won't look at me now. He doesn't reply. But a tear spills out of one eye and trickles down the scarred skin on his face.

Adam

We stay on in London for weeks, first in the field hospital set up in Trafalgar Square and then, when they say I'm out of danger and my burns are starting to heal, in the Hyde Park camp. I don't know what we're waiting for. I s'pose we think that things'll get back to normal soon. But as the days turn into weeks, nothing seems to change, except the queues get longer and our daily handouts of food smaller.

The city's dark at night. The National Grid's still down. We got generators here, but they turn our lights off at ten, and it's pitch black until dawn.

There's five of us in our tent, but it feels like five hundred after another night of the boys messing about, wriggling and crying. It's not their fault. The things Sarah used to see in her nightmares belong to all of us now, even the kids. Especially the kids. When one of the boys starts crying, it wakes the other one up and then they start up too, and we're all awake. Sarah does her best, but it's not her they want in the middle of the night. It's their mum. And she'll never cuddle them better again.

I have nightmares too. I see the same thing over and over again – a slight figure walking away from me into the flames. I can't reach her. She doesn't hear me shouting. She never turns round. I just have to stand there, watching, as the flames take hold of her.

Sarah hardly sleeps, what with the boys and Mia. The thing is, Mia's no trouble. She don't cry. She feeds and sleeps and feeds some more. You'd think a three-month-old baby would be the most trouble of all in a place like this, but she's a doddle: calm, settled, happy even. When I'm right on the edge, when I think I can't take any more, I pick her up and hold her, and I start to feel human again.

The soldiers in charge of the camp start to ration water and I know it's time to leave.

'Where are we going to go?' Sarah asks.

'I dunno. Somewhere where they grow stuff to eat. Somewhere near a river, so we can have as much water as we need. Somewhere near a wood so we can burn stuff and keep warm.'

She sighs.

'You want to move to the country. There's nothing there, Adam. We'll starve. We'll die.'

'Do you call this living? There's cholera in the camp now. They're keeping it quiet, but I heard that three people have died already. We got to get the kids out, Sarah. This is a bad place.'

She frowns and hugs Mia closer to her.

'Are the boys' numbers bad, Adam? What are their numbers?'

My stomach turns over. We haven't talked about the

numbers. I've tried to block them out, not to look at anyone, not to think about it, because when I do, it does my head in. Now it comes flooding back in again, like a dam bursting.

'It don't matter about the numbers, Sarah!' Without knowing it, I'm shouting. 'You can't trust them. Numbers change. A bad number can turn into a good one. A good number can turn into a bad one.'

She puts one hand out and strokes my arm.

'It's all right, Adam. It's all right. Calm down. We'll go. We'll get out of here.'

I try to get my breathing back under control, stop rocking backwards and forwards.

'I'm sorry, Sarah. I didn't mean to get het up. It's just . . . just . . .'

'I know. I know,' she soothes. 'It's too late to leave now. We'll go tomorrow.'

In the morning we quietly pack up the few things we've got left.

'Are we doing the right thing?' Sarah asks just before we leave the camp. There are dark circles under her eyes and her face has got thin. She's still beautiful though. I can't help looking at her and as she searches my face for answers, her number fills my head again, and suddenly I want it to be real. Her number means hope and love and light. Her number makes me want to believe in happy endings.

I cup her face with my hands, and kiss her gently.

'Yeah, Sarah,' I say. 'We're doing the right thing. We'll be all right, you'll see.'

And I want to believe it. I do. I really do.

We take a last look round, then she puts Mia in her sling, she gets the boys to hold hands with her and I pick up our bags, and we walk away.

ACKNOWLEDGEMENTS

I would like to thank everyone at The Chicken House and Scholastic – you've made my dreams come true and changed my life; Barry, Imogen, Rachel, Elinor, Chrissie, Nicki, Claire and Esther, and my fellow writing Chickens – what inspiring people you are. Thank you also Mary and Becky, publicists extraordinaire, and Steve for your amazing cover design. Thanks to my parents, Shirley and David, my parents-in-law Ann and Peter, and all my family and friends for sharing the fun. Thank you to Ali and Pete, who mean more to me than books ever will, even if writing takes me away from you sometimes. Thank you to my friends at Bath and North East Somerset Council and Keynsham Town Council who have taken an interest in my other, 'secret', life and supported me. And finally thanks to the people who read 'Numbers' and took the time to tell me that they liked it – I had no idea how touching your feedback would be.

'You Are Not Alone', with lyrics by Robert S. Kelly (© R. Kelly Publishing Inc, 1994). Produced by Michael Jackson and R. Kelly, and released by Michael Jackson in August 1995 as the second single from his album 'HIStory: Past, Present and Future, Book 1' (© Epic Records, 1995)